John Braine was born in Bradford, Yorkshire in 1922 and left school aged sixteen with no clear view of his future. Following a stint as a librarian and a year in the Royal Navy he wrote his first novel, *Room at the Top* – a bitter analysis of class structure in an English factory town – which was rejected by four publishers before finally appearing in print in 1957 and selling 5000 copies in the first week. By the end of the 1950s it had sold over half a million copies. He wrote eleven other novels, the most famous of which are *The Jealous God* (1964) and *The Crying Game* (1968). He died on 28th October 1986 in Hampstead, London.

The Jealous God

John Braine

HOUSE OF
STRATUS

This edition published in 2001 by House of Stratus, an imprint of
Stratus Holdings plc, 24c Old Burlington Street, London, W1X 1RL, UK.

www.houseofstratus.com

Typeset, printed and bound by House of Stratus.

A catalogue record for this book is available from the British Library.

ISBN 0-7551-0252-5

The jealous God, when we profane his fires,
Those restless passions in revenge inspires;
And bids them make mistaken mortals groan,
Who seek in love for ought but love alone.

ALEXANDER POPE

PART ONE

One

"He was always a little snotnose, that Harry Bandon," Vincent's grandmother said. She frowned at her cup of tea. "It's no wonder he can give a thousand pounds to St Theo's when he charges one-and-eight a quarter for such rubbish." When she frowned, her face became witch-like, the long nose seemed nearly to meet the chin; the frown vanished and her face was smooth and composed again, uncannily young for seventy-eight.

"He's done a lot for St Theo's," Vincent said.

His grandmother laughed. "You're like your father. You'll not hear a bad word about anyone. It's St Theo's that has done a lot for Harry Bandon. If he'd to lose his faith, he'd go bankrupt, God forgive me for saying such a thing."

Vincent smiled, the old contentment settling down over him. "I think all the Bandons would be in trouble if that happened." His grandmother never seemed to change; there had been the time after her operation a year ago, when she'd been mild and temperate in her personal judgements, but it hadn't lasted for very long. For a few days she had lain on the horsehair sofa, a rug over her, gentle-voiced and abstracted, her attention apparently concentrated upon the big wooden crucifix on the wall above the fireplace; but now she was sitting in her Windsor chair again, holding herself so straight that the back of the chair hardly seemed necessary.

When she had complained of a stiff neck ten years ago his father, being flush with a pools win, had bought her the wing-sided arm-chair in which he was now sitting. It was upholstered in plum-coloured Genoa velvet and the back was so high and the sides so long as to protect even Vincent's six feet two from the draughts which, winter and summer alike, seemed continually to plague his grandmother's house; but she had only to his knowledge occupied it once, and that was on the day of its arrival. As his father had said, it wasn't that she felt the chair too good to use, but that it was too comfortable. And, despite its size, it was too feminine for his grandmother's living-room; there should have been a glass-fronted china cabinet, light-coloured floral wallpaper, white woodwork, a great many fragile ornaments and water-colours to set it off properly. It was an intruder in this room with the brown and red stippled walls, the Darkaline-stained floor, the red Axminster carpet, the big oak table and the oak dining-chairs and the oak Welsh dresser and the fireplace with the marble mantelpiece and the mahogany surround. There was a black vase with beech leaves on the walnut occasional table at the window, and the Angora stole which he'd given her two years ago was neatly folded on the sofa.

There had never been any changes in this room since his childhood, except in the direction of a greater austerity. Only the crucifix and the photographs of her husband and her son Matthew stayed in the same places on the wall. There had been other pictures, there had been ornaments, there had been a set of willow-pattern plates on top of the dresser; she had put them all away since his grandfather Dungarvan died ten years ago, the same year that his father died. His mother often remarked upon it – *She's turning queer, there'll be nothing in the house but bare boards and that old Windsor chair soon* – but Vincent knew better. She was travelling light, she needed less and less, she was growing more and more impatient. He felt his eyes closing; the fire was very hot and the sound of his grandmother's knitting-needles curiously soothing. It was already growing dark; his grandmother switched on the standard lamp, heavily and bulbously wooden and nearly six feet high, that stood always by her chair.

"It might be your Uncle Matthew sitting there," she said. "It's strange how you favour him and your brother who was named after him takes after your mother."

Vincent looked at the photograph of his uncle, stiff-necked and staring-eyed in his corporal's uniform. The thin dark face was all nose and eyes and chin, with something about the expression – innocence perhaps – that one didn't seem to see nowadays.

"How old was he then?" he asked, knowing the answer. "That was taken the day after his twentieth birthday, 1918, that was. He hadn't long to live then, poor lad. He'd never talk about what it was like in the trenches, except once he said to me: Mother, I've no business to be alive. And I burst out crying and he was angry with me then; he said he felt bad enough already. And I well remember him waking me up screaming one night and me going into his room and him twisting and turning with the sweat pouring off him, for all it was a bitter cold night. It's a terrible thing to see your own child suffering. You'd give your heart's blood to save them and it's no use."

"He'll not be suffering now," Vincent said gently. She made the sign of the Cross. "They can't do anything more to him. That's what the Canon said, and he got into great trouble over it. They butchered our children, he said, our grand young men, they butchered them to make fortunes for themselves, but now they can't torture them any more. I remember when the Harry Bandon you seem to be sticking up for was against the Canon, as much as he dared. That's when he got his chance to make his money – him and his weak heart!" She snorted in derision.

"That's not his fault, Grandmother."

She snorted. "He's seventy-four now and never a day's illness has that man had. That weak heart hasn't stopped him from making thousands of pounds and fathering six children, though to be sure none of them's up to much. He was mad after Noreen. I remember her telling me about it. 'What shall I do Mrs Dungarvan?' she asked me, her head on one side like a bird. 'He's very little and he has a face like a monkey but he keeps on asking me' – but it was our Matthew she wanted, of course, and that was her way of telling me. And, God forgive me, I'd been against it, because they were both so young, but a heart of stone couldn't have resisted her–"

She smiled. "I can see her now as bright as a button, there was nothing that could put that one down for long. She was an only child and she'd always got what she wanted and she got Matthew and a year after she died, she followed her baby to the grave." Her voice was steady but there was a keening note there, a sadness formalized but not constricted. "I remember her laid out in her coffin and she looked no bigger than a child herself. That was the Spanish 'flu. You know your history but even you won't have heard much about it. They kept it quiet for fear they'd make the soldiers lose heart altogether. I said to your grandfather – " she glanced over Vincent's shoulder as if seeking corroboration from someone else in the room – " Leo, I said, I've wept all my tears. Ah, well, and now Harry Bandon's son is marrying my granddaughter. I thought once she was sweet on you. Not that Delia would have been the right one. Ah, well, it's a great catch for her no doubt. The Bandons have money if they have nothing else. Though the lad seems harmless enough..." Her voice had lost the keening note now, she was back in the present. She suddenly pointed an accusing finger at Vincent. "It's time you were married," she said. "A man of thirty has no business to be a bachelor. I tell you, I'll not be able to die – " there was a note of petulance in her voice as if Vincent were holding her back from a long-planned journey – "until I've seen your children."

Half in annoyance and half in affection Vincent reflected that, no matter how far the conversation might range, his grand-mother had an uncanny knack of bringing it round to the one subject in which she was really interested.

"I don't think it's likely that I'll ever get married," he said.

"Why not? You're not going about with a woman who's married already, are you?"

"Don't be ridiculous, Grandmother."

"It's not ridiculous. You're a man, and the world's full of stravaging harlots. I remember your father, God rest his soul, being mixed up with another man's wife. Her husband was a commercial traveller and a friend of your father's and your father called round one evening on some trumped-up excuse and then it started. He said they were just friends." She snorted, then indulged in the Irish expression which was her nearest approach to an oath. "Muyah! There's no friendship between grown men and grown women, and no one can tell me different."

"You've never told me that about Father before."

"There's a lot of things I haven't told you. I know how to keep my mouth shut. You'll know the woman, a fine big woman with black hair. Mrs – " she snapped her fingers. "I'm getting old. He left his job and they bought a sweet shop in Rodney Terrace."

"I used to buy Odds and Ends there," Vincent said. "A penny a quarter. That'd be before the War. I can't remember the name." He had a vague recollection of a big woman with shiny red cheeks; if he'd even thought of her as a person at all it wouldn't have been in connection with sex.

"You'd have been too young then even for her," his grandmother said. She snapped her fingers again. "Hallsberg," she said. "He was some sort of foreigner, but she wasn't. Poor woman, she never had any luck. Her husband was run over by a lorry not long after they took over the shop, and he wasn't much good after that. I don't know whether the shop's still there, nor her for that matter…"

"You'll find out, Grandmother," Vincent said, grinning.

"I don't often go that way," she said. "You do. It's not far from St Theo's."

"I used to walk it then," Vincent said. "Granville Terrace was a short cut. I bought the sweets with the halfpenny I saved on the tramfare."

"It wouldn't do you any harm to walk it now. That car'll destroy the use of your legs, it will. Don't think you can't get fat,

7

Vincent. That's what killed your father, all this riding about in cars and – " She stopped suddenly. "Never mind. I stopped her capers and he lived to be grateful for it. It wasn't long after that he met your mother, though that's a daft way to put it since she'd been there all the time. You pay heed to me, Vincent, and get yourself married. I knew your father and I know you. Marry or burn, Vincent, marry or burn."

"Some do both," he said lightly. For a second her face looked as if he had slapped her, the grey eyes startled and hurt. "Don't say that, child. It's a silly thing for you to say." She looked past him at the photograph of his uncle. "No matter what your mother thinks, you'll never make a priest. I told her you wouldn't the day you were born. She had the idea in her head even then. The Canon told her at the christening that all she could do was hope. It's God will choose the boy's vocation, he said, not you, Mrs Dungarvan. But she'd not be told."

"I don't want to argue about it," he said. "It's all one in the end, anyway. I'll not do what I don't want to do."

"Perhaps not. That's what your father used to say, God rest his soul. But he always gave way in the end. You're his son."

Suddenly Vincent was weighed down by the sense of the past; in this room the dead were as real as the living, so much so that for an instant he could hardly be sure of his own existence. It wasn't impossible that death should be imperceptible, the least important part of him ceasing to function somewhere between St Theodoric's Grammar School at half-past four and Ten Pelham Street at the time which out of habit he'd identify as six o'clock. In the stories it was always like that; talking to one's grandmother one remembered that she'd been dead for years and then as she smiled and confirmed your suspicion (Yes, my dear, you're one of us now) the door opened and his father and his Uncle Matthew would come in arm-in-arm. There were occasions when he almost wished such stories had some foundation in fact; the simple truth was that he still missed his father.

He opened his briefcase.

"I'd nearly forgotten your library books," he said.

She put on her spectacles; she wore them almost on the tip of her nose, which always irritated him. "Let's have a look at them," she said.

"I wish you'd let me buy you a new pair, Grandmother," he said. "Those damned things make you look like Old Mother Riley."

"Don't be impudent," she said. "I got those forty years ago at Woolworth's and I've never had one bit of trouble with my eyes. They're great robbers, all those opticians with their gold and silver and tortoiseshell frames. Steel's good enough for me." She took the books from him; he noticed with amusement that in order to see them she was forced to look over the spectacles rather than through them.

"I bet you take them off when I've gone," he said.

"Whisht, child! *The End of the Affair. Brideshead Revisited.* Hadn't they any murders?"

"These were the two you said you wanted, Grandmother."

"I hope they're not dirty," she said. "Reading immoral books is a cause of confession." She smiled.

"I'd never give you an immoral book, Grandmother. Why, these are good Catholic authors."

"They're the worst," she said. "That man Greene's terrible. Mind you, he knows about life."

That was the escape clause, Vincent thought. He'd been changing her library books for ten years now; invariably she'd expressed her distaste for immoral books and just as invariably on the few occasions when he'd brought her something innocuous, had rejected it out of hand as being wishy-washy and untrue to life.

"I'll have to be away," he said. He went over to her and kissed her on the cheek. Her skin was smooth and clear, the result, so she always said, of never using anything on her face but oatmeal.

"God be with you," she said.

9

"And you, Grandmother," he said, a trifle self-consciously; he had never been able to find the correct reply to this invariable valediction.

"Are you seeing Clare tonight?" she asked him as he went to the door.

He shook his head.

"Only donkeys shake their heads. Have you quarrelled with her?"

"I've been busy, Grandmother. I haven't seen her for quite a while."

"She'll not be sitting at home twiddling her thumbs. I'd phone her if I were you, Vincent."

"It was never really serious," he said.

"Maybe not for you, Vincent." She had already picked up one of the books. "Take care now, child, the roads are very treacherous." She opened the book; Vincent, smiling to himself, saw that he was no longer with her.

As he went out into the street he saw that there were four Pakistanis standing by the A35. "Excuse me," he said. They fell silent and moved nearer to the car so that two of them actually were pushing their backs against it. They stared at him for a moment; it was not so much the action which irritated him but their expression of fear and bewilderment.

"Excuse me," he said, and they made way for him.

The street lamps came on as the sun disappeared into the west, seeming to be pulled down suddenly by the night rather than to sink slowly. It had started to drizzle again. But the Pakistanis would, he knew, stand there for at least another hour, though none of them wore a raincoat. He was assailed by a momentary pity for their thin bodies and their dark faces which seemed always to have a tinge of grey; it struck him that it would be as well in the next period with the Sixth to point out the analogy between these immigrants, absolutely alien in their whole way of life, and the Irish immigrants who came to this very district with the railways and the Great Famine. Most of you, he would say, had ancestors among those immigrants. Certainly I had. And then no doubt one of the little devils would point out that *their* ancestors weren't black and weren't Mohammedans, and unless he were very careful there'd be a pointless and time-wasting discussion about the colour bar. Most of the Sixth this year seemed to have a positive talent for wasting time; better stick to the syllabus and let them argue about the immigrant problem at the Debating Society.

He drove slowly over the greasy setts; in this part of Charbury, no matter what the weather or the hour, children had a way of appearing from nowhere and under, as often as not, car wheels. The houses, thrown up by the same builder over a hundred years ago, scarcely varied from street to street; one felt unable to escape from the plain oak door, the yellow-stoned doorstep, the three sash windows with their lace curtains which had been white once but now were tinged faintly with yellow.

Now he could hear the bells of St Maurice's; his melancholy increased. It was as if they were tolling for a death rather than ringing the Angelus and it was as if, sentimental though the notion was, they were reproaching him. St Maurice of the Theban Legion, massacred at Agaunum; he had a picture of soldiers standing in the drizzling rain, their arms by their sides, of the archers taking aim or of the axe descending. But it wouldn't have been as tidy as that: massacre had been the word. Patron of dyers, clothmakers, soldiers and swordsmiths, how could you bear it? I have my thoughts for company; they are clever and well informed but not the company of my choosing. Clare wasn't clever. Clare wasn't well informed, Clare had been leading him into mortal sin; but if he'd had before him the prospect of taking her out tonight he wouldn't now be occupying himself with speculations about martyrs of the third century.

There was a smell of chocolate from the Honeychile toffee factory in the next street, coarsely sweet and somehow provocative as if a scent had been made with a *crème de cacao* basis. The smell wasn't generally so strong; the rain perhaps brought it out. There were a lot of girls employed at the Honeychile factory; in the summer they would gather at lunch-time on a patch of waste ground next to the factory, chattering among themselves, playing desultory games which sometimes appeared to be kind of cricket and sometimes a kind of football. He never had looked at them for as long as he would have liked to; he knew very well that involvement, total and hopeless, would follow. They all seemed alike, he thought guiltily, bold-eyed and big-mouthed; like Clare, in fact. When you were going about with a girl, all other girls began to look like her; and when you had broken it off they still continued to look like her. In the early days with Clare, he'd felt that he was going out with every other girl he'd ever fancied or could conceivably fancy; and when it was over it was over with all the other girls too.

Hail Mary, full of grace, he repeated to himself as he drove on away from the sound of the bells and into Hurley Lane, the long straight road which led out of the city, out into the northern suburbs, the Lord is with thee, blessed is the fruit of thy womb...

It was a prayer he used every day and now it had no meaning; it should have driven Clare out of his mind but instead it forced her farther in; it reminded him of womanhood, of the one organ that was specifically female, of the mystery, of that night in Battle Woods and of Clare's resentful expression as he suddenly stood up and said that it was growing late. Her face had been transformed by what could have been nothing else but disappointment, it had become heavy again, the thick eyebrows had frowned, the mouth had pouted and twisted. They had scarcely spoken on the way home.

He stopped the car at the traffic lights; on Markey Road to the left there was scarcely one building standing. The effect was as if the buildings had disintegrated of their own accord, succumbing to some disease peculiar to stone; there seemed to be no plan behind the demolition. Soon the road would cease to exist as a place; he had never liked this part of the city but this evening he found himself staring at the heaps of rubble with a sense of loss, of part of his life having been stolen.

The lights turned to green; he was almost sorry that they should do so. For suddenly the memory was ceasing to hurt. She had said that now he could go home and dream of her – he rummaged in his memory – *you like women but you like being alone better. When I've gone, you'll be able to dream about me, won't you?*

That was it. There were other things too, the smell of her breath that was faintly sweet as if she had been eating herbs but also was faintly acrid, and there was the softness of her face as if a finger would push through the cheeks but push through them only as it would through smoke, being made of a different substance; and there was what he had to be careful about remembering too often, her rising clumsily in the woods, slipping on the autumn leaves, his hand reaching down to steady her, the revelation which was the common-place of comic postcards and pin-up magazines, which was adolescent to dwell upon, but which nevertheless had, no matter for how short a time, taken him above and outside himself: there had been the mystery and he could never be the same again. As he turned to the right into Beckfield Road he smiled to himself; whilst Clare had been beside him in the car there had been no other place where he'd wanted to be, but now that she'd gone, the deepest and the keenest pleasure had begun, a pleasure that couldn't commit him, couldn't puzzle him, couldn't humiliate him; he could dream about her now, he could carry the dream about with him, as portable as a transistor. It was enough, he said to himself as he drove along the stretch of dual carriageway to Beckfield, it was more than enough. One didn't have to pick a flower in order to enjoy it.

It had begun to rain again; he reduced his speed. It was only this morning that he'd seen the wrecked Jaguar on this very stretch of road, about four hundred yards ahead of the turning for Foxley Village; and the roads would be in no better condition since then. The A35 was a nice little car, but it wasn't built for racing; Matthew and Paul were always at him to change it for something better but he knew perfectly well that he was going to keep it for the next ten years at least. The only way to save money is not to spend it, he said to himself; a car is merely transportation… And then he realized as he slowed down for the Beckfield Moor road that he was deliberately making small talk for himself; he'd told himself a lie and now he was chattering aimlessly to cover it up. He was going home to Mother, he was thirty years old and he had never, when it came to the crucial moment, been able to march towards the sound of the guns, not because of fear but because of the desire not to be drawn in, to lose his freedom, to be forced once and for all to disclaim his vocation and to be like the rest. The flower could only be enjoyed by picking it; why was he trying to delude himself?

The windscreen was misting up; he pushed open the window, breathing in gratefully the smell of wet grass and the faintly smoky smell which he always took to be the smell of heather. On a patch of waste ground beside the road a car was parked with its lights off; there was no building nearby or, indeed, for the next two miles. There was a glimpse of a man and a woman in the back seat; Vincent grimaced and accelerated. This unlit moorland road was the shortest route to Beckfield; but in his present mood he wished he'd taken the longest way round along the broad new road which ran through the new Council estate a mile south of Beckfield. The new road was lit by new sodium lamps which took all the colour from the face and turned the lips blue; to make love there you'd need to be not only exhibitionist but necrophilic.

As he approached the lights of Beckfield he found it difficult to forget the man and woman in the car, their heads close together as if forced into contact by some outside agency, oblivious to any consideration except pleasure, a pleasure which he of his own free will had rejected and which wasn't in evidence now anywhere in his own life.

He drove automatically, stopping for a second at the cross-roads past the War Memorial, despite there being no indication of the presence of the main road and, at the steepest point, holding the car on the clutch because putting the handbrake on would mean that he could be stuck there for ten minutes; because of the way in which the back of the Congregational Chapel projected into the road, visibility to the right was non-existent. I am a machine as much as the car is, he thought, and I have made myself so. I am lonely as the car is lonely, being unable to follow any other mode of existence. I had the consciousness of progress once, of working towards an end, of growing somehow better and happier, but now at the age of thirty I can only brood over a glimpse of a girl's thighs and toy endlessly with the notion of myself as Father Dungarvan, Society of Jesus, austere and withdrawn but fulfilled at last, rid of the troubles of the flesh because I shall have gone through and beyond them, I shall have changed, I shall have grown, I shall be a historian, I shall be a theologian, I shall change men's lives...

The fantasy grew, as it always did, Clare and the couple in the car were forgotten, temptations to be expected by all but eunuchs and surmounted by all but weaklings; he drove along Pinley Avenue with a feeling of expansion, almost patronizing the poplars and the stars and then, as he opened the front door and heard his mother's voice he at once diminished; he was Vincent Dungarvan, MA, Senior History Master at St Theodoric's Grammar School and lucky to be that; he could no more change than the A35 could become a Rolls.

There was a smell of cooking from the kitchen.

"You're late," his mother called out. "I was worried sick."

"Just a minute," he said, going into the cloakroom. He knew that he should have gone straight into the kitchen; but lately he had found himself more and more often delaying the first encounter with his mother; there was even an inexplicable shamefulness about it, it wasn't right for a man of thirty to come home to his mother. He pushed the thought aside and sat down for a moment on the WC, his head in his hands. It might, he thought, be the condemned cell: this was the attitude of despair, the black linoleum-covered floor and white distempered walls were the colours of despair. He'd suggested once to his mother that it wouldn't cost much to paper the place in some bright and frivolous design and to have some less funereal linoleum, but she'd decided against it with a great show of feeling. Patterned wallpaper in cloakrooms was not only common, but decadent. He pulled the chain, knowing that if he didn't there would be at some time within the next few hours a remark made about people who hadn't the grace to greet their mother like Christians but must rush straight into the lavatory without doing anything when they got there. There was no malice behind these remarks, and once he'd hardly noticed them, but since he'd broken it off with Clare they'd been penetratingly humiliating. He washed his hands – there might be another remark if she didn't hear the sound of running water – and went into the kitchen.

She didn't turn away from the stove as he came in, but her already stiff back seemed to stiffen still further. "Where in God's name have you been, Vincent?" she asked. "I was on the point of phoning the police."

"I called in to Grandma's," he said. "You asked me to."

"That wouldn't take you five minutes." She pushed a strand of grey hair away from her face. "I expect she was telling you about her wonderful family and all the hard times she had. Ah, she'll bury us all, that one."

"She was talking about Harry Bandon, actually. The old man."

"That cunning devil," she said. "I'd have thought it'd be his son she'd be talking about." She opened the oven. "This pie will have to do you. I'll be late for the PTA meeting if I don't get a move on. It's more than you'd get if you were married to Delia if that's what the black look on your face implies."

"You're being silly, Mother." He began to eat with no appetite; the pie-crust was tough and the peas and potatoes dried and hard.

"Don't think her being your first cousin makes any difference. Though to my mind it's next door to incest. The one she's engaged to is no great catch, for all his money."

"He seems a decent enough little man," Vincent said indifferently.

She ruffled his hair; the quick gesture was more like a cuff than a caress. "A decent enough little man," she said fondly. "It might be your Grandfather Rosslea speaking. Ah, he had the measure of them all."

She smiled, her face becoming perceptibly less sybilline, even the eyes seeming to widen and become more vivid blue. At fifty-five she had the figure of a woman in her forties, her skin had never become withered or leathery, it had always been creamily smooth; her grey hair, which had come almost overnight after his father's death, had made no difference, except perhaps to accentuate this quality of youthfulness.

"You're a disgusting old snob," Vincent said, laughing. "Is there anyone whom you don't consider common and low?"

"Not in Charbury," his mother said. She looked at the plate he had pushed away. "You've not eaten much."

"I don't like eating in the kitchen," he said. He had meant to be facetious but found himself sounding petulant. "A man of my standing eats in the dining-room."

"There's not time," his mother said. "You know how much I dislike being late. Though sometimes it seems I'm the only one who feels like that."

"I'll run you down into the village," he said.

"Don't bother yourself. Mrs Travers is picking me up. Her husband's bought her a car for herself and she's killed showing it off."

"I hope she's not," Vincent said.

"Don't be always picking me up," she said sharply. "You know full well what I mean. Are you going out yourself tonight?"

"I don't know," he said. "I might go over to Matthew's."

"You'll not find him at home tonight. He's off drinking. It's some fool's bachelor night. Maureen 'phoned me today."

Vincent for a moment had a feeling of being excluded, of being shut out of the shouting boisterous male world. "It's just as well you told me," he said. "I don't feel in the mood for that sort of thing."

"I hope you never do," she said. "Matthew's growing a deal too fond of it."

"You're exaggerating, Mother. Matty has to entertain a lot of people – "

"You'll always stick up for him. You always did. Even when you were quite little, Matty could do no wrong."

"He's my brother."

"Your elder brother. But you're the one who looks after him. You've been making excuses for him all your life. You'd do better to tell him the error of his ways."

"His drinking's his own problem," Vincent said. "If it is all that much of a problem. It isn't my business."

Her face assumed an expression which Vincent had a shrewd notion was meant to be both tragic and sardonic, the woman of the world who was acquainted with all human weakness. "It isn't my business," she said, her voice deepening to a throaty contralto. "It isn't my business. And the Lord said unto Cain. Where is Abel thy brother? and he said, I know not: Am I my brother's keeper?"

"Mother, you're wasted as a teacher. There's a great career ahead of you on the stage. I haven't murdered Matthew, you know. That's what the Lord was asking Cain about, in case you've forgotten."

"I forget nothing. That's what your Grandfather Rosslea always said. We forgive, he said, but we never forget." She snatched Vincent's plate and knife and fork and teacup and saucer away and put them in the sink. "Are you going out tonight?"

"I don't know, Mother." Looking at her as she washed up, her movements quick and ferocious and impatient, he felt an enormous fatigue; it was as if her energy were rightfully his, had in fact somehow been stolen from him as soon as he entered the house.

"I don't know," she repeated derisively. "The last refuge of the illiterate. I hear it a hundred times a day at school. You please yourself, my son. But if you go out after I do, please remember just once, just once, I entreat you, to leave the light and the TV turned on. It's the one sure way to frighten off burglars. And for God's sake don't forget the fire-guard – "

He held up his hand

"All right, all right, I'm not a child."

He realized his mistake as soon as he had uttered the words; she looked at him with a brooding tenderness which distressed him more than anger would have done. "Not a child. You're a clever man, but how little you know. You'll be my child until the day I die. Or the day you marry – "

He stood up. He had heard all too often what came next, of how she was only too glad to see her sons married, of how she would never dream of interfering once they were married, of how in any case she would be absolutely powerless to interfere if Vincent's bride were the only true bride for him, the Church; this evening he wouldn't be able to bear it, he could neither cover his face up with his toga and endure the blows nor summon up the energy to fight them. He pushed back his chair, knocking the new vegetable rack over as he did so. Since his father's death the kitchen had been twice redecorated and a great deal of shiny new equipment had been acquired; it was now almost impossible to move unimpeded in any direction and, whenever there was the slightest awkwardness between his mother and himself, all the equipment – vegetable rack, electrical tin-opener, washing-machine, food-mixer, refrigerator, wall-heater, and even the electric kettle seemed to be ranged on his mother's side against him, hard and tangible little enemies. "I'm going out after all," he said.

"You might pick up the vegetable rack," she said. "And those onions. Where are you going?"

"I've no idea," he said, kneeling to pick up the vegetables.

"I have," she said. She elbowed him aside. "Get up, you look ridiculous. You're phoning Clare, you're begging her to have you back. That's what my clever son is about to do. Aren't I right?"

"What if I do phone her?"

"You'll be wasting your time. She's keeping company with Frank Rooley now."

"It'll not be Frank Rooley. She can't bear him."

"That's what she's told you, is it?" His mother's smile was now genuinely sardonic.

"She's told me many a time. Not that I care. Because I'm not phoning her."

"My poor silly son, a girl only mentions a man because she's interested in him. If she really couldn't bear Frank Rooley, his name would never have passed her lips."

"You're very acute," Vincent said. "But I'm not in the least concerned about Clare." The rain was driving hard against the window now; he had the sensation of waiting for something, alone in the outpost checking his ammunition and rations over and over again.

"You're well shut of her," his mother said. "Mind you, God help her taste if it's Frank Rooley she prefers to you."

"If it is Frank, he's a far better bet than me," Vincent said. "He'll die a damned sight richer than I will. I've not seen Clare for over a month now. She'll not sit at home weeping for me, I'm well aware. We weren't suited and that's all there is to say."

"There's nothing but sorrow for you with any girl," his mother said. "I told you a long time ago, you'll not find your bride on this earth. And you know it yourself if you look in your heart."

"I've been into all this before," he said. "I'll decide it myself, Mother. For God's sake stop dramatizing the issue. I've not yet met anyone I want to marry and I don't want to be a priest either."

"Thirty years old," she said. "And not married. And not a priest. So what are you doing? You're making a cheap wife of some poor girl, that's what it is. If it's not that Clare any more, it's someone else. Don't you imagine I won't find out either."

"There's no one," he said wearily. "I almost wish there were." He opened the kitchen door.

She followed him out into the hall. "Swear on the cross there," she said, pointing to the big wooden crucifix hanging over the front door. "Kneel, Vincent, and swear you're not keeping a woman somewhere. I'll believe you then, and not until then."

"You're being utterly ridiculous," he said. "If anyone saw me doing a thing like that they'd think I'd gone out of my head. Goodbye, and God give you more sense."

For a second it seemed as if the hall were as big and dark as once it had seemed in childhood and that his feet, as they had often seemed to do in childhood dreams – and for that matter would perhaps seem to in his dreams tonight – were fastened to the black and red flowered tiles of the floor.

Once outside and in the car the scene was unreal to him, even something to be shrugged off, something to tell Matthew and Maureen. His mother had been in splendid form this evening, but he'd given her as good as he'd got. There was nothing to be done when she was in one of her moods except to endure it; it wouldn't last very long. As he went past the War Memorial, glancing as usual to the left in case anyone on the side road didn't know that he was on a side road, he recognized Mrs Travers at the wheel of her red Mini. Mrs Travers would see his mother's other face, sane and sensible and gently smiling: to everyone except her family Mrs Dungarvan was the widow who had made such a good adjustment to widowhood, who had lived for her fatherless boys but who had let them go without fuss when the time came for them to marry; and if Vincent hadn't married that had been entirely his own choice. Vincent had a vocation, if the truth were to be known; but Vincent, like his father, was obstinate. He was fighting against his destiny. Sooner or later

Vincent would have to give in, sooner or later, she sometimes liked to think, Vincent would acknowledge the known truth, and the Hound of Heaven would catch up with him.

On the Beckfield Moor road the loneliness began; as the headlights shovelled away the darkness, seeming to pile it up like heaps of earth to the left and the right, he tried unavailingly to extract some pleasure from the prospect of an evening out in the city, of his possession of a car, money in his pocket, and freedom from all ties; but as he passed the parked cars and came towards the lights of the dual carriage-way he knew that the journey would be the best part of the outing, that when he arrived in Charbury there would be no alternative to the cinema, the three hours of moving shadows and theme songs as sticky as melted chocolate. Clare had been silly and at times boring, in ten years if not sooner she would run to fat, she referred to magazines as books, she laughed too loudly and used too much cheap scent; she went to Mass every Sunday, but with no real understanding of what was happening, of God in the wafer, of God in the wine; religion, like politics, like books, like music, had not been a subject of conversation between them. She would never have been more than a body to him, there would have been at best a simple animal affection between them; as tirelessly and as mechanically as the windscreen wipers, as the car itself, he discovered reason after reason for being, as the phrase went, well shut of her; by the time he had reached the Odeon and had noted, with a lightening of the spirit, the thirty-foot-high poster of Marilyn Monroe holding, or rather failing to hold her skirts down, he had almost persuaded himself that he was happy. He stopped for a moment at the stills outside the entrance; as he looked at the perfect face, a face dazzled by its own perfection and distraught with distrust of that very perfection, he remembered the first time he had seen the film. That had been five years ago and he had gone to see it alone then. He had seemed to himself then somehow different from the other lonely ones, the bachelors and spinsters whose faces were tight with the struggle to appear self-sufficient, who would never sit next to anyone else if they could help it, who held themselves stiffly so as not to touch anyone else, who never dared look to the left or the right for fear of being misunderstood and who, every last lost one of them, went into the darkness to dream, to relax as far as they were able: *a mess of shadows for their meat.*

As he paid for his seat he was suddenly ashamed of being alone, certain that he detected a contemptuous pity on the face of the girl in the box-office, the girls in the sweet kiosk, the girls at the-hot-dog stand; it seemed a long way to the sheltering darkness of the auditorium.

Two

"I'm sorry, Vince, but I have to wash my hair." Clare's voice was, as usual, transformed by the telephone; soft and intimate, it encouraged him to press her further.

"Tomorrow, then," he said. "I'd love to see you. There's a new night club opening in Harrogate – "

"My God," she said, "what next? But I can't, darling. Because you've just hit upon my very worst week. I'm frantically busy, you really shouldn't have *vanished* from human ken for such an *eternity…*"

It was the note of dismissal, made no more palatable by the special telephone voice and the outdated idiom; Vincent listened gloomily to her voice, now trilling, now cooing, and finally said goodbye, conscious of having lost face, of having achieved no more than to inform her that he was still on the hook.

There was a slight but unmistakable smell of urine in the telephone kiosk and the grubby directory had lost its cover. Vincent propped the door ajar with his foot, letting in the cold night air and the smell of wet grass. There was not one light showing at any of the dozen houses which comprised the hamlet; from somewhere in the yard of the farm across the road, a dog barked loudly then stopped as if intimidated by the silence around it. This was the last stretch of arable land until Sarnley, five miles farther north. The moors could not be seen from here, nor the hills beyond them; but they existed, he wanted to possess them, he wanted somehow to match himself against them, walking through the night; if he took the path through Battle Woods, two miles down the road, his feet need never touch tarmac until he reached Sarnley. Loneliness wouldn't matter, loneliness being a word that had no meaning on the moors where even the cairns which marked the path seemed to have no connection with human beings.

As he picked up the telephone to call Matthew he was still toying with the idea; and then as he felt the coldness of the concrete floor strike through his thin shoes, he knew that he wouldn't go anywhere that evening except on four wheels. And, he realized as he talked to Matthew, a solitary walk taking at least three hours wouldn't have been what he needed; last night had been enough and more than enough, and then at least he'd been assured of some sort of escape from himself even if only with the shadow of a dead woman.

"I'll be there in a quarter of an hour," he said to Matthew finally. "Be good, then."

"I've no bloody option," Matthew said. "Take care of yourself, boy. They haven't done any repairs to that road since the Romans left."

As he started the car Vincent was surprised to find himself looking forward to the evening; the area in which he and Matthew could meet was almost daily diminishing, their relationship was kept alive because of shared memories and force of habit rather than common interests, but there was a warmth about Matthew that shone through his words, that made even his laboured witticisms touching; it was like a dog bringing one a dead mouse, it was the intention which counted.

So now the quietness around him, the small loneliness of Battle Woods and the bigger loneliness of the moors, dark now in the moonlight, were nothing to be afraid of, the journey had a purpose. When he looked at Battle Woods he was able, for the first time in years, to think about the battle which, if the stories were true, had given the woods their name some nineteen hundred years ago; he pulled in by the side of the road for a moment and stared up the hillside, trying to visualize the first rush of the Brigantes on to the Roman trenches, the wild yells and the trumpets, attack after attack breaking upon the front line, twelve hundred javelins thrown as one, the air turned silver; and then the sudden parting of the front line, the regathering of the Brigantes, their last charge, the closing in of the second and third Roman lines, their shields locked together; defeat slowly tightening its grip. On that patch of ground in daylight it was a deeper green; but that was what was always said about old battlefields.

He pulled down the window and took a deep breath; it was as if he were assimilating the trees, the steep hillside sweeping up to the moors, the undulating hills against the skyline, the grey tatters of cloud over the new moon, the sense of winter coming and the sense of remoteness, of departure from human concerns. Now that the engine had stopped, he could hear the sounds of the woods, the faint rustlings, the creaking of branches in the breeze, an owl hooting far away, then nearer and louder and longer, and then what might have been the scream of some small animal; there was violence here and pain and terror but without fuss, it was as beautiful in its way as the Roman encirclement of the Brigantes must have been.

Then there was the sound of a woman's voice and a man's voice answering, rough and pleading; Vincent frowned and turned the ignition key. It was all out of tune now, he thought savagely, the real animals are here, the worst animals, the destroying and fouling animals, the animals with neither the intelligence to understand nor the instinct to act completely and with grace; he drove off, surprised at the intensity of his hatred for the unknown couple who, he saw in his mirror, were now disappearing into the woods by the same stile that he and Clare had used a month ago.

He turned to the right into the Sarnley road which ran ruler-straight for ten miles. It had been made by the Romans but the settlement of Sarnum with which it connected hadn't been in existence for very long before it had been overrun from the

North. The legions had left Britain, but they hadn't bothered to tell the garrison at Sarnum or, what was more likely, their communication system had broken down. Translation: the courier would have been killed, because there wouldn't have been the men to spare for an escort. The road wouldn't have changed much in fifteen hundred years, except to get a line of cat's-eyes and a layer of tarmac; and the moors which bordered the road still belonged to the sheep and the curlews rather than to any human being. It didn't take a great effort of the inward eye to see over the next rise the glimmer of Roman helmets under the new moon: when he and Matthew and Paul had come here as boys that had been exactly what they'd always hoped for; though Paul had once pointed out that only officers wore metal helmets in the Roman army. Matthew had lost his temper and accused Paul of always spoiling things; but it was Paul's nature to be precise, just as it was his own nature to be dreamy. And Matthew's too: for him all the soldiers would have shiny helmets and all the horses would be white Arabians. If it came to that, he could only have chosen Sarnley to live in because of their boyhood cult of all things Roman; property values were sky-high there, and it was a fifteen-mile drive to Silvington Mills.

A big car came suddenly out from the left and turned to the right, lurching over on its springs, trailing behind it the sound of music like tinsel on the black and silver silence of the moors. Vincent breathed sharply and blew his horn; this was commuter country, dotted with dream houses and weekend cottages and every year the cars grew bigger and the driving more lunatic.

He put the car into second gear as he came to the top of Battlement Hill; here the road became narrow and winding as it veered to the left towards the town; the Roman road continued towards the site of the fort and then across the moors to join the road at Blackstone Edge. There was nothing to be seen now except from the air; the Sarnley Urban District Council wasn't interested in the past. But it was something to know that it once had been there, that there had been helmets, metal or leather, that there'd been some link with a wider world.

There was still room for research, there were still discoveries to be made about the Romans in Britain; by the time he had reached Matthew's house, he had done all the research and made all the discoveries and, not very much older, had accepted a fellowship at All Souls and a title. Sir Vincent would do to begin with; later on Lord Beckfield.

When the housing estate where Matthew lived had been built, just before the war, it had been something of a sensation, the first of its kind in Sarnley. The concrete was blotched with damp now, the flat roofs gave the impression merely of the houses not being finished; the war had prevented the roads from being made up, and when eventually they were each resident's share of the cost would be at the very least in three figures. Matthew's house wasn't one of the most expensive houses in Sarnley and its value hadn't gone up as much as others in the district; but it was more than Matthew could afford. There was more than one kind of dream, Vincent thought complacently: his own dreams cost nothing.

He pressed the bell-push which once had been luminous and, almost immediately, his sister-in-law opened the door. She was wearing a tight red dress which he hadn't noticed her wearing before; something about the way that she stood, one hand on her hip, reminded him of Clare. The dress, he could see now that his eyes had grown accustomed to the light, was close-fitting because of many washings: it would be what women described as *that* old thing, and if he expressed his admiration of her appearance, she'd suspect him of being ironical. Her blonde hair, too, was dishevelled, and streaky where the tint had worn off; he couldn't admire that either but suddenly, shockingly, he wanted to touch it, she was a woman whom he could imagine undressing, going to bed, she was a woman just as Clare was a woman, she was a woman whom he'd known before her marriage, whom he'd never taken out but who, he was certain now, wouldn't have said no to him.

"Hello, Vince," she said. "Tell me you've come just to see me even if it's a rotten lie. I feel like something the cat's brought in."

This flirtatiousness was invariable; this evening, remembering what had, after all, been a downright rejection by Clare, it was difficult for him to answer in a similar vein.

"You look absolutely entrancing," he said, aware of not sounding particularly convincing. "Of course I've come to see you. It would be impossible for me to keep away from you."

"Liar," she said. "You've not been near us for months." She smiled. "How's Clare?"

"I haven't seen her lately."

"How sad," she said still smiling. From upstairs there was the sound of splashing and children screaming.

"Oh my God," she said, "they're drowning the poor child." She ran upstairs. One of her slippers came off and fell at Vincent's feet; he picked it up and took it into the lounge where Matthew was watching television.

"You're late Vince. Drinking time is slipping away." He turned the volume control down, his eyes still on the blonde in the low-cut dress leaning forwards towards an old man who seemed more frightened than pleased. "It's best like this," he said. "I make the dialogue up. Grandad, she's saying, don't you wish you could manage it? Don't you wish you were a fine man like Matthew Dungarvan?"

A man in an evening suit, smiling broadly, suddenly replaced the blonde. Matthew yawned and turned the set off sharply. "Bloody rubbish," he said. He lit a cigarette and almost immediately began to cough. "The damned things are killing me, you don't know how lucky you are, Vince. You look fitter every time I see you, by God you do."

"I'm younger," Vincent said.

"Six years. I feel as if it were sixty." He ran his hand through his hair. "I found a bald patch today. Or rather my dear boss Larry Silvington did." He mimicked effeminacy. "My dear, you're moulting. Positively moulting. You used to have such nice thick ebony tresses."

"I can't see anything," Vincent said. But as he said it he saw the small white patch on the crown of the head; he saw too the way in which his brother's features had begun to be blurred with fat.

"Larry can," Matthew said. "My dear, dear boss Larry is *very* sharp. He has every last detail off pat. Mind you, he's like them all, crying poverty. Told me he'd been to an auction in Bradford – they were selling off a lot of machinery, old stuff. If I'd had forty thousand in cash, he said to me, I'd have bought that machinery, run it twenty-four hours a day for two years, and then I'd retire and live in the Bahamas." Matthew inhaled deeply and coughed again, even more rackingly. "Larry, I said to him, if I had forty thousand in cash I'd retire and live in the Bahamas."

"So would I." Vincent sat down. The fire was very hot: it seemed to bring out a great many smells. Tobacco, talcum, dust, bacon, and most strongly of all, woman's hair. The chair he was sitting on must be Maureen's chair. He pushed it away from the fire and then found his buttock encounter something sharp. He reached down and picked up a heavy metal bracelet. "So would I," he repeated. "You've nothing to complain about."

"You wouldn't," Matthew said. "You'd go on teaching. You'd even go on at St Theo's. You like your job. I don't like mine. It's a way of earning a living, that's all. You'll not get very far in the wool trade if you're a Mick, either."

"You'll have to turn Methodist," Vincent said.

"Maureen wouldn't wear it. Besides everyone would know why you'd done it. And even if they thought you were absolutely sincere, it still wouldn't change your name and you'd still have the same father."

Vincent laughed. "You'd still have the same face too." At the moment Matthew looked the stage Irishman to the life; emotion seemed to elongate his long upper lip and to redden the tiptilted nose.

"It's all right for you," Matthew said. "You'd pass for an Englishman or anyway a Jew with that big conk of yours."

Maureen came into the room dragging her right foot. "Who's got my slipper?"

Vincent held it up. She bent down and put it on, using his shoulder to support herself.

"You'd forget your head if it were loose," Matthew said. "Last Saturday she went to the Old Boys' Dance without her pants. She forgot the bloody things. It's a wonder she remembers to dress."

Vincent fixed his gaze above the fireplace. He had a feeling of physical sickness; he could hardly believe that Matthew wasn't deliberately trying to provoke him. How did Matthew know, unless after the dance she'd thrown off her dress in one movement – she would surely undress like that, impetuously – how would he be so certain unless he'd looked? He forced himself to speak.

"Have the children settled down?"

"Eileen's settled down," Maureen said. "She sets them all off. But it's just the last flare-up, she plays the devil for ten minutes and then she goes out like a light. I haven't told her you're here, otherwise she'd find the energy to stay up an hour longer and she'd be going around all day tomorrow like a little ghost."

Matthew's fingers began to drum on the chair-arm. "How about a drink, Vince?"

"For God's sake, he's not been here five minutes," Maureen said. "It's always the same, he comes to see us, you sit there hardly able to contain yourself, and then you drag him out for a drink. Didn't you get enough at your bloody hotel lunch?"

"I lunched with a Methodist. He didn't drink so neither did I. Do you take me for an alcoholic?"

Matthew had always lost his temper quickly and as quickly regained it; but there was something about his face now which disquieted Vincent. His anger was reddening his face alarmingly, a vein was swelling on his forehead; he was not so much losing

31

his temper as being lost by it, the red face, the beautifully polished brown shoes, the grey and brown and lovat green checked suit with each colour seeming to carry overtones of the other colours, all seeming to be involved in his bad temper too.

"Vincent would rather have a cup of tea," Maureen said. "He's got ten times as much sense as you."

"Don't tell Vincent what he would rather have," Matthew said. "Or me, either. Jesus God, I've spent the whole bloody day working my guts out for bloody Larry Silvington, I didn't even have a break at lunchtime, looking at Whernside's sour face watching every bloody word – he'd steal the shirt off your back that one, and then cry like a baby because he'd not stolen your vest too. Am I not to have any relaxation?"

"I haven't heard that Larry Silvington drinks very much," Maureen said.

"He isn't married," Matthew said, his good humour returning. "He doesn't need to. Besides, I want to talk to Vincent."

"You can talk to him here. If I disturb you there's another room."

"You'd have to light a fire," Matthew said.

She shrugged. "Do as you like then. But you'd better take the key, because I'm not waiting up for you till all hours."

"I could get some beer at the off-licence," Vincent said. Despite the shabbiness of the room, with its shabby slab-sided blue three-piece suite and grey carpet upon which hard wear had imposed what always seemed at first sight to be a pattern of black, he felt comfortable in this room; even the litter, left by three children – the musical rattle, the rag doll, the four Dinky Cars all without tyres – even the grubby imprints of hands upon the pink flowered wallpaper, didn't detract from the feeling of being in the proper place, of being somehow both protected and protecting. The sudden fit of desire had vanished now; but he still didn't want to leave Maureen. She was once again his brother's wife but she was also a woman, he was glad to be with her, to listen to her, to look at her, to enjoy without the sense of sin her actual presence, the laddered stocking and the pink fluffy slippers and the round face which should have been bold and brassy to have matched the tinted hair but which was always soft and responsive and open as a child's.

"They don't have off-licences in this town," Matthew said. "Too bloody low. Anyway, I don't like bottled beer. We'll bring Maureen back a Babycham if she's good." He levered himself out of his chair and put his hand to the small of his back. "I've got rheumatism, I shouldn't wonder," he said, and pecked Maureen's cheek. "I won't be late back, love."

"So you always say."

"Don't worry," Vincent said. "We'll go in my car." He smiled at her. "If I were him, wild horses wouldn't drag me away from you," he said.

She squeezed his hand. "You're the only one who says nice things to me."

Matthew, already at the door, laughed. "That's because he's not married to you."

Maureen switched on the television. "It'll be a lucky girl that marries Vince," she said.

Vincent looked at her, startled; the gaiety and friendliness had left her face. When she returned his look her face was set in a frown; it was almost as if she hated him, the tone was as if she were ordering him out of the house.

As they went down the short concrete path which the estate agent had once described as a broad sweeping drive Vincent had the feeling of deserting more than Maureen; it was as if the house itself needed him in order not to crumble away in the rain, as if in the tiny front garden beside the drive, without his presence, no flowers would ever grow again. But, he reflected, the whole estate, perched as it was on the hillside with the moors surrounding it, had an air of impermanence; it was like a military camp on the eve of a battle which everyone knew they couldn't win.

"It's not very cheerful," Matthew said, echoing Vincent's thoughts. He levered himself into the Austin, swearing as his knee hit the dashboard. "Why on earth don't you get a decent-sized car, Vince?"

"It suits me," Vincent said.

"If I were a bachelor I'd get something bigger," Matthew said. "You feel every little bump in these damned things. I could get you a lovely Humber Hawk, only two years old, runs like a sewing-machine–"

"No." Vincent slowed down to circumnavigate a pothole. "I hope you're not thinking of it either. Particularly if it belongs to a friend of yours."

"My God, I can only just afford to run the one I've got." Matthew swallowed. "That's really what's on my mind. It's been the hell of a year, Vince. Silvington's pay me a reasonable salary, but it's the commissions I depend upon to put a bit of jam upon my bread."

"What's on your mind exactly?" Vincent knew that his voice was cold, knew too that Matthew was chilled by its coldness but, driving along the rocky and winding roads of the estate to a drink or more than one drink, which he did not want, he was not disposed to make things easier for his brother.

"I was just telling you, everyone in wool doesn't make a fortune. We won the war, you see, and we've still got all the old machinery. The bloody Continentals have had to buy new machinery. So we've missed the boat…"

"They always do in Charbury."

"They're no better in Bradford," Matthew said. He lit a cigarette; Vincent opened the window at his side, letting in a stream of cold air. "Or Halifax. Or Huddersfield."

Vincent glanced at the half-full car park of the pub on his left. "Where would you like to go?"

"Nowhere in this dump," Matthew said. "Let's go to the Hibernian."

"I've just come from Charbury –" Vincent began, then stopped. Ten miles driving would mean twenty minutes less drinking, "All right, if you really want to. But it's pretty dead during the week."

"It makes a change," Matthew said. "God, I remember when Father first took me there. Mother played the devil, but he didn't care. If Matt's going to have a drink, he said, let him have it in decent company. He'll not get robbed nor get a dose at the Hibs. Of course, he didn't use those very words about the dose, but he as good as... I wish we'd never left Charbury."

"You could go back."

"You kidding? Vince, you're a true bachelor. You don't know the first thing about marriage. Let me tell you about Maureen – "

He told Vincent about Maureen for the rest of the journey, his financial worries apparently forgotten; Vincent listened with only half his attention, his mind, despite himself, returning to Clare, to the cool voice on the telephone, to the white flesh in Battle Woods, to the mystery, to the offer and the rejection; it was with relief that he saw they were approaching the Hibernian Club.

The Hibernian Club occupied the first floor of a large Victorian mansion in Cord Street, a stone's throw away from his grandmother's house. Except for the club it was a street in which there was no evidence of life after six in the evening when the offices and consulting-rooms and showrooms had all closed down. No one, least of all the solid professional men for whom it had been built, lived in Cord Street any longer, and within the next two years it would be razed to the ground; the demolition gangs had already arrived in the next street but one and the air was heavy with the smell of stone-dust and old plaster and half-rotten wood. A breeze sprang up as they went into the clubrooms; the smell was stirred up and thickened rather than dispelled. Vincent ran up the stairway ahead of Matthew, his handkerchief to his nose and, as he was running, wondered why he should be so eager.

There would only be the usual people, respectable and responsible Catholics, mainly middle-class. He and Matthew would know most of them by their Christian names and those they didn't know would know them, because they'd be pointed out to them. Or at least Vincent would be pointed out; there was only one Catholic grammar school in Charbury or indeed within a radius of twenty miles, so that if the visitor were a Charbury man Vincent would be to some extent that man's property. *We pay your wages, don't forget,* one visitor had said to him in his cups and though he'd been quickly hushed, he had pretty well summed up the feelings of everyone present.

As he had anticipated, the club was empty except for two middle-aged men standing in silence by the bar; Matthew's expression changed with an almost comical rapidity from gay to lugubrious.

"Where the hell's everyone?" he asked Vincent fiercely, rather as if Vincent had somehow spirited away the large and uproariously convivial company which had been eagerly awaiting his arrival.

"I told you this was the wrong night." One of the four windows overlooking the street still had its red plush curtain undrawn; he endured the lack of symmetry for a moment, then went over to the window. The weighted cord which operated the curtain wasn't functioning; he went back to Matthew feeling more irritated than was reasonable. In his father's time, he thought, there wouldn't have been any curtains that couldn't be drawn or any unsteady tables or worn carpeting or unpolished brass; the club was going down hill along with the neighbourhood. He had the feeling this evening of being forgotten, of being not properly maintained, of being good for fifty years with care but not receiving that care; he went over to the window again and tugged harder at the cord but could not make it move. There seemed to be a great many people standing about in the street and the Pakistani grocery was still open. Even the moon was different here; the wind blew black smoke over it so steadily that one never expected it to be clean again.

"What the hell are you staring at, Vince?" Matthew asked. "There's nothing in Emmett Street but blacks and nothing in Cord Street but offices." He joined Vincent at the window. "Don't tell me you fancy a bit of black stuff, Vince. You might get your throat cut –"

"Don't be disgusting," Vincent said sharply. In the harsh glare of the overhead light his brother's face seemed even fatter, more tired, as blotchy as the distempered walls; he laughed, and his teeth, though still strong and unblemished, were yellow rather than white.

"You're human too, Vince, what's disgusting about that?"

The door opened; Matthew looked at it hungrily as if, Vincent thought, expecting to see a noisy influx of drinking companions, perhaps even the companions of his bachelor days. Matthew pouted childishly with disappointment. "It's only Tom Ardrahan," he said. "Set your watches. It's eight-thirty precisely."

They watched Tom Ardrahan slowly walk over to his seat in the far corner, slowly take off his hat and overcoat, slowly sit down, and then waited for him to tap the floor with his walking-stick. Jack Herning, the barman, was already drawing the pint of bitter almost before the walking-stick touched the floor. He carried the drink over; Tom Ardrahan inspected it in silence then pushed half a crown over the table. Jack Herning fumbled in the pocket of his white jacket. Tom Ardrahan's face grew scornful as once it had when faced with Vincent's limping excuses for scamped homework; slowly and tremblingly his hand outlined the gesture of rejection and Jack Herning said loudly: "Thank you very much, Mr Ardrahan."

"The ritual's over," Vincent said. "The night he doesn't come here he'll be dead. Or the bomb will have dropped."

"Forty years he's been coming here. I don't suppose I shall." He nodded at Tom Ardrahan, who returned the nod after a pause, the pale blue eyes puzzled and suspicious.

"Let's sit down, Vince. I'm shagged out." He glanced at Tom Ardrahan again as they sat down at the table nearest the bar. "He'll make old bones, will Boots. A salary cheque every month when he was teaching and two thirds when he retired… A pint of bitter, Vincent, since you're so eager for me to have one."

When Vincent brought back the drinks, Matthew emptied half the glass at one pull. "That's better," he said. Vincent saw that his face seemed almost instantly to have grown more even in colour, smoother and healthier; it was as if wax had been injected under the skin by a plastic surgeon, a miraculous transformation had taken place; Vincent, his own drink still untouched, almost envied him. He took a mouthful of his own drink; and as always with the first taste remembered his disappointment at its bitterness when as a child he'd surreptitiously drunk from his father's glass. He looked at the faded photograph of James Connolly over the bar, side by side with Michael Collins and De Valera; there had been trouble about the display of each of the pictures once, but no one cared now, and the majority of the members wouldn't even know who Connolly and Collins were.

"The Hibernian's not what it used to be," he said.

"They go to the Knights or the Irish Club," Matthew said. "As my Da used to say, God rest his soul – " the brogue was half-unconscious, half in jest – "the blackbeetles never liked the Hib. The coppers did. They knew where to find the IRA men."

"That's a long time ago," Vincent said, wondering why it was that the Romans had always seemed more real to him than the IRA and the Free State, why even the still living De Valera seemed dead in a way the indisputably dead Caesar wasn't; Matthew's eyes were alive with interest now and he himself could only summon up whatever patience he possessed to wait for closing time which, he thought glumly, was always an elastic hour at the Hibernian.

Matthew finished his drink. "I needed that," he said. "I told you, Vincent, I had lunch with old Whernside today and he won't do business with anyone who smells of drink." He held up two fingers to Jack Herning. Vincent shook his head and Herning brought over one pint.

"Did you do any business with him?" Vincent asked.

"No. I paid for the bastard's lunch, though. It hasn't been my day." He glanced at Vincent's half-pint. "Are you sure you won't have another?"

"You know I don't like it very much."

I wish to God I didn't, Vince. It shook me today, seeing that old sod. Seventy-five, and he doesn't walk, he runs. Skin like a baby's, straight back, and he's a damned sight sharper than me. Mind you, he's a nasty old pig and it's time he was dead, but it makes you think. He kept needling me too. Asking me how much I weighed and how old my father was when he died."

"You'd think he'd have known," Vincent said.

"Of course he knew, the old burk. Of course he knew. But he wanted to hear me say that he was only fifty-one and he died of a heart attack."

"Father died because he'd worked too hard all his life," Vincent said sharply. "He wasn't a drinker."

"No, he certainly wasn't a drinker." Matthew smiled. "What exactly are you driving at?"

"Nothing. I'm agreeing with you. Don't I always?"

The smile had disappeared but there was an expression on Matthew's face which, if Vincent had been his superior officer, he'd have called dumb insolence. It was Vincent's own face, six years older, fleshier, redder, the blue eyes bloodshot, the archetypal Mick.

"He was my father, too," Matthew said. "I'm not saying anything wrong about him. He's been in his grave for ten years now, so let him rest. You never cared about him all that much, anyway. He was too bloody vulgar, like me. He worked night and day when he was young. He'd take on any job to earn something extra and he'd give it all to Mother. I've seen him pour it into her lap in new half-crowns and he's never got so much as a flicker of a smile from her. I think she was pleased when he became the manager at Silvington's but she wasn't pleased enough. Christ, he was about the only Catholic in the wool trade who was anything more than an overseer. You didn't notice; did you, Vince? You take after her side of the family, you're like dear Father Cyril and dear Aunty Felicity and dear Doctor Hubert who's always inviting us to his house in Berkshire when he's not quite so frantically busy. Hubert – I wouldn't call a bloody bike Hubert. You wouldn't notice whether your father was happy or not, would you?"

His speech was becoming more and more blurred, his gestures more sweeping; Vincent, remembering his capacity, looked at him in suspicion. "You've had something to drink before you came out." Matthew shook his head: the movement was so jerky and exaggerated that he seemed to have difficulty stopping it. "First today. Absolutely – my first... Get me another, you mean old sod."

"If you must," Vincent said. He suddenly felt enormously dejected. He went to the bar, glad to be away from his brother if only for a moment.

"A pint of bitter, please," he said to Jack Herning.

"You hardly need to tell me. Aren't you having anything yourself?"

"No. You have one though."

"You're like your father," Jack Herning said. The pale ageless face with the white hair combed forward in an Edwardian quiff briefly indicated approval. "Matt's got something on his mind, hasn't he?"

"He'll not make it any better here," Vincent said. When he returned to the table Matthew had slumped back in his chair, his eyes half-closed.

"I'm sorry, Vince. You know I'm sorry." His eyes opened but seemed to have trouble in focusing. "You're the best of the bloody lot. Better than Paul. Do you know he wrote me a letter? Said I had to pull myself together. Wonder he didn't charge me six and eightpence for the good advice. He phoned, too. Said he was worried. Isn't that splendid? Paul's worried."

"I'm not," Vincent said. "You're big enough and ugly enough to manage your own life. You're not in trouble with the bookies, are you?"

"Never mind," Matthew said. He hiccuped. "Never mind. I'll manage, as you say, I've always managed. I don't need any help from anyone."

"For God's sake have a bit of sense. What the devil did you drag me out tonight for if you didn't want help?"

"I thought I did."

He went over to the bar and came back with a glass of rum. "I thought I did. But there isn't anything you can do. That bloody old Whernside got under my skin, you see."

"Pull yourself together," Vincent said impatiently. "Why should you care what that old fool said?"

"Paul's words, Paul's very words. You're enjoying yourself, aren't you? They always said you should be the elder brother. You're the clever one, you see. And you're the one who keeps sober. You've more sense than to get married, haven't you? You don't have any wife to nag you, you don't have any kids to worry about."

"It's about time you went home," Vincent said wearily.

"Go home? Go home to be played hell with? Jesus God, do you know what it's like? I go home with a smile on my face and Maureen wipes it off. Listen, I'll tell you what she said to me tonight. Don't bother to come back, she said, don't bother to come back..."

Vincent stifled a yawn as his brother's voice, perceptibly thickening with each mouthful of drink, continued in a monotone that at times became totally incoherent. At a quarter to ten he rose and tapped Matthew on the shoulder. "It really is time to go," he said.

"It always is. When you're in bed it's always time to get up, and when you're up it's always time to go to bed. She's a good girl, though, is Maureen. If I lost my job tomorrow, she wouldn't give a damn. She'd go out to work. She'd love that. Yes, she would." He turned his head to look at the large picture of the Pope. "That's the Holy Father, Vincent," he said. "He won't go home to be played hell with. He'll have a bit of respect." He took out his packet of cigarettes. "Empty," he said. "I was going to give up when I'd smoked these." He went over to the bar and returned with a pint and a new packet of cigarettes. "Maureen's very demanding, you see. Did you know that, Vincent? How could you? If I do tonight, I'm a drunken monster. A sex-maniac. If I don't I'm a bloody eunuch and I don't love her anymore."

"You'll be sorry tomorrow," Vincent said.

"I always am. I always am. Vincent, I've not eaten breakfast for the past three years." He inhaled deeply then coughed. "I'm going to give up," he said when he had recovered. "I'm going to give up. Vincent, I'm going to ask you a favour. It's been on my mind for a bit now – " He stopped and scratched his head. The black hair was lifeless and greasy. He shook his head in irritation. "Dandruff now," he said. "I've got a horrible cough and there's a boil on the back of my neck and I can't keep anything down. If I were a dog they'd destroy me. Where was I?"

"You were going to ask me a favour," Vincent said.

"You know where you can put your bloody favour. And you can take that smug smile off your face, you creep. Mummy's boy, that's what you are. You never notice anything, do you?"

"It's time to go home," Vincent said.

Matthew did not answer but stared over Vincent's shoulder, his fist clenched. There were beads of sweat on his forehead and the black tufts of hair high on his cheekbones seemed as if stuck on with spirit gum

"Rooley" he said. "Frank Rooley. Rooley-Dooley, the big man. The bookie of the bloody year. And your girl."

Vincent turned to see Frank Rooley and Clare; there was a moment of blind rage as he observed the way in which she looked at Rooley, her hand on the sleeve of his jacket, her face lit up in a

42

way it had never been for Vincent; then he saw merely a dark-haired rather plump girl in a bright red coat and a white fur hat and a tall man with a loud voice and a fawn corduroy motoring jacket and fawn whipcord slacks and dark brown ponyskin shoes so richly glitteringly hairy that they seemed to cover hooves rather than feet.

"Hello, Frank," he said and took the outstretched hand. "Hello, Clare. What are you doing in this part of the world?"

"Just been to the flicks," Frank Rooley said. Clare grinned impudently at Vincent; he remembered their phone conversation and was divided between anger and admiration. She was so enormously pleased with herself that he couldn't help but like her; and once that particular feeling, cool and friendly and not far from paternal, entered into it, there wouldn't be any jealousy. Matthew was glowering, his fist still clenched.

"Have a drink with me," Frank Rooley said. "It's not often we meet. You're not a gambling man, are you, Vincent?"

Looking at him intently Vincent was maliciously pleased to discover that when Frank Rooley smiled there was at each corner of his lower lip a glint of metal and that there was a slight variation in the colour of the centre teeth in the upper lip. The realization that he had not only a partial denture but caps on his teeth made him seem for a moment more human, even capable of failure.

"I'm just going, Frank," he said.

"Nonsense. And I'm sure Matt could do with another little drink." He punched Matthew playfully in the arm; it was a habit of long standing, and Vincent, remembering from his schooldays how painful those playful punches could be, moved out of range.

Clare opened her coat a little, revealing a white dress; as she did so she diffused her personal aroma, warm, moist, of flowers growing rather than flowers cut; briefly her presence as a woman rippled through the room, jerking even Tom Ardrahan's head in her direction.

"I didn't know you went boozing at the Hib," she said.

"I'd rather have been out with you." He looked at her black hair, piled high in a beehive arrangement. "It's wonderful how quickly your hair's dried."

She laughed delightedly. "Ah, Vincent, it's sweet of you to pretend to be jealous. But you don't really care a rap about poor little me. Do you?"

The impudent grin flashed at him again; he smiled back at her, ruefully acknowledging to himself that what he felt for her was far from being paternal, that he was with every minute becoming more and more jealous of Frank Rooley, who was now engaged in what seemed uncommonly like a heated argument with Matthew.

"All right," he said to Clare. "Perhaps I'm still on the hook. I'll phone you again, if I may–"

He heard Matthew shouting and turned quickly. "Those are bloody pansy shoes." Matthew shouted. "Bloody pansy shoes, why don't you wear a bloody skirt, Mrs Rooley-Dooley?" His fists were flailing but not touching Frank Rooley, whose face had now turned hard and pale and serious. Jack Herning stepped round quickly from behind the bar; his expression was identical with Rooley's, watchful, not angry, even rather sad. Vincent took Matthew's arm. "Sorry about this," he said, his eyes on Frank Rooley. "Come on, Matthew. You don't know what you're saying."

Matthew shook off Vincent's hand. "You bloody well hit him. He took out your girl."

"She's not my girl," Vincent said. "The worst he's done to you is buy you a whisky. Which you've drunk." He took Matthew by the arm, more firmly this time and led him to the door. Matthew's free arm was still flailing ineffectually and he was muttering incoherently; by the time Vincent had put him into the car he had fallen asleep.

When they reached Matthew's house all the lights were off. Vincent held Matthew up as he pressed the doorbell. Under the moonlight the house seemed smaller rather than larger; the white paint on the framework of the glass door and even the glass seemed to be dingier. Matthew muttered something, then slid to his knees, stretching out his arms. His head hit the wall, narrowly avoiding the protruding door-handle. Vincent was helping him to his feet when the door opened.

"Merciful God," Maureen said. "He's bleeding."

"He's all right," Vincent said.

"He's drunk," she said. "You've got him drunk."

"Never mind that. Let's get him inside. He's going to pass out."

One on each side of Matthew they struggled into the lounge. Grunting with the effort, Vincent put him on the sofa and unloosed his collar.

"I ought to slap your face," Maureen said. In a grubby white towelling dressing-gown and with her hair dishevelled she seemed the central figure in some music-hall sketch, the shrewish wife waiting for her errant husband with the rolling-pin not very far away.

"You ought to thank me," Vincent said. "He wanted to fight Frank Rooley." The fire had died down; there was a smell of damp walls and stale tobacco smoke and stale biscuits in the room. There was another smell too, of soap and bath salts and talcum; he tried to keep his eyes on Maureen's face.

"Why would he want to fight Frank Rooley?" she asked. "He doesn't bet with him." She glared at Vincent. "Of course you broke it up. The big man. You're not drunk, are you? You just get your stupid brother drunk – "

She bent over Matthew, who had already begun to snore. "It's only a graze," she said. "I'll boil some water." She took a cigarette from her dressing-gown pocket. "Give me a light, will you, Vince?" The front of her dressing-gown opened a little as she leaned towards him; he felt his face reddening.

"I'm terribly sorry," he said. "About Matthew, I mean."

"Don't worry," she said. "It would have been worse if you hadn't been with him." Her hand was holding together the front of her dressing-gown now. "I'm sorry I lost my temper, Vince."

"He seemed to get drunk so quickly," Vincent said. "It took me by surprise. I asked him to take it easy, but I couldn't stop him – "

"No. Of course drinking doesn't tempt you, does it, Vince? I don't know what does."

"Shall I help you take him upstairs?"

"When he's had some hot tea he'll take himself up. I'd leave him there, but I don't want the children to see him sleeping on the sofa. Eileen's very sharp, and she's just at the age where she tells everyone. Eileen'll take his side. Kids are funny. Michael's not bothered and Kevin's too young to bother anyway, but Eileen's all for her father. She wants to marry him when she grows up. I wish to God she could now." She put her hand up to her hair. "I'll boil some water. You stay there with your big brother, Vince."

When she returned with the tea-tray she had changed into a blue quilted dressing-gown and her hair had been brushed.

"There's some cotton wool and a bowl of hot water in the kitchen," she said. "Fetch them in, Vince."

As he rose to obey her, he was struck by the expression on her face. It was all too calm, all too undisturbed, all too decided; he had never seen her like that before.

She bathed Matthew's graze quickly but thoroughly, the expression on her face unchanging, and stood over him whilst he gulped down a cup of tea. "Bed Matthew," she said. He pulled himself slowly to his feet and left the room.

When the sound of his footsteps had receded Maureen gave Vincent a bright, curiously social smile. Her eyes were moist.

"Drink your tea whilst it's hot, Vince," she said. "Matt'll be off to sleep as soon as his head hits the pillow."

"He's worried about something," Vincent said. "He didn't get round to telling me about it."

"He hasn't got round to telling me either. Whatever it is, drinking won't make it any better. It's a funny thing, he's never been the same since your father died. He never used to drink like that." She lit another cigarette. "I ought to stop," she said, looking at the cigarette. "I don't at all when I'm alone in the house. But as soon as Matthew comes in – "

"I'm not Matthew," Vincent said.

"No, you're not," she said. She looked at the threadbare patch on the grey carpeting. "Not thick enough," she said. "It's for a bedroom, really. Matthew got it wholesale. He never buys anything straight out. They must see him coming. This damned suite's bankrupt stock and no wonder, for it's falling apart. And did you ever see such a shade of blue outside a horror film? And the wallpaper's peeling, and the sooner it all drops off and I don't have to look at those pink and yellow flowers the better. And the TV's an unknown make. It was dirt cheap because they don't make them any more. So it costs twice as much to have the thing serviced. It's a wonder he's got a car that's still on the market, but Silvington's bought it for him. But he's longing to get a Czechoslovakian one, of all things. Don't you like your tea, Vince?"

"I'd better not keep you up any longer," he said.

She poured his cup of tea into the slop basin and gave him a fresh cup. "You're not keeping me up," she said. "It's nice to talk with a man; Matthew isn't in much these days."

The telephone rang. She picked it up. "Yes. Yes of course they're here. He's just going. Do you want a word with him?" The social smile returned to her face and she began to tap her foot. The slipper fell off and she kicked it away impatiently. "About five minutes," she said. "Yes, I'm fine, thank you. Kevin's a bit crochety, though. Don't worry, he's tough. I'm keeping him in a bit. See you tomorrow, then. Goodbye." She put the receiver down with such force that it slid across the table and nearly fell on to the floor. As she walked over towards Vincent's chair he thought for one moment that she was going to sit on his knee. She looked at him intently, the social smile disappearing, then sat on the hearthrug beside the fireplace, hugging her knees, her hair over her eyes.

"Your mother, Vince," she said. "She didn't know you were here and was worried because you were so late. It's nearly a quarter-past eleven. You said you'd be in for ten, and there's a terrible amount of traffic on the roads. I told her you were all right and drinking tea."

"I'd better be going," Vincent said. "She does worry ever since Paul had that accident last year."

"That's right," Maureen said. "Even Paul had a bump. And there's not a more careful man living than Paul."

Vincent put down his cup. "I've a busy day tomorrow," he said. From upstairs he heard the sound of a snore.

"You're in a great hurry," Maureen said. She shifted her position; he looked at her bare leg then looked away again. "Was Frank Rooley with anyone?"

"Clare. Not that I give a damn."

"I wonder what you do give a damn about," she said, more to herself than to Vincent. "I should have tried to find out before, shouldn't I?"

"Maureen," he said. "Maureen, can't I – "

She stood up and came over to him so that their bodies were almost touching. "Can't you what, Vincent?"

"Can't I help you? If there's something I can do – "

Perhaps Matthew will wake up, he thought desperately. And then, with equal desperation, he hoped that Matthew wouldn't wake up; it wasn't possible that there should be so much pleasure from the mere proximity of a few yards of pale blue quilted satin with a woman's body underneath it. He didn't want to touch that body, he was quite content simply that it should be there; but he knew that in another moment he would be pushed as if by some outside force into contact. He reached out his hand slowly to touch her hair; then there was the sound of a child's voice from upstairs and he stepped quickly away from her. There was an acrid taste in his mouth and an actual physical pain at the pit of his stomach.

"That's Eileen," she said. "I thought she'd wake up." She turned away from Vincent. "I won't keep you any longer, Vince. Your mother will worry until you get home. Of course you can't leave her on her own. That'd be terrible, wouldn't it?"

"I'll let myself out," Vincent said. "Goodnight, Maureen."

"Goodnight, Vincent." She put her hand on his; it was dry and hot. "Tell your mother not to worry so much about you, Vince. You're a grown man. Aren't you a grown man?"

Three

"O'Hara, when did Henry the Eighth publish the Act of Succession?"

O'Hara, a stocky boy of fourteen, looked up from his desk. "I *did* know, sir."

"I'm delighted, O'Hara, delighted beyond measure you knew, but more important things have crowded the date out of your mind." He suddenly turned from the blackboard and put his hand on O'Hara's desk.

"Don't move, O'Hara," he said. "This is like the last chapter of a thriller. The murderer is about to be unmasked." He picked up a piece of blotting-paper; underneath it was a sheet of writing-paper. "The mystery is solved," he said. "Mr O'Hara has been meditating about a different kind of contest from the one which I've been doing my poor best to discuss with you. Mr O'Hara has been planning the composition of the England football team. Being a young man not handicapped by false modesty he's awarded himself the position of centre-forward."

There was a ripple of laughter; nowhere else but in the classroom, Vincent thought, was it so easy to make people laugh. He handed the paper back to O'Hara. "All right, O'Hara. Never mind about the date of the Act, though one day you will have to worry about it. Stand up and tell us all about the Act of Succession in your own words."

"Henry wanted to be supreme, sir." O'Hara's eyes were half-closed, his face screwed up as if in pain. "Henry didn't want

50

anyone over him, sir. He hadn't any money, so he wanted to be supreme king so he didn't have anyone arguing about how he spent the money. He wanted to destroy the Catholics too, sir. So he passed the Act of Supremacy..." O'Hara's voice trailed away.

"You may sit down, O'Hara." Vincent sighed gustily and theatrically. "Well, you certainly were in there trying, boy. But never in all my life have I heard such a farrago of nonsense. Of course Henry wanted to be supreme. That's what being a king meant in the sixteenth century. And of course he was chronically hard-up. But the real reason for the Act of Succession – not Supremacy, O'Hara – was that Henry wanted to make his marriage to Anne Boleyn valid." He threw the piece of chalk he was holding at the boy in the corner; it hit him on the nose and he yelped as if hurt. "I'll throw something harder and heavier next time if you don't stop giggling, Conlon," he said.

He walked over to the side of the room which overlooked the street; the whole of the building opposite was occupied by Furnett's, a mail order firm; the windows were painted dark green, so dark that only on as bright an Indian summer morning as this was the green apparent, leaving only a quarter clear, and as they were unusually high, nothing of whatever activities went on inside was visible. He bent down to put his eyes on a level with Conlon's and saw at the window directly opposite a girl's head. She had short fair hair and was laughing at someone below her out of sight. He was probably holding the ladder, his hands on her ankles, Vincent thought; women don't laugh in that way at other women. The girl's face disappeared from sight. Vincent straightened up. "Back to the sixteenth century, Conlon," he said. "Henry the Eighth wanted to make his marriage to Anne Boleyn valid. He could only do this by having his marriage to Catherine of Aragon made null and void. Once his marriage to Anne was declared lawful it followed that the children of that marriage were legitimate and the children of the marriage to Catherine of Aragon illegitimate. That meant that Mary, his daughter by Catherine of Aragon, was disinherited. When she ascended the throne she was in consequence less than tolerant. Of course, Henry wanted a son, and Catherine didn't give him a son. Neither did Anne Boleyn. Some historians consider that this is the real reason for his having Anne executed."

He paused. It was ridiculous to envy the dead, but Henry the Eighth, like Charles the Second, was all too real a figure in his imagination. Henry had the power too. Henry not only took whatever women he fancied, but had them killed into the bargain. It's curious that I should earn my living by talking about these monsters of uncontrolled appetites, he thought; I'm like a dyspeptic chef.

"Didn't Henry behave in a very cruel way towards the Catholics, sir?"

That was Simon Kelly who was doing his best to be teacher's pet and who everyone said had a vocation.

"He did, Kelly, but the Catholics weren't the only ones he was cruel to, and we're not really discussing his morals. Henry was a very wicked man, but we can't, you know, judge him by our standards. In fact, Henry couldn't have afforded what we'd consider to be humane standards. But he could have been a great deal worse. He had a conscience of sorts and always had to give his actions the colour of legality. Some kings in his position would have arranged a fatal accident for Catherine, and that would have rid him of all his problems. But Henry thought of himself as being a good Catholic, indeed an exemplary Catholic. He went to Mass every day of his life, in fact…"

He had their attention now: they all could understand Henry the Eighth. The real test was whether one could make Walpole or Lord North or Peel interesting; but that was a bridge he'd cross when he came to it.

The dinner bell rang, and almost simultaneously with the sound there was a faint odour of meat and barley. He would have known it without the odour; the dinners at St Theo's were always predictable. He quietened the class with a wave of the hand. "I shall expect from each and every one of you by the next time

I have the pleasure of seeing you – " he paused – "not what you've been expecting, an essay on the Act of Succession, but an essay on St Thomas More. An *original* essay on St Thomas More. Class dismissed."

He stayed behind for a moment after everyone had gone: he was more and more beginning to value these moments when he was by himself, all the more acutely by himself because of the voices of the boys in the corridors. The actual fabric of St Theo's was of no great age: it had been built as a block of offices some eighty years ago. And St Theo's itself had been founded only in 1922, but the classrooms, uniformly cream and beige with windows and ceilings which were too high ever to keep decently clean, had a quality of timelessness about them. There'd be a new school one day, the site was already earmarked not very far from his own home at Beckfield. They didn't have schools in the centre of cities any longer; but because St Theo's was in the centre of Charbury it belonged to Charbury in a way that the new Grammar School five miles out on the edge of the Beckfield Moors never would. This too, he thought, looking out into the street, was the quarter of Charbury into which his great-grandparents had come, well over a hundred years ago, ragged, stinking, and starving. And most of the boys' great-grandparents for that matter. He walked over to the place where Conlon had been sitting; no blonde head was visible. As he went out of the classroom he found himself glad that she wasn't there; he would have been forced to wave at her, he would even have been forced to wait until she came out of the building at half past five. He imagined the texture of her blonde hair under his fingers: it would be agreeable to touch because it couldn't possibly be other than genuine. Dyed hair couldn't reflect back the sun as her hair did; but what was he going to say to her? He felt someone touch his shoulder-blades and turned to see John Trummery, the junior science master.

"Didn't you hear me yelling out your name?" Trummery asked. He put a heavy arm round Vincent's shoulder for a moment. "Why are you always going about in a dream, man?"

"I think deeply about deep matters," Vincent said. "And I zip my fly all the way up."

"Why, I thought those little devils were sniggering about something," Trummery said. Though he had put in a great deal of work on his accent since he came to the school a year ago, he couldn't quite keep out the Northumbrian lilt. He tugged at the zip, holding in his breath. "It's my big belly, man."

His fiancée, whom Vincent had met at the Garden Party dance, was scarcely more than five feet tall, even in high heels. Vincent had a momentary vision of Trummery's fifteen stones covering that small, thin body; there wouldn't be any two ways about her being covered either, he thought wryly. He was surprised to find how much he resented the idea of Trummery, or anyone else, being engaged. Firmly he erased the picture.

"You'll have to watch out," he said. "Or you'll run to fat and die early of thrombosis."

"I know. Rosemary's made me go on a diet. No sugar, no cakes, no bread, no beer. And I've given up smoking. There's only one thing left and then not until you're married and you'll do it with a thermometer and a calendar and a slide-rule. And that reminds me. I stopped you to sell you a ticket for this play she's in. Saturday night, St Tom's, all for a good cause. A hilarious wholesome comedy, that's what it is. Do you the world of good."

"I'll let you know," Vincent said. They were nearly at the dining hall; he put his handkerchief to his nose.

"You ought to take up smoking," Trummery said. "The combined smell of boys and Irish stew is a bit too much."

"One becomes accustomed to it," Vincent said. They turned to the right and went towards the staff room where the predominant smell, he knew, would be tobacco smoke and old books; but he had never become accustomed to it. That was another lie: the smell of stew, the harsh metallic smell of the boys, the smell of tobacco and old books, a girl's blonde head in the sunlight, were all being encountered by him now for the first time. The more he tried to make sense of it all, the more entangled he became: it was like trying to work out an equation in which the figures continually changed not only in number but in colour. There had to be something more to living than merely to be bombarded by physical impressions, and the body had to be merely the container of the intelligence instead of, as it had been yesterday, as momentarily it had been this very morning, a shambling overseer with a whip. He knew there was something more, he knew the way to give that something shape and habitation; he knew, above all, that there was nothing more important than penetrating to this core of meaning; he wanted, as it were, to unwrap the sandwiches and eat, but couldn't bear to take off the wrapping. It wasn't because he wasn't hungry, he thought, but because he liked the wrapping too much. On an impulse, he took out his pocket diary. "I'm free next Saturday after all," he said to Trummery. "Get me two tickets."

Trummery raised his eyebrows. "Two?"

"Yes," Vincent said. "Why not?"

Six hours later as he sat in the Charbury Public Library he was beginning to regret his impulse. He told himself that it wasn't very important and turned his attention back to Harton's *History of Charbury in the Seventeenth Century*; as he assiduously made notes, the face of the blonde at Furnett's became dimmer; what mattered was the amassing of facts and the shaping of those facts into something original.

The Reference Department, a large circular room with radiating bookshelves, had always been one of the places in which he could find what was, when he came to think of it, literally a kind of sanctuary. It was a place where no one could make any demands on him, it was a place where, more often than not, he would simply sit still, a pen in his hand, not thinking, not even sometimes aware of himself as a person. There was nothing to distract the eye and nothing to offend it: only the books and the huge mahogany tables and the catalogue cabinets and the service counter. You emptied your mind of the irrelevant, you sat there quietly and then, sometimes, there was a glimpse of the relevant.

There were only about ten other people in the room this evening; generally every table was filled with students from the University. There seemed to be no one there tonight younger than himself: he found the fact unaccountably depressing. He sighed and took out another book from the pile in front of him. It was his own fault, he thought, I should stick to what I came for and look for the other thing in the proper place.

Query, population distribution as compared Bradford, he wrote and saw that what he needed wasn't there. He was tempted for a moment to stay where he was, to continue to make notes from the books already by him. Then he looked towards the counter and saw that the young man who had been on duty when he had first come in had been replaced by a young woman. He looked again; she had been there on the last two occasions he had visited the Reference Department. She had a great deal of black hair, worn long, past her shoulders, and large eyes which seemed to change colour from green to hazel as he looked at her; even under the harsh overhead light her skin was a warm olive.

He was appalled to discover that his hands were beginning to shake. He wasn't going to do any more work that evening: his plans for two hours' research in the library, followed by an hour of listening to records, followed by a walk before an early bed, were completely ruined. He had an hour and a half left before the library closed, during which time he was irrecoverably bound to staring alternately at the same paragraph in *Harton's Charbury in the Seventeenth Century* and at the girl with black hair. And when he went home he would put on a gramophone record, he would, for that matter, put on several, but he wouldn't enjoy them. Whatever they were, the total effect would be wistfully erotic, he'd be like a character in a film listening in tears to Our Song.

There'd be the walk, but the walk would be only as far as the Green Crown, not for the drink, but in order not to be alone. He had, in short, been content; now, one way or another, discontent had begun. The smell of books and floor-polish now seemed not simply without life but positively dead and decaying; he would have preferred the sharp, inky smell of brand-new books, and the aromatic smell of wood with the sap not yet dried out. If it came to that, he thought, he could do without the books: there had been too many of them and there had been too many quiet evenings alone. He rose abruptly and went over to the catalogue and slowly looked up half a dozen titles. He filled in three request slips. As he noted the titles of the books he kept glancing in the direction of the black-haired girl. There was no ring on her left hand but she had a heavy gold man's signet ring on her right hand; she caught his glance and looked away from him at a pile of forms in front of her.

Unexpectedly the hunter's instinct was stung to life; half annoyed, half amused at himself, he frankly stared in her direction, knowing that she would inevitably look up again. She brought her head up slowly and for a second he was conscious of himself simply as a not particularly handsome young man staring rudely at a pretty girl; he wanted to drop his eyes, not to look at her again, to close the poetry book and put it away, to switch off the record player and turn the music into a portable silence. The hunter stayed by him and he continued to look at the girl, not staring at her now but appraising her unhurriedly; there was the feeling of there being some kind of struggle between them, of instant defeat as the consequence of his looking away. Suddenly and surprisingly she smiled at him and he scooped up the forms and went over to the counter as if in obedience to a signal.

She was still smiling when he approached her; to his consternation he found himself unable to speak. She was a person, he thought in panic, she was real, he was not the hunter but the observer, he must not be involved; and then he heard his own-voice – loudly, even coarsely self-confident – saying: "I'd be

57

obliged if you'd get me these." He glanced at the lettered block on the counter. "You're not Mr Tomkins, surely?"

She put the block under the counter. "Mine isn't ready yet. Laura Heycliff."

"You haven't been here long, Miss Heycliff."

"Not in this department, Mr Dungarvan." An elderly man in an alpaca jacket emerged from the staff enclosure behind her, peered mistrustfully around him, and disappeared again.

"I thought I hadn't seen you," he said. "I don't generally notice the assistants' faces, though."

She put her finger to her lips and went into the staff enclosure, to emerge a moment later with two books. She handed him back a form. "It's at the binders, I'm afraid. If it's urgent, we can get it for you from another library." Her eyebrows were very thick but not heavy, thinning to a fine point at the outer edges. From a distance they appeared as if painted; close to, he could almost count each fine hair.

She handed him a form; he took out his pen, then put it back in his pocket again. "It doesn't matter," he said. He cleared his throat. "It isn't long till closing time." He suddenly found himself beginning to stammer, his self-confidence dwindling before her official composure. "I'm sorry but – "

"But what?"

She was smiling again; and, speaking quickly to run ahead of his stammer, he blurted out: "Would you like to have a drink with me? I'll meet you outside the library – "

She shook her head, still smiling. "Not the library. Somewhere else."

"The Espresso Nevada? It's just opposite."

She nodded and then looked at the form and back again at him, her face expressionless. "I'll certainly make inquiries about it, Mr Dungarvan," she said. "It's really the best book on the subject."

She glanced behind her; the elderly man in the alpaca jacket had appeared again, and was walking slowly towards her. "Excuse me." She turned away from Vincent.

Vincent returned to his table trying to keep the grin off his face. He opened the two books at random but made no real attempt at working: the population distribution of Charbury as compared to Bradford had lost its interest ever since Laura Heycliff had come into the room. He wondered for a moment whether or not she was angry with him – after all, he was, not to put too fine a point on it, picking her up – but then his instincts reassured him. She'd be there in the Nevada at eight and when she was there everything would change. He was at last going to feel what he always pretended to himself that he'd feel with a girl. It was too good to be true; it wasn't possible that he should be about to take out a girl who not only spoke well but who was pretty in an acceptable way, not tartish, not twitchily refined, not dowdy and quiet, but someone about whom he could dream without finding it necessary to make her into something which she was not.

The Espresso Nevada, just opposite the main entrance of the Public Library, had, somehow or other, possibly because its prices were higher than those of any other espresso bar, acquired a certain air of respectability. Under its former management it had regularly been the scene of fights after the pubs had closed and there had been rumours that it was a place where one could buy reefers, girls, or even, just before it closed down, boys. It had changed its name, been redecorated to match the new name, and the new proprietor, Jack Moonan, never allowed any rough stuff, nor had any rough stuff been attempted since he broke the jaw of a youth who tried to sell him ten thousand Capstan at two shillings for twenty. Moonan hadn't reported the youth to the police but everyone knew, almost at the instant that the youth's head hit the floor, that the good old days were over. The youth after a minute got to his feet and attempted to say something; since his jaw was hanging loose, he only managed a few inarticulate noises, half-way between groaning and retching, and then put his hand to his jaw to hold it in place and shuffled out into the street. Moonan, his face expressionless, went back to the counter. What had made the incident frightening had been the suddenness of the blow; the youth had buttonholed Moonan by the counter and almost before he had finished speaking Moonan had struck.

He was there tonight, dressed as usual in a black pin-striped suit of good material but an old-fashioned cut, tight fitting with broad lapels. His stiff white collar and black tie added to the effect as of an undertaker waiting for custom: his hands were resting in absolute immobility on the counter. They were very large hands with thick fingers and incongruously manicured nails and appeared as if they belonged to him and yet were not part of his body, like guns. He smiled at Vincent as he came in. "Good evening, Mr Dungarvan," he said; Moonan made a great point of addressing his regular customers by name.

"Good evening, Jack. A white coffee, please."

"One cappuccino," Moonan said. He seemed to like the word as much as Vincent disliked it; he shook his head reprovingly at Vincent, his black oiled hair glistening underneath the fluorescent light. His parting was geometrically down the middle; the general impression was of a sealskin skullcap rather than a head of human hair.

"You're slack tonight," Vincent said.

"I don't mind," Moonan said. "There's a girl short tonight. A grumbling appendix, she says. I know those grumbling appendixes. They cry all night and they're wet at both ends." He glanced at Vincent's bulging brief-case. "You've been working hard, Mr Dungarvan?" His accent was of no definable locality, though at times there was a trace of Birmingham detectable, thick and adenoidal.

"I've been grubbing among the bookstacks," Vincent said. "I don't know whether it'll come to anything."

"It comes to more than hanging about the pubs and the billiard halls," Moonan said. "If only I'd applied myself more to the books when I was a lad I'd be doing something better than keeping a coffee-bar now."

"There's more money in what you're doing than what I'm doing," Vincent said.

"That's not everything," Moonan said. "I'm fifty years old and I know what I'm talking about. Respect, that's the thing to aim at." The pale smooth face wrinkled momentarily. "That's what you've got, Mr Dungarvan. They respect you."

"I'm not so sure," Vincent said. He had never heard Moonan talk at such length about himself before.

"I am," Moonan said, and then turned away to serve a customer.

Vincent took his coffee to a seat by the window and settled down to watch the Library entrance across the street. Here in this room, decorated with Colts and Remingtons and old posters, everything was going to change. Everything in the room was pretending to be something else: the guns were plastic, the posters were printed in Charbury, the stone and timber walls were photo-lithographic wallpaper, the whisky bottles behind the counter were filled with coloured water; but what he felt at this moment was real. He was off the treadmill, he was walking on his own two feet.

She came out at last, stopping for a moment to say something to the young man who had come out with her. She was wearing a bright red raincoat; the colour was all the more festive because of the contrast with her companion's clerical grey gabardine and the blackened stone of the library. The young man walked away slowly, his shoulders hunched: she looked across at the café, saw Vincent, and smiled at him. Again he thought with foreboding: it's too good to be true.

He opened the door for her, noticing with pleasure that the other people in the cafe were all watching him.

61

"I shouldn't have kept you waiting," she said. "Arnold wanted to take me out. But I couldn't. He's too young. It's a shame for the poor boy, though; it's taken him two months to pluck up courage to ask me."

"I'm sorry," Vincent said. "Would you like a cup of coffee?" He half rose; Moonan, catching sight of him gestured to him to sit down and came over to the table.

"Espresso, Miss Heycliff?"

"Please, Jack"

She took out a packet of cigarettes and pushed them over to Vincent.

"No, thanks," he said. "I've never begun."

"I wish I hadn't," she said. "Perhaps it keeps me from worse things."

"You've not been here for long," he said. Now that she was here, a private person only a few feet away from him, he couldn't think of what to say.

"Six weeks," she said. "Before that I worked at the special library in Harlham; it was all terribly hush-hush and I got tired of it." She sipped from the small cup of black coffee which Moonan had brought her. "I suppose you've lived here all your life?"

"I was born here. I'm very dull, I'm afraid."

"Don't cry yourself down," she said sharply. "Tell me about yourself."

"There isn't very much to tell. I teach English and History at St Theo's, and I live at home. I have two brothers and they're both married. I went to the University here for four years and got a fairish degree and my DipEd and eventually I got the job at St Theo's."

"Do you like it here?" In the softer light he could now see that her eyes were hazel with flecks of green and when she asked a question she had a trick of widening them so that they appeared to grow larger.

"If I didn't, I wouldn't do it," he said. "It's hard work but every now and again you come across a boy who uses the brains the good God has given him. And then it's exciting."

"It makes a change," she said.

"What makes a change?"

"Meeting a man who likes his job."

"I told you I was very dull."

"I told you," she said. "Call yourself dull and you'll become dull. You don't seem in the least dull when you look at me."

"You've noticed, then."

She laughed. "I could hardly help but notice."

"I'm sorry if I embarrassed you."

"It'll embarrass me much more if no man bothers to look at me. You do it rather well, actually. Wistfully, and rather sternly, but not lecherously. I should think you rather like women."

He looked at her, gratefully confirming her newness as a person, her unlikeness to any girl he'd ever known before, the way in which she was already turning the dry shreds of his life into something as rich and nourishing as the label on the packet promised. There was a drawback: what came with the goods under that label – Love at First Sight or, if that was too sentimental, simply First Meeting – was awkwardness, mumbling, averted glances, long silences, the feeling on both sides that it was best not to reveal too much. And then, incredulously but soberly, he realised that there wasn't going to be any sort of shyness between them, that this new relationship wasn't, as it were, in need of being run in but could immediately be driven at full speed.

He said: "I like being here with you. I don't want other women now. I'm glad we're alone."

"That's bad," she said. "At your age you should like them all."

"I do. But I only *warmly* like one woman at a time."

"What's your father like?" she asked.

"He's dead. Ten years ago. Heart."

"I'm sorry," she said. "I'm too nosy. All women are nosy. I didn't mean to upset you."

"You weren't to know. As a matter of fact, I rather like talking about him. Mother never seems to, I don't know why. Father was what they call a card. He knew everyone in Charbury and he loved company. He worked like a black when he was young – he went to school half-time and then to night-school to fill in the gaps. He was the manager at Silvington's. Everything was different when he was alive, there was more daylight about the place, if you see what I mean."

"Yes, I do."

"He was naturally cheerful. He could never believe that anything really dreadful could happen to him. So it never did, except once; not that dying's dreadful."

"Isn't it?"

"That's what you're born for," he said. "It's nothing to be afraid of. I think about it every day of my life."

"You're very odd," she said. "I try never to think about it at all."

"That's bad," he said. "That's very bad. It's a fact of life and you mustn't try to dodge it." He frowned; despite all that he'd said, the longing to see his father again had begun to hurt. "Never mind. I mustn't talk to you as if you were one of my pupils. And I asked you to have a drink with me, didn't I?"

"I'm having one," she said.

"I mean a proper drink."

"I'm not really bothered," she said. "Unless you need one. But I'm rather hungry."

"We'll go somewhere else, then. There's not much choice here."

She read the items from the wheel-shaped menu. "Spaghetti Bolognese, Goulash, Club Sandwich, Egg and French Fried and a lot more things with French Fried. I'd love some spaghetti. But we'll go somewhere else if you really want to. I wouldn't want to come between a man and his pint."

"You won't be," he said. "I'd just as soon stay here." He rose to go to the counter, but Moonan was already there at the table.

She ate neatly but with enormous enjoyment; when she had finished she mopped the plate clean with her roll and then ate the roll.

"Thank you, Vincent," she said. "I was resigning myself to something out of a tin tonight. The girl I share the flat with has gone out and she's the one who does the fancy cooking anyway. I haven't the heart to cook for myself, have you?"

"I've never tried," he said. "I can make tea and that's all. I don't think my father could even make tea. Mother won't let anyone but herself into the kitchen. In fact, I'm absolutely useless about the house."

"I'm glad," she said. "I don't like men who can cook and who potter around in old clothes mending things and putting things up." Her eyes were sparkling and her face flushed; it was as if she'd discovered that they both belonged to the same revolutionary movement. She caught his wrist, squeezing hard. "You don't wear old clothes and mend things either, do you, Vincent? Or bath twice a day? Or use aftershave or talcum?"

He looked at her suspiciously; it seemed to him that now she had got over her first delight at discovering he was in the same movement – whatever it might be – and was checking his credentials.

"No. Does it matter?"

She lit a cigarette and blew out a series of smoke-rings before speaking. Her face lost its animation and became inscrutable. He wanted suddenly to shake her; momentarily, embarrassingly, she seemed to have been taken over by another woman. "It does matter, Vincent. It matters terribly. But it's all right." She took his hand and put it to her nose. "You smell of carbolic, and you wear a splendid old-fashioned shirt with a stiff white collar and a suit with a waistcoat and shoes with toe-caps." She stroked his sheep-skin jacket on the chair beside her." I wish you didn't wear that thing, though. It's very nice, but it isn't you. A real overcoat is more your style."

"You're making fun of me."

"No, Vincent. I'd never do that."

Suddenly he felt a premonition of disaster. It was like seeing a wisp of black smoke when driving up a hill; you slowed down and there, when you reached the crest, was the burnt-out car and the fire-engine and the bundles in blankets at the roadside.

"Not much you wouldn't," he said. "But I don't care." The premonition passed; he was driving along an empty road now. All his life he had wanted everything to change, he had wanted to rush on into a new life; he had hoped for it, desperately needed it, but had not really believed in it until now when, merely by speaking a few words, he had gone into the new life. He wasn't even sure that he liked Laura Heycliff, he wasn't sure that she'd bring him any sort of comfort; what he was sure of, he realized exultantly, was that he could fall in love with her.

Four

He was quite content sitting there beside Laura in the half-light of the cinema, his hand resting lightly upon hers. On the screen the Roman soldiers trotted through the forest, their mouths talking a different language from their voices. Suddenly the Gauls, furred and bearded, dropped from the trees; horses whinnied, men screamed. Laura clutched Vincent's hand tightly, her eyes rounding like a child's. The alternative to Romans versus Gauls had been Ingmar Bergman; Laura had without hestitation rejected Bergman. Looking at her now as much as at the screen, Vincent thought that he knew why. It was escape she needed, escape to a more innocent world: surprised by his own perspicacity, he realized that it was her father's hand she was holding.

He did not know whether to be sorry or glad, whether or not to emulate the man to the right whose arm was now round his girl's shoulders or whether to relax still further, to join in the pretence completely, to imagine himself as protective, sexual but sexless, going farther and farther into the world of fantasy. The eyes were a child's eyes, she was frightened that the barbarians would leap out of the screen at her, the sharp but rounded profile was childish, even to the slightly parted lips, but the full neck and the impertinent breasts weren't childish, nor was her smell. It was different from Clare's which had a certain smokiness about it, attractive but not far from being acrid, or Maureen's, which was lighter, almost of spring flowers, but tired, desperately tired.

This smell was clean but not aseptically so; it was fresh, it was not so much excited as expecting pleasure.

Outside in the street he still kept hold of her hand. It was raining hard; as they crossed the street and walked in the direction of the Espresso Nevada his head was already uncomfortably wet. Laura did not speak, but kept pace with him, her face grave. As they passed a shop window, their reflections were as of policeman and prisoner; she intercepted his glance and smiled and he knew that she had had the same thought.

"I enjoyed that," she said as they were sitting at the table at the Espresso Nevada which by now he thought of as theirs.

"The film or the walk in the rain?"

"Both," she said. She put her tongue to her lips. "The rain tastes of hemp and coal. I'd forgotten it. In the South it's concrete and dust. The rain brings the smells out."

"Hasn't it rained for you until now?"

"I hadn't noticed until now. I've been so busy settling down in the new job and now I'm flat-hunting... And then tonight suddenly I noticed. I've been in, well, a sort of limbo, not feeling much at all. I'm still living out of a suitcase, but now I've started to plan again."

"I thought you had a flat."

"Ruth's putting me up for the time being. This girl I went to the Library School with. But I don't like sharing a flat. She's terribly possessive."

"She'll be lonely."

"So am I sometimes, but I don't want to end up sharing a flat with Ruth ten years from now. She's even vexed at me going out with you tonight. She'd planned to take me to visit some friends of hers at Sarnley. She warned me against you. She says you don't look serious. You are serious, aren't you, Vincent?" She smiled.

"Yes," he said. "I'm very serious. Serious to the point of tedium."

"I wouldn't mind," she said. "I wouldn't mind if you were a good old-fashioned wolf." She sipped her coffee and pulled a face. "It tastes horrible tonight. This isn't a real Espresso, it's just coffee without milk. Jack isn't here. I think he terrorises his staff so much that they go to pieces when he's not there. Like the barbarians when the Romans had gone." She giggled. "He's a Roman of the old school, as someone said in that film tonight. You didn't like it very much, though, did you, Vincent? I could see you scowling at that awful dubbing. They kept on opening and shutting their mouths after their voices had stopped. My twin brother and I used to go and see films with Romans in when we were kids, but there weren't very many then. So I'm making up for it now."

"Have you got a flat of your own yet?"

"I'm seeing an agent tomorrow. But there shouldn't be much trouble in this part of the world. If I don't get somewhere very soon I'll go into lodgings. Ruth's driving me up the wall. It's worse than being married. She's got it into her head that I'm delicate and she's always preparing huge meals for me. When I can't finish them she looks hurt, and there's a scene. I can't bear scenes, can you?"

"She sounds a bit queer," Vincent said. "Hasn't she a boy-friend?"

"I don't believe she's ever been out with a man. I don't think she likes men at all – " She laughed. "Vincent, don't look so horrified. Ruth's a most moral girl. Goes to church every Sunday, morning and evening, and sometimes in the week as well,"

"Don't you go?"

"I wouldn't mind going sometimes." Momentarily her face became less vivid and he noticed for the first time the beginning of what one day might be harsh lines from the nostril to the corners of the mouth. "If it were what it's supposed to be it would be exactly what I've always needed. I want something hard and definite, but I want to be looked after – I want a sort of trade union for the weak and the stupid. Living's so damned – oh, *regimental* now. You've got to be sensible. You've got to look at the small print, you've got to be well adjusted. Everyone you ask tries to understand. But I don't want to be understood. And I don't want to have doubts either… You Catholics don't have any doubts, do you?"

He had known almost as soon as he'd met her that she wasn't a Catholic; now that it was finally confirmed he felt both disappointment and relief. Once again he hadn't found the nice Catholic girl, marriage to whom as an alternative to the priesthood had been recommended to him as long as he could remember; but if he didn't want to marry her, the excuse was there ready-made.

"I often have doubts," he said. "My brains weren't washed away when I was baptized. I'm not a very good Catholic really. The women are the best Catholics." He tapped his forehead. "I believe it here." He tapped his chest. "My mother believes it here."

"Vincent," she said abruptly, "why have you never married? Or is it that you've been married?"

"Good God! I've never been married. Everyone in Charbury would know if I had. The fact is that I've never met anyone I wanted to marry."

She looked away from him towards the Wells Fargo bills and the plastic rifles and pistols. "Doesn't your mother want you to get married?"

"She wants me either to get married or become a priest. One thing or the other, according to her mood. The balance is in favour of me being a priest."

"Why is she so keen on it?"

"God knows. I mean, literally God knows. She thinks I'm the clever one. I'm not, actually. My brother Paul, the solicitor, has all the brains and all the money. He lives in Harrogate. Matthew's in wool."

"You haven't ever wanted to be a priest, have you?"

"It's a bit late now, anyway. A lot of Catholic mamas have the idea. It adds to their status. My mama's very hot on status."

"Do you really care what she wants?"

"No," he said. "I'll do what I think best for myself."

"I thought you would. She must be quite a character."

"You'll have to meet her," he said.

"It's a bit late now," she said. "I will soon if you really meant it. But you might get tired of me first."

"Never," he said. "I'm frightened of you running away sometimes, that's all."

"I'm quite good at running away," she said. "I've run all over the country."

"You've stopped now," he said. "The trains don't go any farther."

"I hope I have," she said. "I'm twenty-seven. When I think of it, I'm not so sure that I'm in any condition for running." She put down her cup. "Let me give you some decent coffee. Ruth won't be back yet."

"Let me buy you a drink," he said as they walked over to his car.

"I don't very much like alcohol," she said. "Neither do you." She touched his hand. "You're not afraid of me, are you?"

"Perhaps I'm afraid of Ruth," he said.

"I'll have a place of my own soon. Turn left here, Vincent. It's Charlton Road, Number 12A."

"I know it," he said. "My grandfather Rosslea used to live there. It's not far from the park."

"This is only the second time we've been out together," she said as he drove out of the city centre.

"Is that good or bad?"

"I feel as if I've known you for longer," she said.

He knew the opening gambits but always before he had been the one to employ them. He wasn't used to the woman taking the lead; nor was he used to talking to a woman who, sooner or later, didn't betray some lack of perception, some essential vulgarity.

"I felt that the first time," he said. "Though we didn't really talk as much then. Were you nervous?"

"A bit," she said. "Isn't that your school over there?"

He nodded. "Do you come to work by bus?"

"I sold my car. I don't really like driving."

"I'll look out for you," he said. "Will you wave?"

"I might wave at the wrong man."

"I might wave at the wrong woman. Then I'll lose my job."

"I wouldn't want that to happen," she said. "Stop the car here."

"This isn't Charlton Road."

"I know."

They were in a little side street by the park, almost as broad as it was long, There was only one gas-lamp and to the right was a patch of grass and a straggling line of bushes. The four big houses on the left showed no sign of life.

She turned towards him. He kissed her gently.

"Yes," she said. "It's all right, Vincent." She stroked his hair. "It's lovely, like wire wool."

"It'll be a good thing to remember," he said. "You can hardly hear the traffic and it's stopped raining. But you can hear the rain running away down the gutters and off the trees."

His kiss was less gentle this time; she returned it fiercely then broke away. "There's someone coming," she said.

"It's only the wind."

"We'd better go. You know I'm not teasing you, don't you, Vincent? But I can't be certain whether or not Ruth will have come back."

He started the car.

"There's not really anywhere one can go in Charbury," he said, trying to keep the relief out of his voice. Another moment, he thought, and it would have happened, would have happened despite the possibility of a policeman tapping at the window of the car; the difficulty was that the reality of sin was much more attractive than the idea. He wondered why it never seemed to be possible simply to stop at the moment one enjoyed the most, why, when it came down to it, he was no different from the rest. Her next words took him by surprise.

"I don't want to rush things," she said. "Not in a car in a side street. I just wanted you to kiss me. Sometimes that's all one does want."

He stopped at his grandfather's house, tall and square with the ridiculous small turrets on each corner. Inside the arched doorway – a faithful copy, his grandfather had told him, of one of the fourteenth century – he could see six bell-pushes. "My grandfather was a lawyer," he said. "He got mixed up in Irish politics and came here to look after his countrymen. He made a lot of money and he spent it all. My mother wanted my father to buy that house, but by the time he could afford it, it had been converted into flats." He turned the ignition key. "Where's your place?"

"It's here," she said. "I told you." She laughed. "You're marvellous," she said. "No wonder you teach history."

"I never thought of it by a number," he said. "Much less Twelve A. My grandfather would never have stood for that. It was always Daniel House. After the Liberator."

"It's better than calling it Twelve A," she said. "Or Number Thirteen, come to that."

They went up the broad stairway, covered now by a dingy buff carpeting. The whole house appeared to have lost its identity; the walls were white and bare and the heavy mahogany banisters had been replaced by an arrangement of steel and rope. He could have found his way about blindfold once; now open spaces had been boxed in and crimson and mahogany and green and gilt had been replaced by staring white and dingy buff.

Laura kissed him. "Come in," she said, opening the door on the first floor which once had been his grandfather's study. "Less of the nostalgia, Vincent."

"That's splendid," he said. "You've used the word accurately. Not many do."

She took his raincoat from him and hung it up. "Wouldn't your grandfather have been pleased to have me living here?"

"He was never very pleased about anything," Vincent said. "He was a cantankerous old devil if the truth were to be known. No one liked him."

"Did you?"

"He was very old when I knew him. Scared of dying, I think. He was a lot gentler. Like a tiger with its teeth drawn. He used to talk to me here about the Great Liberator and Robert Emmett and Parnell and the rest." He looked around him. "There wasn't a kitchenette or a bathroom here then. Or a pink carpet. There was a huge Indian rug and a desk about twenty feet long and bookshelves all round and a leather sofa and a swivel chair and a couple of basket chairs."

He followed her into the kitchenette and put his arms around her waist. She arched her back, her buttocks surprisingly firm and resilient. He put his face against her hair, suppressing a desire to touch her breasts.

"There was a big table here," he said. "About eight by four, but you could put extra sections in. Say sixteen by four. He was very keen on miltary history and he used to put his maps there."

"You admired him, didn't you, Vincent?" She released herself from his grasp and took down a percolator.

"He was a good lawyer," Vincent said. "But I never fancied the law myself. My brother Paul did. My grandfather wanted me to be a judge, actually. My mother's side of the family are all very bossy." He saw the maps again, almost always maps of Eastern Europe thick with unpronounceable names. Understand Eastern Europe and you understand history, his grandfather had said; but what his grandfather had said about war was oddly overlaid with the festive smell of cigars and hot whisky and lemon. "I nearly became a military historian, though."

"Were you in the services?" The percolator began to bubble.

"The Education Corps. It was very dull. Then I got a job at St Maurice's in Charbury which was rather fun. Mostly I taught thirteen-year-olds. Then the job at St Theo's came up." He sat down on the Formica-topped table. "I rather like it, to tell you the truth. Did I tell you that before?"

"I don't mind. Pass me that tray on top of the refrigerator, will you?"

"You don't say fridge. Is it because I'm a teacher?"

"Just a habit," she said. She opened the glass-fronted cupboard above her and took down a packet of cigarettes and a box of matches. She lit a cigarette. "I hide them so I won't smoke too much," she said. "They're all over the place." She put cups and a milk jug on the tray. "Hand me that double-boiler from the shelf behind you, will you, Vincent? And give me a bottle of milk from the refrigerator. I'm doing everything out of order."

In the bottom of the refrigerator was an array of little bottles and tubes. She saw him looking at them.

"Ruth's," she said. "Her doctor always gives her the sort of drug with a long name which has got to be kept in a cool place. She's the original Miss Neverwell. You ought to see the bathroom. You don't care very much about your health, do you, Vincent?"

She smoothed down her dress nervously. The material seemed to be a fine wool; like her eyes, it was difficult to tell whether it was green or brown. Suddenly he left the table and knelt down before her, his face in her belly. Her hands tightened round his head. This, he thought exultantly, is what it's all about. Her flesh was taut but at the same time surprisingly soft and at this moment everything was permissible but everything meant not curiosity, not lechery, but a kind of reverence: it was an act of homage that was taking place and for the first time in his life there was no hurry, no division in his mind, no sense of sin. The cloth of her dress seemed very warm to the touch: he heard Laura catch her breath and then she moved away and he was left kneeling there, noticing for the first time the coldness of the linoleum.

"It's Ruth," Laura said. "Damn her eyes." He rose and dusted his knees. She was smiling. "You didn't think about it," she said.

"That's what I like, you didn't calculate, you didn't manoeuvre. Open the door for me, darling, it always sticks."

She was setting out the cups on a small table when Ruth came in.

"I heard your scooter," Laura said. "This is Vincent Dungarvan, Ruth. We've been to the pictures."

Ruth shook Vincent's hand firmly. "Is there a cup for me, Laura?"

"Of course."

"There's no milk." She snatched up the empty jug, stalked into the kitchen, and reappeared with it filled with warm milk. "Double boilers do boil dry, dear," she said. "Just because you like yours black, you always forget."

She took off her sheepskin jacket, flung it over the studio couch opposite Vincent's armchair, and let herself down stiffly beside the jacket.

"Did you have a pleasant evening?" Laura asked, taking her across a cup of coffee.

"Very quiet. We just had a good old natter and listened to some records."

Laura stubbed out her cigarette and lit another. "We went to one of my Roman films," she said. "Lots of fighting. We were very naughty, Vincent had tickets for an amateur show but we didn't really fancy it."

Ruth laughed. When she laughed, her mouth seemed to become square, as if invisible fingers were stretching it at the corners.

"Leo and Shirley said you would. 'Dear Laura won't miss a blood-and-thunder if she can help it,' Leo said. 'She hasn't changed.' " She rubbed her hands together then held them out in the direction of the gas fire. "They send their love. Leo's on the short list for Cataloguer at Bradford."

"I do hope he gets it," Laura said. She sat on the arm of Vincent's chair, her hand on his shoulder.

"He jolly well deserves it," Ruth said. "He's been stuck on APT One for long enough. Of course this is Greek to you, isn't it, Mr Dungarvan?"

He found himself not able to answer her immediately; the lisle stockings, the suede bootees, her pervading sexual unattractiveness, at first evoked a strong revulsion then an equally strong compassion. "I'm a teacher," he said. "I expect our salary problems are the same."

"I wish they were," Ruth said. She took a small metal box from the pocket of her tweed suit and extracted a minute white tablet. "It's not the same as sugar," she said, putting it in her coffee. "You don't diet, do you, Mr Dungarvan?"

"Not yet."

"Call him Vincent," Laura said. "Do you know we're living in his grandfather's house?"

"No, I didn't. All these houses round the park were somebody's grandfather's, though. Would you like some biscuits or cake or something, Mr Dungarvan?" She had a square face, reddened by the ride through the rain; the squareness seemed to extend even to her hips and breasts. Vincent felt obscurely that he should be ashamed of himself for liking her so little; and then, observing the way in which her eyes followed every movement of Laura's, he began to feel vaguely disquieted.

"No, thanks, Ruth. I've got to be off, anyway. I've still some essays to mark."

Ruth stared at him for a moment as if considering the validity of his statement. "I must have an early night myself," she said, looking again at Laura. "Good night to you both." She went out of the room, her coffee cup in her hand.

"I'll let myself out," he said to Laura.

She kissed him. "You needn't be in a hurry."

He put down his coffee cup and pointed at the door through which Ruth had left. "She puts me off," he whispered.

She nodded. "It won't be long now," she said.

77

"I'll see you tomorrow," he said. "It'll be the first Sunday I've really looked forward to for months."

She came with him to the door, her hand in his; when he opened it, she hugged him convulsively. "Thank you, Vincent."

"It's nothing," he said.

"It was marvellous," she said. "I'd say fabulous, but such a lot of people use the word."

"I don't want to go," he said.

"Tomorrow then. Don't forget what I said." She hugged him again and gently closed the door.

As he drove off down Charlton Road he tried to remember the feeling of Laura's body and the texture of her dress. The fine wool under his fingers, he heard her quickened breathing; when he saw, superimposed upon the picture of Laura and himself in the tiny kitchen, the Roman soldier with an arrow in his throat.

Five

Vincent was dozing off, the *Observer* in his lap, when he heard Paul's voice, then his mother's, then a confusion of children's voices. He stretched himself and yawned and was levering himself out of the armchair when Paul burst into the room, his hand outstretched, as if, Vincent thought sourly, he hadn't seen his brother for years, and as if, moreover, he were somehow forgiving him for it.

"The deadly sin of sloth," Paul said, shaking Vincent's hand vigorously. He looked at the *Observer* over the top of this heavy horn-rimmed spectacles, his lips pursed. "And still taking that anti-Catholic paper."

"It isn't anti-Catholic," Vincent said.

"No Catholic can be an editor of the *Observer*. What's that but anti-Catholic?"

"Never mind," Vincent said. "I don't want to be the editor. Anyway, they changed that."

Paul sat down heavily, pulling up his fawn whipcord trousers at the knee. Like Matthew, he was putting on weight and his hair was thinning, but unlike Matthew he had about him an aura of complacent good health, as palpable as carbolic. He took a large briar pipe, the stem bound with a silver band, from the pocket of his tweed jacket.

"Shame you never smoked a pipe, young Vincent," he said. "Not cigarettes, mind. A pipe. Makes you more human."

"I'm human enough," Vincent said.

"So I hear."

Vincent flushed. "You'd better tell me what you hear."

"You've got a girlfriend. A Protestant." He waved with his pipe-stem at the drawing-room door. "Ma didn't tell me, if that's what you're thinking. A friend told Jenny. Don't ask me, dear brother, who told the friend."

"I think they communicate with smoke signals like Red Indians," Vincent said. "What's the fuss, anyway? You married a Protestant."

"She turned," Paul said. He dabbed his forehead with a large yellow silk handkerchief. "You keep a good fire here."

"I'm not so well-covered as you," Vincent said. "You're not going to preach me a sermon on mixed marriages, are you?"

"I think I may say I know my own brother better than that," Paul, said heavily. Then he smiled as if to acknowledge his tendency towards portentousness. "Good God, what are we supposed to do? Live in a sort of ghetto? I thought I'd warn you, that's all. You're rumbled, lad."

"I've only been out with her four times," Vincent said. "For heaven's sake, it's a bit previous to talk about marriage."

"I didn't use the word first," Paul said. The pipe was drawing well now; he puffed out smoke noisily. The tobacco had an extraordinary pungency but Vincent found himself enjoying the smell. Since his father had died the room seemed to have become by degrees all too neat and feminine and pastel-coloured; the smell of pipe tobacco seemed to make it more comfortable, more lived-in, more like a room in a home and less like the Warden's room in the YWCA. Paul's accent grew more preposterously refined, his clothes more County, his self-esteem more overweening, each time he saw him; but he was a man living with a woman upon whom he'd begotten three children. And, unlike Matthew, he wasn't in any kind of trouble; Paul could be a crashing bore but there was something enormously reassuring about him.

"I wasn't really thinking very hard about marriage," he said. "But it's in my mind. She's great fun."

"There's more to marriage than fun," Paul said.

Vincent's feeling of affection suddenly disappeared. "Continue," he said. "Pray continue. Tell me that marriage is a serious business."

"It's a sacrament." Paul said. "It's for a long time. As long as you both shall live. You're better unmarried than married unhappily. Or a priest."

"I've almost given up that idea," Vincent said.

"I hadn't heard."

"No doubt, since you live nearly fifty miles away." He recovered his temper. "You'll have to meet Laura some time, and then you can judge for yourself."

"I'd like to very much," Paul said, his composure unruffled. "Or you could come and see us at Harrogate sometime. She's a librarian, isn't she?"

"You're well informed," Vincent said, feeling his temper rise again.

"If she's qualified, she'll always be able to earn enough to live on. Jenny always says that she's no need to worry if I snuff it. She can always earn enough to support her and the kids."

"Oh God, don't have poor Laura widowed already! Let's get married first."

"It's always best to pick someone on your own level. Look at Matthew now. I'm not saying that Maureen isn't a nice girl, but what can she do if he leaves her unprovided for? Shop assistants don't even earn enough to keep themselves."

"I don't expect he worries about it overmuch. Or Maureen either."

"That's the trouble with those two. I hope you haven't lent him any money, by the way." Paul's eyes wandered away from Vincent to the engraving of the martyrdom of the Blessed Edmund Campion which hung over the mantelpiece. The soldiers at the foot of the scaffold had all the same face, moustached and bearded and impassive; the masked executioner towered over Campion and over the minister who was pointing to an opened Bible. There was a smoking cauldron and an array of knives on a block. The faces were uninspired, even Campion's lacking expression, but the knives and the cauldron and the block were drawn with a disturbing accuracy; the block even had meticulously cross-hatched grooves.

"I hate that bloody picture," Paul said. "I saw an SS man disembowelled once. Once they started you had to let them finish, you'd have done no good to yourself interfering." He walked over to the window. "Indian summer weather," he said. "We should go out for a walk."

"Why mustn't I lend Matthew any money?"

Paul did not seem to hear; this evasion of awkward questions Vincent reflected, had now become second nature to him. He had never heard about the SS man before; but it was a typical wartime anecdote of Paul's, demonstrating as it did that Paul was not only extremely sensitive but tough as well.

"Your hollyhocks are coming along very nicely," Paul said. "By Jove, those purple ones by the front gate must be seven feet high."

"Why mustn't I lend money to Matthew?"

"You wouldn't be doing him a kindness, believe me. It's the very worst thing you could do to him."

"And they say that lawyers haven't any human feelings. I'm ashamed of myself, Paul, when I think of your generosity. That decision must have cost you a great deal."

"It'd cost me a great deal more if lent him any money," Paul said sharply. "I've got a wife and three children."

Vincent began to laugh. "You won't lend him any money because you think you wouldn't get it back. Admit it, Paul"

Paul began to laugh too. The door opened and Jenny came in, her finger laid to her mouth. "You're making too much noise," she said. "The baby's just gone off to sleep. Hello, Vincent." She briskly kissed his cheek. "You're looking extremely well." The kiss and the statement about his personal appearance were invariable, one as dry and accurate as the other. If Jenny had said I looked as if I were going to die in the next twenty-four hours, he thought, I'd make my will; looking at the round and rosy but severe face with the delicate fair eyebrows and the prim mouth, he was sure that if she thought anyone was going to die she'd have no hesitation in telling them so.

"I'm feeling extremely well, Jenny," he said. "All the better for seeing your pretty face."

She acknowledged the compliment with a faint smile. "I would have shown you it sooner but Bernard had a slight internal disaster. Grandmother's now consoling him. I wondered if two men would like to take Bernard and Shane for a walk. They're looking awfully peaky."

"I was just saying we ought to," Paul said. He rubbed his hands together nervously.

"If I don't nag him, he just sits around at weekends," Jenny said. "He's frightfully lazy, Vincent. He even drives to the postbox and it's scarcely three hundred yards away."

"We'll have a walk through Twine Woods," Paul said. "We don't want to overtire the boys."

"I wish you could," Jenny said. "They haven't been sleeping at all well recently." She pushed a strand of hair out of her eyes; it was as if it were made of something of an enormous heaviness. She seemed to have lost weight since Vincent had last seen her; it was as if the thin body were held up by the thick tweed jacket and skirt.

"We'll take them away before they break something," Paul said.

"Do that," Jenny said. She sat down with the *Observer.*

When Paul and Vincent went into the drawing-room his mother was rocking the baby in her arms and the two boys were reading, stretched out on the hearthrug.

"I think we'll move into the living-room," his mother said. "Switch off the gas-fire, will you, Vincent?" She touched the baby's cheek lightly. "Hasn't he the delicate skin? Not old leather like his father's."

"My back's broad enough to bear it," Paul said, picking up the Karricot and its stand. "Grandma says he's all Dungarvan."

His mother sniffed. "She would. No, he's his mother's son, this one. He'll be fair, if not ginger. It's Bernard and Shane that take after you."

Vincent looked at the small red face, the eyes screwed tight as if in anger: he was astounded to feel a great tenderness not only for the baby but for Paul and Jenny and his mother and the two boys. "He's marvellous," he said. "Look, he's smiling in his sleep."

"It's wind," Paul said. "He's too young to smile."

Shane, the elder boy, suddenly rose and threw himself Vincent. "Are we going for a walk, Uncle Vincent? Will you buy me some ice-cream?"

"I'll consider it," Vincent said, ruffling the boy's dark hair.

Shane punched his leg. "Don't consider it, Uncle. I don't like consider."

"Neither do I," said Vincent. "I'm rather tired of the word."

Shane poked Bernard in the ribs with his foot. "Come on, Barney. We're going out for some ice-cream."

"I want to read," Bernard said.

"You can't read. You only pretend-read. I can read, can't I, Uncle?"

"You're seven and he's five," Vincent said. "It isn't surprising, is it?"

"I could read when I was four, couldn't I, Grandma?"

Vincent's mother stood up, holding the baby still more tightly to her. "You'll not go through the world unnoticed, will you, child."

"It's the best way to be," Vincent said. "Look at him, Mother, he's like a little bull."

His mother sighed. "He'll need a firm hand, that one." She smiled at Shane. "Be a good boy now, Shane, and take good care of your little brother. His legs aren't as long as yours. And don't be calling him Barney. You know Mummy and Daddy don't like it."

Vincent picked Bernard up. "I bet you can walk faster than Shane," he said. "And you'll be able to read when you're as old as he is." Bernard didn't answer, but stared at Vincent with large blue eyes. "We'll see if there's any ice cream in the shops," Vincent said. He felt unreasonably sad at being unable to coax a response from the child, and puzzled that he had never felt like this before. The last time he'd seen the children, it had been as usual: Shane, the eldest and the brightest, had been the only one he'd had any interest in, and Bernard and the baby were no more than animated dolls. But Bernard was a person, Bernard had feelings, Bernard wanted to be like his elder brother, Bernard wanted to be taken as much notice of as Shane.

"I can read," Bernard said as Paul came in with the coats. "I can read too, Uncle Vincent."

"I'll tell you some stories," Vincent said. "About when Daddy and Uncle Vincent and Uncle Matthew were little boys."

As they went out Bernard took Vincent's hand. "That's Daddy's car," he said, pointing to Paul's shooting-brake. "He wants a new one."

"A mobile slum, that's what it is," Paul said. "Five years with that model and it begins to fall part."

"I was sick in it," Bernard said.

"Nothing to be proud of," Paul said. He paused at the front gate. "By Jove, those hollyhocks really are splendid." He took a deep breath and thumped his chest. "Marvellous day," he said, looking down Pinley Avenue and towards the moors. "You can smell winter though." He picked up two dead leaves. "No good for twankers," he said. "Remember playing that at school every autumn term?"

"They still do," Vincent said.

"It's funny to think of you still being there," Paul said.

"I go to other places. Italy, Spain, France, Switzerland."

"Don't remind me," Paul said. "We went to Scarborough."

Pinley Avenue was short and lined with cypresses, almost as broad as it was long. Outside three of the houses cars were being washed; this was part of the Sunday ritual.

Paul grimaced. "I swear I saw that thin man with the moustache kiss his on the bonnet," he said. "They do the same in my part of the world."

They turned down Thacker's Snicket, their feet stirring the fallen leaves. The boys ran on ahead towards the woods, pausing to yell and dance round each other in circles, their arms outstretched.

"No one seems to go for walks here any more," Vincent said. "Once upon a time you could hardly move for people."

"Standing or lying," Paul said. "They must do it at home now." The children were nearly out of sight over the brow of the hill. "Bernard! Shane!" he shouted. "Come back!" The children did not seem to hear; Paul broke into a run. He ran heavily and clumsily, his head strained back as if caught from behind. The children stopped; Paul, panting, took hold of their hands.

When Vincent drew level with him his face was still red. "You've got to watch the little devils," he said. "They can disappear in a minute. There's some damned funny customers around these days. Boys are no more safe than girls. Do you hear, Shane? Do you hear, Bernard?" He cuffed Shane on the back of the head, then Bernard, his face momentarily contorted with anxiety. The blow was light, more admonitory than punitive, but Bernard started to cry. Shane looked at his father with no change in his expression. "We wouldn't have run away, Daddy," he said.

"All right," Paul said. "But just you remember there are bad men about." He laughed. "They say children keep you young," he said to Vincent. "But I never knew what worry was until I became a father."

Bernard sniffed; Vincent bent down and gave him his handkerchief. "Stop crying," he said gently, "and there may be something nice." The tears stopped, and they walked on in silence for a moment, Bernard taking hold of Vincent's hand again.

"He seems to like you," Paul said. "He's a funny kid. Dreamy. You were dreamy, not that you'd remember." They came to the steps which led into the woods; they seemed almost perpendicular.

"We used to run up those steps," Vincent said. "There's three hundred of them."

Paul took out his pipe. "Are you seeing this girl tonight?" He looked embarrassed.

"As a matter of fact I am."

"You could bring her to our place sometime. Or why don't you bring her home tonight?"

"I don't think she'd enjoy being under inspection," Vincent said coldly.

"There's nothing wrong in you bringing her to see Jenny and me, is there? Besides, I think Jenny knew her at the Library School."

"She hasn't said anything to me about it."

"Damn it, Vince, don't be so suspicious. Jenny wasn't married then, and in any case they didn't know each other all that well. It might be that Jenny got her name wrong."

They had reached the fiftieth step now and Paul was slowing down a little.

"Mother's been saying something to you," he said. "She's been ominously quiet about the whole thing,"

"She thinks it a bit queer that you don't bring the girl home. She doesn't mind you having a girl."

"Not much she doesn't," Vincent said. "I know what she wants me to do."

"Don't be so daft. You wanted to be a priest once and she was happy if that was what you wanted. Then you changed your mind."

"I don't want anyone to interfere," Vincent said. "I've a good mind to get a place of my own in Charbury."

Paul stopped. "You? Why, you couldn't even boil an egg. You couldn't manage for even a day without someone to look after you. You've never even lived in lodgings, you can't have any idea what it's like."

"I was in the Army," Vincent said stiffly.

"That's different. That's a picnic, anyway. In the Forces in peacetime, they look after you twenty-four hours a day. You were forced to do your National Service anyway. You're not forced to leave home. Besides, what would people say?" He paused, breathing heavily. "You've got to admit, Vince, it would look very odd."

"I wouldn't do anything that would make people talk," Vincent said. "Of course not." There had been many arguments like this, he thought wearily, and Paul had always won; for Paul always accepted things as they were, he had no wish for his life to be any different. For over a quarter of a century now he'd been making attempts to break out, and Paul's big guns had beaten him back, so that now he hardly knew what it was he really wanted.

"Mother's worried," Paul said. "I know she hasn't said much to you about it, but she's a bit hurt. See if you can't bring Laura in tonight, if only for a cup of tea. You're not ashamed of her, are you?"

"I'll see," Vincent said. "But don't let's make a big dramatic issue of it."

"What's dramatic?" Bernard asked.

"It's rather difficult to explain," Vincent said, and heard his own voice going on to explain it as they walked on towards the top of the hill and the three-hundredth step.

When he called for Laura that evening she answered the door immediately, her raincoat over her arm; almost before he had opened his mouth they were running down the steps and into the car.

"Let's be off," she said. "I wouldn't have stayed there another minute if you hadn't been coming." She kissed him quickly. "I was so afraid you'd be late."

"You should have phoned me. We could have met somewhere else. Or earlier. Or you could have come to my house."

"I couldn't do that," she said.

He helped her into the car. "Why couldn't you?"

"Your mother. She wouldn't like me."

"You can't possibly say that until you've met her."

"I've had more experience than you have," she said. "I've never been any Mum's favourite. I'm too much the bird of passage. You're not a bird of passage, are you, Vincent?"

"I've been to more countries than England," he said. "Living rough, too. When I was at the University, my father never let me take a job in the vacations. I wanted to, because he had to pay for me, but he more or less threw me out of the house. I've walked all over Europe."

"That isn't what I meant," she said. "You still live in this place, you always come back to it. You have relations, you have a family, you have a religion. I haven't anything. At least, not as much as you. I don't often go home, you see. My parents don't really approve of me; I'm wild and hard, I don't go to church any more."

"I'm sorry," he said. He was too intent on negotiating the right-hand turn into the Sarnley Road to look at her; but the bitterness in her voice made him imagine a face pale and grimacing; wild and hard; it wasn't what he had wanted this evening.

"Do you mean you're sorry I don't go to church, Vincent? I thought a Protestant would be the equivalent of a pagan to you."

The voice was definitely hard now; but it was an assumed hardness, it was the hardness of someone who had been hurt.

"A priest was excommunicated not so long ago for saying that. It's your own business anyway. I only meant that I was sorry you didn't hit it off with your parents."

"It's not as bad as that. I *do* see them. But you don't approve of me, Vincent. Not really. You think I ought to see them regularly. That's what I hate so much about you. You're so damned rigid, so black-and-white."

"I try not to be," he said stiffly. He stopped the car. "I thought we might go to the pictures."

"I don't want to go to the pictures." Her mouth was pulled down at the comers like a sulking child's. "I can't talk to you in the pictures."

"We'll go to the Country Club at Sarnley. Have you eaten?"

She shook her head.

"You're a silly girl, aren't you?" She nodded vigorously, smiling for the first time; in her shawl-necked white dress her face seemed defencelessly small and young.

"I don't go there very often," he said. "But I don't drink much, so I can't bear pubs. I used to go to the Green Horn in Sarnley a lot once, but they started having fights there. Not my idea of fun."

She stroked the back of his neck gently, her hand running upward. "What nice short hair you have. You're always clean, Vincent."

"I do my best," he said, turning the ignition key. They had stopped in the same spot near the park where they had stopped on the first occasion he'd gone to her, or rather Ruth's flat: he had the sensation, because of Laura's presence, because of her explicit interest in him as a person to talk to rather than an escort to pass the evening with, that the dark green laurels, the blank windows of the big houses, the leafless trees in the park visible against the skyline on the right, were not so much ordinary three-dimensional objects as objects beyond dimension, the lines of a poem which he'd forgotten but was now remembering. He kissed her lightly and all the way to the Country Club tried not to moisten his lips so that the taste, not of lipstick but of her mouth, wouldn't be lost.

"I've been longing to see you all day," she said as they sat in the bar of the Country Club. "I told Ruth that I'd got a flat of my own and the balloon went up. You've no idea of how possessive women can be. One would think –" She hesitated.

"One would think what?"

"One doesn't want to shock you," she said.

The bar was filling up with young people, their dress curiously uniform – Italian cut suits for the men and sheath dresses for the girls; the girls moved to the bar and sat on the stools with a designedly unselfconscious display of leg, the men ordered drinks in high voices with a snap of the fingers, seeming to strut even when standing still. To his surprise, Vincent found himself enjoying them along with the gilt mirrors and the pale yellow walls and the thick red carpet and the reproductions of Rouault and Dali and Picasso: they bore the same relation to the young people he knew as Klee's fishes and cats did to real cats and fishes, they belonged less to the West Riding than to London and less to London than New York and Paris and Copenhagen and West Berlin, they were people who showered rather than bathed, whose clothes were stage properties rather than covering, as easily taken off as put on: he would never live in their world and didn't want to, but at this moment, smelling Laura's Gauloise and sipping his gin and tonic he could be grateful to them simply because they weren't dingy or fat or poor, because they wouldn't make any demands upon him, or, for that matter, anyone else: they simply were themselves without guilt or fear, the magic fishes which would never lose their glitter.

"I'd rather liked to be shocked," he said. "I'm well over the age of intellectual consent."

"One would think we were lovers," she said. "One would think I'd sworn eternal fidelity to her. She's stamped about the flat all day with a face as black as thunder. I suppose she's having a good cry now. Actually, I don't think she's equal to sex of any kind. You can't imagine it, can you?"

Vincent pulled a face. "I don't want to."

"She's terribly lonely," Laura said. She frowned at the menu the waiter had brought them. "*Entrecôte* and salad, please. French dressing."

"The same for me," Vincent said. He looked at the wine list. "Half a bottle of Bordeaux, please, Number Thirty. All right for you, Laura?"

"I haven't anything against it," she said. "You don't make a ceremony of it do you?"

"My grandfather used to lecture me about it. He said that stout and spirits were the curse of the Irish and put us at the mercy of the monsignors and the gombeen men. He got through a bottle of whisky every day just the same. If only he'd practised what he'd preached I'd probably be with that lot at the bar."

"I doubt it," Laura said. "You're much too solid. You don't care, do you?"

"No. Why should I?"

"I didn't think you would. I don't suppose you'd have lost your temper with poor silly Ruth, either. She doesn't mean any harm, and she feeds me so well that I'm sure she can't make any profit out of me. She brought me a present last night because I said I'd been looking for it for a long time. Rilke's *Duino Elegies.* Don't say you know them if you don't."

"I'd have lent you mine," he said.

"I can always borrow them. But I wanted a copy of my own. She blushed when she gave me the book, it was a big moment for her. I'd been going to tell her that night and not put it off any longer, but then I had to put it off till today. She's started to plan our holidays for next year. I'd rather spend them by myself in darkest Blackpool if it came to the choice. At least I'd get a man there – "

She looked at him anxiously. "I have shocked you after all. I bet I shock you all the time."

"I know all the facts of life," he said. A girl at the bar was talking to a young man, unaware that her shoulder-straps were slipping. Her voice was breathless and piping, her shoulders and hips narrow; only the unbroken smoothness of her throat and the length of her hair saved her from boyishness. The dress began to slip; she continued to talk to her companion. Vincent drew in his breath, trying not to look at the white back; a girl came up to her and whispered something and slowly the thin hands came up and replaced the shoulder-straps.

"You appear to be fascinated," Laura said. "Perhaps I should have put on a different dress."

"I don't like the Lolita type," he said. "I'm astonished they let her in,"

"She's drinking tomato juice," Laura said. "The law says people under eighteen can't drink alcohol in licensed premises, not that they can't enter licensed premises."

Startled, he recognized the authentic note of jealousy. It seemed to make not only Laura feasibly available but all the other women in the room: the chalk dust was being washed off his fingers, the dryness was dissolving.

"I'm here with *you*," he said sharply. "I've told you I don't like little girls."

"You do," she said. "At least you like this one. Not that she's really a little girl. You're a man, you see." She ran her index finger very lightly over his lips. "You've got the wrong kind of mouth not to like women. They like you, Vincent. I wonder sometimes if you realize it."

"I don't think about it," he said.

"You do. You think about it a great deal. And you come to the conclusion that they aren't really interested. I suppose that's why you never married. God knows how you plucked up the courage to ask me to go out with you." She stubbed out her cigarette, took out the blue packet from her handbag, then put it away again. "You don't really like to see me smoking, do you?"

"That's your business."

"I won't stop, but I'll try not to smoke so much when I'm with you. You make me nervous, you see."

The waiter came in and signalled in their direction; Vincent rose and pulled Laura's chair back for her, glad to leave what she had said unanswered. Over dinner he deliberately kept the conversation impersonal; he wanted time to think, to put the proper name to the relationship which was growing between them. When they were silent, it was as if she were thinking the same thoughts; over the coffee, he caught her looking at him with an expression which was of complete acceptance.

"I'll be moving into the new place next week," she said suddenly. "Then I've got to go home on Friday, but I'll be back on Sunday. I'll give you the address now. Forty, Warden Avenue. Phone eleven hundred. It's in Marlcliffe. Do you know it?"

He wrote the address down in his diary. "It's a long way from the Library."

"That was the idea. I'm a country girl really." She laughed. "No, I'm not. I want to be as far away from Ruth as possible, that's all. I hate possessive people, they drain your strength. I'd rather be absolutely alone – "

"No one is," he said. "Or rather, no one can be."

"They can, Vincent. Anything's better than living with someone who won't leave you alone, who tries to devour you, who's pathetically glad if you say a kind word, and who starts to cry if you as much as wrinkle your forehead."

"Is she as bad as all that?"

Laura was not looking at him as she spoke; her gaze was moving restlessly from person to person in the big dining-room; she seemed to be searching for someone.

"Is who as bad as all that?"

"Ruth. You were grumbling about her."

"Oh." She looked at her reflection in the big mirror to her right. "I didn't mean Ruth." The dining-room was decorated in the same style as the bar except for a small patch of floor by the orchestra stand; the pictures were all Utrillo street-scenes, and Vincent, with a disproportionate warmth of feeling, decided that the colours, in a room of this size, weren't bold enough. The orchestra stand was empty: there was never any music and dancing on a Sunday night in the Charbury area. When he had first entered the place it had seemed full ; now he saw that half the tables were empty. He had to go home soon; never before had he found the fact so intolerably depressing.

"Who did you mean?"

"Just people in general. Neurotics. The unhappy ones. Men. Men one doesn't love but feels sorry for. That's the worst thing that can happen to a woman."

"Do you feel sorry for me?"

"I don't think that I ever will." Her eyes seemed more green than hazel under the light of the chandeliers; her tone was coolly speculative, a tone used in a world very different from Charbury, a world in which, he thought, one might well discuss the value of different kinds of experience, in which one well might live with a man out of pity as much as out of desire; she was telling him, in short, that she wasn't a virgin. He was surprised to discover how much the knowledge hurt him.

"I wonder what kind of a man you take me for."

"Very respectable. Very moral." She touched his mouth lightly. And, as if I hadn't already told you, very sensual. I sometimes honestly think – never mind." She looked at her watch. "I'm frightfully tired. Will you take me home?" She grimaced. "To coin a phrase."

His mother was sitting by the fire when he went in, her hands over her eyes. The room was lit only by the small table-lamp with the blue Delft base which he had brought her back from the school trip to Holland; the fire was nearly out. He put his hand on the wall switch; something about his mother's attitude depressed and irritated him.

"No," she said, sharply. "My eyes hurt."

"You should get some glasses," he said.

95

"I don't need glasses. My mother didn't and she was seventy-five when she died. I've been sitting here alone, thinking and worrying and praying about my children."

"You needn't pray for me," he said.

She took her hands away from her eyes. "It's you I pray for most of all. You who were the apple of my eye, God forgive me. You who still are. Not Paul, who's worth a dozen of you, not poor silly Matthew who needs all the help he can get, but you."

He sat down. "Mother, there really isn't any need for amateur dramatics. I'm going to bed."

"You don't want anything?"

"No. I've had something."

"May I ask where?"

"The Country Club."

"That's a fine place. Full of drunkards and whores. No, not whores. Whores' robbers. That's a fine place for a teacher from St Theo's to be in on a Sunday night. You couldn't stay in just for once, could you? You couldn't go to Benediction, could you?"

"Oh God, don't be so ridiculous! It's a perfectly respectable place. You talk as if it were a brothel."

"So it is," she said. "A place for men with more money than sense and girls with no sense of shame. Who were you with, if I may make so bold as to ask?"

"Laura."

"That's the first time I've heard her name from your lips. Other people told me. Oh, they enjoyed telling me. 'Your son's never away from the Library, Mrs Dungarvan.' 'I see your son's got himself a girl, Mrs Dungarvan' and them grinning all over their faces, because they know full well you've kept it dark." She stood up, her hand stretched out accusingly at Vincent. "And why haven't you told me? Because she's a Protestant. That's why. Because you know she's the wrong girl for you, that's why."

"There's nothing in it," he said. "I don't have to marry a girl just because I take her out to dinner."

"You're just going to lead her on." She shook her head slowly. He found himself blushing, not from shame but from vicarious embarrassment; the slow shaking of her head, which he knew from experience was meant to indicate sorrow, was even more grotesquely false than its precursor, the accusing hand. "Poor girl. Poor girl. She'll think you're serious – after all, you're not a silly teenager and neither is she. And then you'll drop her just as you dropped Clare. Mind, I don't say that I was all that keen on Clare. She's common, you can't deny it: But she's a good Catholic, and she comes from good decent people. You didn't do right by her, Vincent."

"Clare gave me up," he said wearily.

She laughed; again he felt an embarrassment that was now close to nausea. There was no amusement in the laugh; it was a snort of derision which only a trained actress could have made anything else than grotesque. "That one'd never give you up. Why, you'd be the biggest feather in her cap, and her family's cap – they'd think they'd died and gone to Heaven. Her mother's never got over her going to St Felicity's and getting an office job – she was the first one in that family to be anything better than a mill-girl. You were lucky to get away with it, son. She was quite capable of suing you for breach of promise."

"Mother, don't talk in that ridiculous way. You're living in the twentieth century, for God's sake. Who are we to look down on anyone?"

As he said it, he knew that he didn't believe it, that he had found certain traits of Clare grating upon him more and more, that if he had married Clare he would have had to leave Charbury because he couldn't find any point of contact with her family. But this knowledge didn't diminish his anger but increased it: his mother was acknowledging what he didn't want to acknowledge.

"Oh, you're the great democrat," his mother said quietly. "You've a soul above these petty distinctions, Vincent. Many's the time I've watched you with other children, and I know what you're thinking. I've seen you standing apart from them like a little king. And they know it, and don't imagine that they like it. They know that you don't belong with them. And you don't belong to Clare or to Laura or to any other woman. You belong to the Church, Vincent. Why do you fight against it?"

"That's enough. It's my business whether I become a priest or not. And I'm sure I won't. I'm not going to become one just because you want me to."

She shook her head slowly. The fire was nearly out now: the room had become very cold. "No, Vincent. Don't do anything to please the woman that bore you in pain and anguish." Her hands were trembling, he noted sourly; but that seemed as false as the slow shaking of the head. "Do nothing to please me. Break my heart, Vincent. You know the story of the young man who fell in love with a bad woman" – she spat out rather than spoke the adjective – "and who promised her anything she wanted. And she said, *Cut out your mother's heart* – "

"I've heard it," Vincent said. "And he stumbled as he was carrying the heart and the heart said *Did you hurt yourself, my son?* You'd be more likely to say you hoped I broke my neck. Come off it, Mother."

She smiled reluctantly. "You're a hard devil," she said. "For all that, I don't like you going about with this Laura. You don't know anything about her."

"You'll remedy that deficiency for me," he said. "I think I'd like a cup of tea." This, he thought, was her most insidious form of attack; she was going to be calm and quiet and reasonable.

"Where does she live?"

"She's sharing a flat with another girl. At Daniel House, in fact. But it's just temporary."

"That's a queer arrangement. Women living together who aren't related."

"For God's sake, Mother, it's perfectly normal."

"You needn't think I'm ignorant of the world, son. There was that woman next door to us when we lived in Beaumont Terrace.

Of course, you'd be too young to know what was going on. She ran away with another woman. Left her husband and her two lovely young children – "

"Oh God, you make me sick," he said. "I swear to God I'll leave this bloody house. You don't know Laura, and you don't know Ruth. She's getting a place of her own anyway – " Despite himself images were forming in his mind, augmented by memories. He could see again the unmistakable look of jealousy on Ruth's face that evening she came into the flat to find him there with Laura. Wasn't there altogether too much fuss being made about Laura finding a place of her own? Wasn't Laura altogether too disturbed about Ruth's attitude? Why, being presumably a woman of some experience, hadn't Laura refused Ruth's offer in the first instance? He looked at his mother and detected the triumph on her face. "No," he said. "No, Mother, I know what you're hinting at. You'll not get your own way this time."

"I don't care about getting my own way," she said. "I only want to save you unhappiness."

"You'll not save me unhappiness by blackguarding a girl you haven't even met."

"Ah, you're on her side already." She rose slowly, levering herself up by the arms of her chair. She usually leaped to her feet; this simulation of approaching age was the last shot in her locker. She sighed and put a hand on her back in the attitude of a sufferer from lumbago. "I'll make you your tea," she said. "That's one thing your poor old mother can do. Make tea and wash your shirts and cook your meals." She rubbed her back. "I'm not as young as I was," she said. "I won't always be here." She sighed again and shuffled out of the room, her head down.

Vincent stretched his legs and yawned. Another Sunday was ending: he would drink his tea and finish reading the *Observer*, he would go to bed and five minutes after saying his prayers he would be asleep. No more would be said about Laura tonight; these scenes with his mother, whatever their cause, ran always to the same predictable pattern. Those who lived under the shadow of a volcano grew used to it; he was even at this moment quite near to contentment. He picked up the paper and then suddenly flung it into a corner of the room. He was lying to himself and it was habit that made him lie; he disliked himself for it, he would ask to be forgiven for it later, but what he felt for his mother was something near hatred. He picked up the paper again; but when he heard her footsteps – light and quick and impatient now – outside the room he was appalled to find that he dreaded seeing her again.

Six

During the next five days there was an uneasy truce. Vincent took Laura to the cinema on Tuesday and to a concert on Thursday; each night when he came home his mother had already gone to bed and the morning after made no reference to the fact of his having gone out the night before. On the evenings when he stayed at home she went out, once to Matthew's and twice to the cinema; Vincent in his turn went to bed early and the morning after made no reference to the fact of her having been out the night before.

It was exactly as if he were sharing the house with a stranger; suddenly they became coldly, meticulously polite to each other. He had the impression that she went out only because he was staying in; the house had become too small for both of them. It wasn't the most comfortable of arrangements, since she also stopped taking her meals with him; but it was infinitely preferable to the kind of scene they'd had on Sunday night. Afterwards he was to look back upon those five days with regret. The truce was an uneasy one, he couldn't delude himself that the fighting wouldn't start again at any moment; but his evenings with Laura became entirely enjoyable. In the quiet house he would make himself tea and remember every detail, however small: on the Tuesday she had worn a cherry-coloured dress with white cloth buttons, they had sat in the second row of the upper circle, she had had a strawberry ice at the interval, on the Thursday they had sat downstairs, she had worn a maroon wool dress with a high neck, they had a gin and tonic each afterwards at the Royalty Hotel American Bar: there had been nothing finally beyond a quick kiss in the car, but this hadn't mattered. On Sunday night his mother had almost spoiled everything, he had almost been ready to believe his own worst fantasies about Laura; now, sipping his tea, he was a solid and sane research student of pleasure, of pleasure untainted by guilt.

On Saturday morning he went into Charbury immediately after breakfast. He had no clear idea of what he would do with himself for something like fourteen hours; Laura had gone home on the Friday evening and he would not see her until Sunday. He only knew that the day was his own. The Indian summer, against all odds in this part of the West Riding, had continued; there was coldness in the air but the sun seemed to transfigure the city, almost to gild it.

He parked the car in Westman Street, a cul-de-sac a little out of the centre of the city, and stood for a moment in what was almost a trance. A habit had been broken: for five years now his habit had been to do most of the weekend shopping in Beckfield, to lunch at home, and then, and only then to go out. As often as not he only went as far as the garden in the afternoon and the cinema or the theatre in the evening: occasionally he would visit Matthew or Paul or his grandmother or his Uncle Peter, or more rarely, his Uncle Luke. There were some visitors, but not as many as when his father had been alive, in fact it was precisely the friends and relations his father had liked the best who didn't come any more. His mother hadn't been heavy-handed about it; but it was, for instance, at least six months since they'd seen his Uncle Simon and his Aunt Rosa. He could live without seeing them but the reason why they didn't come any more was simply that they'd been frozen off on their last visit. They were common; uncle Simon's fingernails were black and Aunt Rosa had a loud laugh and made lavatory jokes. And, above all, his father had liked them. They were Dungarvans, of course, which was a count against them to begin with: but now that Vincent came to think of it, his Uncle Louis and his Aunt Bernadette didn't visit them any more. Louis was her own brother, a prosperous accountant who had regular manicures, and his Aunt Bernadette had been a teacher, of all things, of elocution. His father had liked Louis and Bernadette: after the first five minutes and a whisky Louis would tell mildly improper jokes and Bernadette's vowels would open out and she'd begin to giggle and to stop pulling down her skirt every five minutes.

A West Indian girl came out of the house opposite and leaned against the door, her eyes on him. The house, like all the others on Westman Street, was down-at-heel, its paint peeling, its brass doorknobs unpolished, its lace curtains grey, its front garden a small wilderness. The windows were still whole: the next stage was cardboard to replace a missing pane and after that the demolition gang would move in. Before the war his uncle Louis and Aunt Bernadette had lived in the next street; it had still been possible then for a professional man to live in the district. The girl yawned, stretching out her arms: it was as if she were in the act of love, the thin body seemed to ripple stiffly in the sunshine. The lilac of her dress was of a shade not often seen these days; when he'd been taken by his father to see Uncle Louis and Aunt Bernadette his aunt had been wearing a dress of exactly that shade.

Through the open door a voice yelled something at the girl There was a smell of something cooking, hot and milky and at the same time peppery: the girl looked at Vincent once again and then walked into the house, slamming the door. He walked down the street into George Road, still seeing her thin dark body and flat impassive face; it was almost as if he had slept with her. That now would be something for his mother to worry about, he thought, grinning to himself. Supposing I found a West Indian girl who was a good clean-living Catholic and I wanted to marry her?

He put the thought firmly out of his mind as he walked down into the centre of the city. Today his mother didn't exist, today he was free of the habit of five years. At breakfast he'd simply told his mother that he was going out for the day and she'd said that she was going to Paul's and would do her shopping in Harrogate. And that had been that: instead of walking about Beckfield with a shopping-list he was strolling about the city free and unencumbered. It was never going to be the same again.

He stopped outside W H Smith's to look at the display of records and was drawn in not so much by the records as by the curiously exciting smell of printer's ink which always seemed to emanate from the shop. It was odd, he thought dreamily: no other newsagent and stationers had quite the same smell. He bought half a dozen Penguins and was paying for them when he heard a woman's voice call his name. It was Ruth, faintly perspiring in a green tweed suit.

"Hello," he said. "Aren't you working?"

"They let us off the leash now and again," she said. She came closer to him as she spoke: he caught the smell of sweat and talcum and camphor.

"You work behind the scenes anyway, don't you?" he said.

She laughed suddenly, almost as if tickled. "I'm an admin bod," she said. "*Eminence grise*, that's me. Brains of the establishment. Laura prefers working with the public. She's jolly good at it, actually."

"I should imagine she would be," he said.

She took out a pair of heavy black horn-rimmed spectacles from her black shoulder bag, put them on and stared at him. "You should know," she said. The spectacles seemed to make her pale blue eyes paler and harder. "She's jolly good at dealing with people. All sorts of people. Now *I'm* always putting my foot in it. I speak my mind, you see. I can't dodge the issue. I've always been like that."

"It's a commendable attitude," Vincent said.

"You don't really think it's commendable at all," she said. She put her hand on his arm suddenly, grasping it firmly as if about to take him into custody. "Come and have a coffee with me. You don't mind being seen with me, do you? I won't tell Laura." She laughed again. "I don't like drinking coffee by myself."

"I'd be delighted," he said automatically. "I was just going to ask you, in fact."

She released his arm. "Oh no, Vincent," she said. "You weren't. But it's nice of you to say so."

He followed her out into the street; the sunlight had become stronger now, and he shaded his eyes against it. "There's Rodger's Tearooms just a hundred yards away," he said.

"You don't suggest the Nevada," she said.

"If you really want to – "

"Rodger's is quite nice," she said. "Dark with little booths. You won't see anyone you know there." She took off her spectacles and rubbed her eyes; with repulsion and with pity saw that they were red-rimmed and that the eyelids were dry and flaky

"They have rather good cakes," he said. "And they don't use that filthy homogenized milk."

"That's what I need," she said. "Cakes and full-cream milk. Laura drinks her coffee black, doesn't she?"

"I don't," he said as they went into Rodger's Tearooms. "And I eat cakes too. And I take at least five lumps of sugar."

"You probably diet in secret," she said.

He laughed; to his consternation the laugh was as false as Ruth's, a nervous cachinnation to disguise the fact that he had nothing in common with his companion. "I'm a Mick," he said. "We thrive on sugar and carbohydrates."

He beckoned to the waitress who, like all the waitresses at Rodger's, was middle-aged and inclined towards plumpness. "Coffee and cakes, please," he said.

"I won't eat them," Ruth said. There was a grotesque suggestion of coyness in her voice.

"You must," he said. "Everyone else is. It's rather Germanic here, isn't it? I remember being in a cafe in Stuttgart once at eleven in the morning and I saw three fat middle-aged men eating mounds of whipped cream. This place has been here for fifty years. They have a string trio here at teatime. I suppose they've been here for fifty years too."

"Have you been to Laura's new flat yet?" she asked abruptly.

"As a matter of fact, I haven't."

"I wondered whether you had."

"I've put you straight then, haven't I? I'm wondering why you should ask me. So you'd better tell me."

The cakes and coffee arrived; abstractedly she took a meringue and dug her fork into it.

"I'm worried about Laura," she said. "I've known her a long time. We went to school together: I've always tried to look after her."

"Isn't she old enough to look after herself?"

"I sometimes wonder. Laura's a wonderful person, really wonderful, but she has a wild streak. This flat of hers – it's far too expensive. She was far better off sharing with me."

"You were on your own before Laura came, weren't you?" he said impatiently.

"I'm on a higher grade than Laura. And I don't have quite such expensive tastes. I suppose you're serious about her, aren't you, Vincent?"

He pushed his chair back and stood up. "I've no intention of being cross-examined by you or by anyone else."

"I'm sorry," she said. "I always put my foot in it. Please sit down again."

"Why did you ask me?" He looked at her intently: he had always imagined women of her sexual inclination to be more masculine, more sophisticated, more exotic; then, slowly and reluctantly, he recognized the truth. There was no passion in Ruth's face, there was no real jealousy: there never had been any sex there. She wouldn't have looked out of place in a gym slip, she was the Captain of the Fifth telling him something for his own good.

"I had a good reason," she said. "You're a Catholic, Vincent."

"Don't tell me that Laura isn't. I know already."

"I've thought a lot about it. I asked the vicar about it and he told me not to interfere. He said I should be quite certain of my own motives first." She took an éclair. "But if I don't speak out then a lot of people are going to be hurt. Mind you, I could have done it a different way." She glanced at the éclair; the cream was faintly yellow. She took a little on her fork and licked it off with a surprisingly pink tongue. "I could just have let it slip out. Because it isn't really a secret. I know because my mother and father know her mother and father. She comes from Silbridge."

"That isn't a crime," he said.

"She never liked it. She goes to see her parents whenever she gets a long weekend, but I suspect it's strictly from a sense of duty."

"I gathered that," he said.

"I thought you were just another wolf at first," she said. "Not that I've met you all that much. But then from things that Laura's let drop I've discovered that you're not."

"It's decent of you to say so," he said, trying to keep his voice neutral.

"Laura hasn't generally very good taste in men. She's very romantic, she lives in a soap opera world. But a very superior soap opera. She's terribly impetuous and untidy and impractical. She's very clever and she gets on terribly well with people, but she doesn't know whether she's coming or going half the time." She looked in surprise at the remains of the éclair and, frowning, selected a piece of chocolate cake.

"I suppose you're right. But if you're warning me against her I really ought to tell you that it won't work. You see, I don't really care." He glanced at his watch. "You'll have to excuse me, I'm afraid."

"I told you she didn't have very good taste in men." Ruth's attention seemed to be directed towards the chocolate cake rather than towards him. "There's been some awful ones, really awful."

"This is becoming ridiculous. I've known some awful women, come to that." He beckoned the waitress. "The bill, please"

"Her husband was the worst." She took a mouthful of chocolate cake.

"You're making this up. She would have told me." He felt an actual pain, a squeezing of the bowels, and a desire to hurt someone physically.

"She generally does. At least, as far as I know. She's divorced, of course. She's been divorced for two years. But you don't recognize divorce, do you?" She continued to eat her chocolate cake; it was as if the situation had become tangible on her plate, and that she were enjoying the taste in precisely the same way.

"You shouldn't have told me," he managed to say at last. "It isn't fair. She'd have told me."

"She'd have been forced to, I expect. But it would have been far worse." She sipped her coffee, made a face, and put in two spoonfuls of brown sugar.

"You're enjoying this," he said. "I've made your bloody day, haven't I" He automatically took the bill from the waitress and rummaged in his pocket for change. "You haven't thought of the effect upon Laura, have you?"

"I always do the wrong thing," she said. She took off her glasses again: it almost seemed as if the redness and dryness around her eyes had disappeared. "But I know what's right and what's wrong, Vincent." She straightened her back. "You'd be wrong to think harshly of her. I know that Robert hurt her very much. When it was over she went back to her maiden name and she took this job in the South. She was dreadfully hurt. If it's any consolation to you, she wasn't the guilty party. Not that that makes any difference to Catholics. You're very black-and-white, aren't you? If you were a little less rigid, you'd understand."

"It's not me who's rigid." he said. It was eleven o'clock, he thought: how would he pass the rest of the day?

"I wish I hadn't told you now," she said. She pushed her plate away. "But if she's thinking of marrying again, you're a likely candidate. I wouldn't want either of you to be hurt."

"You don't want her to get married at all," he said. "You've enjoyed hurting me. You'd always enjoy hurting a man." He put a shilling under the saucer. He knew now who he wanted to hurt and how he wanted to hurt them. "The trouble with you," he said, "is that you want a man and can't get one."

Almost as soon as he had said it, the guilt began: she did not answer him, but merely looked at him, her eyes beginning to moisten. It was as if she would have welcomed a blow. "I'm sorry, Ruth," he said. "I shouldn't have said that."

"I didn't choose my face," she said in a low voice.

"I'm sorry," he said again, and walked quickly out of the room. Outside in the sunlight the guilt began again.

Seven

As he drove towards Marlcliffe he kept pretending to himself that nothing had happened the day before. He hadn't met Ruth; so far as he was concerned, Laura had never been married. He would be in the village in another ten minutes and then he would be alone with Laura; it was raining heavily but they wouldn't have to go to the cinema or a pub or sit in a café, he would at long last on a wet Sunday night be alone with a woman in comfort. He would at long last be free, he wouldn't be torn apart any longer by desire and guilt; there would be no sin because he intended to marry her, because he might even make her understand that it would be better if they waited.

He had, the day before, looking over gramophone records in Smith's, made his mind up. The sin had been committed in the mind, awake and asleep; there was nothing more to be done, since he couldn't bring himself to regret it. The actual physical act would be no more than a crossing of the t's and a dotting of the i's; and there was always the chance that it wouldn't happen, that the promise of marriage would content her.

He stopped the car and peered to the left to make certain of the road. Marlcliffe was foreign country, a small village with two mills and nothing to recommend it but its Norman Shaw parish church visible now at the end of the street, and a seventeenth century weaver's cottage on the village green. The bells were ringing now, their sound muted by the rain. Third right past the church, second left; he drove slowly down the empty street.

Laura's flat was on the first floor of an unexpectedly spruce-looking semi-detached house. The street was well-lit and broad and the houses, assorted though their styles were, belonged to the pre-1939 period rather than the pre-1914 period. The door opened and Laura ushered him into an entrance hall which was not unlike that of his own home.

She kissed him lightly. "It's marvellous to see you, Vincent."

He swallowed. "I've missed you. How are they at home?"

"Fine," she said. "Grumbling like mad but otherwise fine. I've put on at least ten pounds."

As he followed her into the lounge he noticed for the first time her extreme slimness. It was as if she had lost weight; and her face seemed paler than usual.

He pulled her to him; her body felt unexpectedly fragile. "What's happened?"

"Nothing," she said. She detached herself from him and went over to a small coffee table near the window. "I must give you a drink. You're the very first visitor. I couldn't have you here before because it was such a frightful mess. It's my furniture, you see." She waved her arm around. "There's a bedroom, and this room, and a kitchen, and a bathroom. It's a shower actually, because there isn't room for a proper bath. The carpet and the curtains aren't mine, but I'll change them if I stay. And it shouldn't be hard to paper over that rather grim yellow distemper. But it's nice, isn't it? I mean, it's *me*."

"Yes," he said, sitting down in a basket chair, "it's you, Laura." He closed his eyes, feeling suddenly tired. Despite the yellow distemper, the nondescript grey carpet and the blue chintz curtains, the room was Laura; the studio-couch with the gold-coloured loose cover, the two basket chairs, the white-framed pictures, the three crammed bookcases, the large radiogram, and the open record rack, all added up to Laura. He would like the pictures, he would enjoy the books and the gramophone records: if she left him alone in the room he would be contented until she returned. There was a smell of Gauloise tobacco and flowers and in the background a smell of coffee. It was different from the rooms he was accustomed to, except for the blazing fire; it was less cluttered, giving the impression that Laura had carried it round with her from place to place, each item numbered. He opened his eyes again and smiled at her. "I feel as if I want to stay."

"Stay as long as you like, Vincent," she said. "Gin and tonic?"

"Just a little," he said.

"There's ice and lemon."

He nodded. "Why didn't you ask me to help?"

"The removal men were very kind. I didn't want you to see it until everything was just so. You can help me redecorate if you like." She brought over his drink.

"I can't afford it really," she said. "I'll have to give up something."

"You could share with another girl."

She grimaced. "That's just what I don't want to do. It never works out. If you only share with one then sooner or later she gets too damned possessive. And if there's more than one sharing, the place becomes an absolute pigsty. And there's always one who won't take her turn at washing up or who doesn't pay up at the end of the month. Don't worry, Vincent, I'll manage."

She went over to the radiogram. "I brought back some of my records," she said. "Would you like to listen to some nice melancholy music?"

He nodded, his eyes half closed. This, he thought to himself, was the actuality of sin. He was alone with a woman he knew to be married, a woman whom he had kissed, a woman he knew was fond of him; the room was warm, he was listening to a piece which, whatever its subject nominally was, nevertheless always had an erotic effect upon him. He should not be here at all: he should have left a note yesterday. Her plain blue dress made her seem extremely young; virginal was the word he might have used before he'd met Ruth yesterday. He had got now what so often he had dreamed about: the girl, the blazing fire, the rain against the window, Tchaikovsky's *Winter Dreams* playing softly. The sin had already been committed in his imagination, long before he'd even met Laura, listening to this very record which wasn't, despite its title, about winter, but about a lonely man wanting sex. The girl sitting opposite him on the gold-covered studio couch had sometimes had red hair, sometimes blonde hair; the room had been smaller, the room had been larger, but always in the end the girl had been naked, crying out in terror and delight underneath him, and afterwards there had been no complications, he'd got up, put on his hat, and walked away. A man had taken his pleasure and that was all there was to it.

Now it was real, now the girl could be seen, could be touched, now he could break out of the circle: it was a sin but no more a sin than any other. There are seven deadly sins; the Protestant heresy is that there is only one or at the most two. I've already taken off the blue dress, I've already sinned; he went over to the studio couch and kissed her, his hand touching her breast with a feeling of inevitability.

"I love you," he said. He half heard the theme on the violas, heard it diminish in tone, then forgot to listen to it. The music was for the guilty dreams, the solitary adolescent yearnings; Laura was a person, Laura's nipple, stiff under his hand, belonged to a woman who could bear children, he was back at last in the human race.

"Are you sure?" Her face seemed for a moment almost stupid; the bright alertness had vanished. "You don't have to say it just to make me take my clothes off, Vincent." She pulled away from him and stood up and unbuttoned her dress. Her eyes upon him, she let it fall to the floor. She sat down beside him again. "You can do the rest," she said. "We don't have to hurry. It's as if we were married – "

He stood up suddenly. "You are married," he said. His throat was chokingly dry. "I shouldn't have come. If only you hadn't lied to me – "

"Who told you? No, you needn't say. It'd be Ruth, wouldn't it?"

"I was going to ask you to marry me," he said, surprised to find that tears were coming into his eyes.

"I am divorced, you know," she said sharply. "If you married me you wouldn't be committing bigamy."

"Why didn't you tell me?"

She picked up her dress from the floor and buttoned it up again.

"I was scared. I didn't want to lose you. I know what you bloody Papists feel about divorce. I'm surprised you came." She put out her hand. "That's not it. Oh, your body's ready. It's just your damned conscience – "

"You're married," he said. "If I'd known, I wouldn't have asked you to go out with me." He picked up his rain-coat. The pain at the centre of his body was now almost making him cry out.

"Vincent, where are you?" She dug her fingernails deep into his wrist. "Listen. We're human beings, Vincent. You know you love me. My husband was no use to me, Vincent. It's all over. I've never taken a penny from him. I could have ruined him if I'd wanted to: but I don't hate him, even now." She hit him across the face. "Can't I make you feel, can't I make you into a real person? What are you going to do now, Vincent? Are you going out in the rain to be miserable? Why can't you stay here, why can't you let me explain to you just how it was? Why do you think I won't even use his name?" She kissed the cheek she had struck. "Hit me if you like, Vincent, but don't go away and leave me alone. It's so crazy – "

The record had ended, there was a discordant whirring sound from the gramophone. She switched it off and looked at him appealingly, the tears rolling down her cheeks.

"I'm sorry," he said, beginning to weep himself. "It isn't me, Laura, it isn't me – " He ran out of the room and out into the street. "It isn't me," he said, as he unlocked the car door. "It isn't me." He looked at Laura's window, half hoping for the curtain to part. "It isn't me," he said, still weeping.

Eight

"I suppose you're going out now," his mother said, speaking for the first time that evening. "The old woman has made your tea and you've eaten it and now you're off out to wherever it is you go to. You are going out again, aren't you?"

Vincent put down the newspaper. "I'm going out. I wasn't intending to go out immediately, but now I shall." He stood up.

"You're going out with that bloody Protestant woman again, aren't you?"

He didn't remember ever before having heard her swear: the word on her lips was so much out of character that he would have been less surprised to see her drunk.

"I'm not answering you," he said. "I'm old enough to choose my own company."

"I've something to tell you first," she said. "It's about your charming little Protestant girl."

"I don't want to hear it," he said.

"You will hear it, Vincent. I had a phone call from Jenny this evening." She smiled. "It's a funny thing, but converts are a deal more full of the grace of God than cradle Catholics are. Jenny was shocked. You see, Jenny knows what's right and decent. She's a good friend to you and she doesn't want you to go headlong into mortal sin. She's found out what your Laura's real name is. It's Mrs Palworth. Your girlfriend's divorced. Married, I should say; her husband's still alive. Now are you still going to see her tonight?"

"That was very kind of Jenny," Vincent said. "I bet she went to a lot of trouble. Did she make a special journey to Silbridge to pursue her inquiries?"

"She wasn't doing any more than her duty."

"She can mind her own business for a start. She'd get a real kick out of it, the interfering little bitch. Why didn't you set a private detective on to me when you were about it?"

"She's done more for you than ever that Maureen whom you like so much would do for you. She's warned you of your mortal danger. If you had the least little particle of manhood about you you'd ring her up and thank her."

"Thank her!" he shouted. "Thank her for meddling in my private life! You tell her from me that I'll never speak to her again." He went to the door, surprised to find, as he put his hand on the doorknob, that the figure of speech was true; for a second there was a haze before his eyes that if not red was tinged with red. There was a pain in his chest; his anger and his physical distress were so great that there seemed no way of obtaining relief but by physical violence.

His mother clutched him by the shoulder; he shook off her hand. "Get out of the way," he said. "Get out of my way."

"Where are you going, for God's sake?"

"Away from you and this damned house."

She backed away from him and slumped into the nearest chair. "Oh God," she said, "God have mercy upon me!" She flung out her arms. "He's going off to that whore, that dirty little whore. My fine handsome son's going off to the arms of a married woman. My pride and my joy, my fine clever son who I thought one day would even be one of God's holy priests." She suddenly left the chair and flung herself on her knees. Still on her knees she shuffled over to Vincent and clutched his ankles. "Vincent, Vincent, my son. I beg of you, don't go to that woman. She's a bad woman, Vincent, she'll destroy your immortal soul." She began to weep. "Vincent, I'm on my knees to you humbly, the mother who bore you in pain and suffering is asking you to do this one thing. Not for my sake, Vincent, but your own sake. She'll destroy your career, Vincent, you'll lose every thing you have – "

He looked down at her coldly: the grey hair, he noticed with revulsion, had traces of dandruff, the face that was turned up to him was blotched red where the tears had washed away the powder.

"Get up," he said. "You look ridiculous."

Her weeping became noisier.

"You're the cold one," she said. "You're the cold one. You're the sort of man who crucifies Christ again."

She stood up with an effort. "Get out then. Go to her. You're no longer my son. Go and live with your whore, go and lose your job – "

"I'm not going to see her," he said. "I haven't seen her for nearly a week. I found out she was divorced. Her friend told me. So it's all over: Jenny could have saved herself the trouble."

"You didn't tell me. You didn't tell *your own mother.*" Her voice became a contralto throb with the last three words; he no longer felt anger but a weary boredom and distaste.

"I don't like admitting I've been made a fool of. I would have told you, though. In my own time."

"So I was right all the time," she said. "Oh, she made a fool of you, my son. A lie would be nothing to her. She's committed one great sin, so what's another little one to her?"

"Getting divorced isn't a sin," he said impatiently. "She sees things differently from you. It's not her fault she's a Protestant."

"Ah, that's the fashion these days. Nothing's anyone's fault. I suppose you know she was only married two years when she left her husband?"

"I suppose she had good reason," Vincent said, trying to keep his voice steady.

"Oh yes. He took another woman to a hotel. He sinned right enough, but it was her duty to forgive him. Some women forgive their husbands their whole lives through." She was speaking very quietly and sadly now and her face seemed for a moment to have

117

a dignity which before it hadn't possessed. "Jenny says he was a nice young man of a good family. She used to quarrel with him all the time, even in public, Always showing him up."

"Mother, for God's sake! You haven't the least idea what the facts really are. You're just prejudiced and that's all there is to it." He thought of Laura as he had last seen her, letting the blue dress fall to the floor, her eyes downcast, smiling faintly, he saw her head jerk up and her mouth open but he couldn't hear her words. "She's a human being," he said. "She's a human being – " but he couldn't go on.

"An animal," his mother said. "She's an animal, and that's what everyone is who lives without God. You should know it, you who's read so much history, you who should be an example to the children you teach." She suddenly put herself against the door: her tone and her gestures had become theatrical again and his boredom and distaste had now become a frantic desire to be free at all costs.

"I'm going out," he said. "Would you mind moving?"

"Tell me where. Tell me where. Tell me you're not going to that woman again. That's all I ask." She clapped her hands to her head. "Oh God," she said, her voice turning into a wail, "I'm going mad. This is my own son Vincent, my favourite son, stupid woman that I am, my own son turned hard and cold and cruel."

"I'm going out because I can't stand it here a moment longer. It's like being in prison. I don't want to watch TV and you won't let me read or even listen to the gramophone without bellyaching about Laura. Or else you just sit with a face like thunder and that's almost as bad as your bellyaching. Now move out of my way."

When he was outside he began to shiver; it was a cold night with the smell of frost in the air. His sheepskin jacket was in the hall; he hesitated outside the front door, then went to the garage.

He discovered himself at the Hibernian Club without knowing how he had reached it or why he should be there rather than anywhere else. He ordered a pint of bitter and then suddenly felt hungry. He added a pork pie to the order and sat in the corner by the picture of the Pope. There seemed to be no one else in the club except Jack Herning, who was dusting the bottles behind the bar, boredom written in every line of his body. Vincent parted the red plush curtain and peered out into Emmett Street, not quite knowing why he should do so: there was nothing there that hadn't always been there, unless you counted the Pakistani grocery, which after all had been a Polish grocery before and, originally, one of Cloneen's groceries, if not the first of the Cloneen groceries. The Irish move out and the Poles move in, the Poles move out and the Pakistanis move in; it's still the same dirty street and I'm still leading the same dirty life; I still want her, I still can see her standing there in her white slip, I have possessed her again and again. I have sinned again and again and I know it's a sin and not any the less a sin for only being in the mind. But I haven't had her, I have done everything else but I haven't had her. He took a bite of the pie; it was very cold and the jelly was so hard as to be rubbery.

It hadn't been so long since that he could always find someone to talk to here at this time, even on a week night; now they'd all gone away. He tasted the beer: he didn't want that either. He had never wanted it, but only the feeling of being one of a group. Now there was no group; for the group he'd been a member of was the bachelors' group and they were now all married men. He didn't belong there, simply because he wasn't married; and he didn't belong with the bachelors either, because he was too old. Men can't make new friends at thirty because men don't choose new friends except as children. They're issued with friends at school and university and work: when you're thirty you're either married or, as they say, on your tod. He looked at his glass and found it empty: simultaneously there was ignited somewhere within him a small spark of cheerfulness.

He took his empty glass to the bar. "Bitter, please," he said. "It's quiet tonight."

Jack Herning grunted. "No money about." He jerked his thumb to the right in the direction of the television room. "When they do come, the buggers spend the whole night in there. Half a pint all damned night; they daren't order a drink for fear they'll miss something."

"It's a curse," Vincent said. "The kids can't get on with their homework for it."

"I won't have it in my house," the barman said. "Though no doubt my wife and daughters'll persuade me in the end. You're not married yourself, are you. Mr Dungarvan?"

Vincent shook his head.

"You're a wise man, a very wise man. Ah, priests and nuns know what they're doing. You look at a nun's face, an old nun's face. As smooth as a baby's. They've no worries, you see. I've a cousin who's a nun – "

Vincent recognized the tone; Jack Herning was ready to reminisce all evening about his cousin the nun and, by easy stages, his cousin the bookmaker, his cousin the taxi-driver, and, brightest jewel in the family crown, his cousin the gynaecologist who was the finest brain in the profession and who would have risen even higher if he'd been willing to forget his faith. Vincent made vague noises indicative of polite interest; he went out to the urinal in an attempt to put the barman out of his stride but when he returned the flow of reminiscence was taken up again at the point where it had been interrupted.

At half past eight Tom Ardrahan came in and took up his usual place in the corner near the radiator. He was followed by a group of middle-aged men who gave their orders to the barman and went straight into the television room: the bar man sighed and banged down six glasses on the counter.

"Square-eyed sods," he said.

"Give me two pints," Vincent said. He took them over to Tom Ardrahan, who was staring at the picture of the Pope, his hands folded on the table.

"Very kind of you, Vincent," he said slowly. "Very kind. You always had a nice nature. Not quite as nice as your brother Matthew's, but nicer than your brother Paul's. Not that I don't like Paul. Dear me, no. He's an example to us, every one of us Papists." He nodded in the direction of the television room. "Do you not like the – the *telly*, Vincent? Are you not an addict of the goggle-box?"

"I watch the commercials occasionally," Vincent said. Tom Ardrahan had been his form master at St Theo's nineteen years ago ; he had remained a spruce fifty for fifteen years and then, on his retirement four years ago had suddenly added those fifteen years to his age. He used a stick now and the booming voice that had given him the nickname of Boots had lost its rich reverberations and was merely gruff. The face that had once been taut and alert now sagged in every direction; even the bald scalp seemed to be wrinkled. He looked suspiciously at Vincent. "You watch the commercials?" He put out his hand very slowly, lifted up the pint and took a mouthful. "I don't understand, Vincent."

"It's a joke," Vincent said. "I watch the advertisements because they're generally better than the programmes."

"Are they? Are they honestly?" There was no irony in his tone, only, Vincent saw with pity, an honest bewilderment.

"I mean simply that the programmes are terrible," Vincent said.

"To think that I taught you English. The programmes do not inspire terror; therefore they are not terrible. I expected better from you, Vincent." He levered himself to his feet and began to take, off his overcoat. It was chocolate brown and very long and heavy, as thick as a blanket, with a quilted silk lining; when Vincent had hung it up for him the old man looked at it fondly. "They don't make overcoats like that now, Vincent. Nearly thirty years old and as good as new." He unwound his two scarves. "Buy the best, Vincent, and you spend the least in the long run."

Vincent stifled a yawn. The room was beginning to fill up now; but there was no one he knew or wanted to know, except possibly the rather plump woman with red hair who had just gone up to the bar with a young man; she had a hoarse, stridently self-assured voice and unexpectedly slender ankles and even from where he sat he could sense, under the cheap scent, her availability, the fact that, not to put too fine a point on it, she liked it. He looked more closely at the young man with her and deduced from the identical colour of his hair and the difference in age that he could only be the woman's son.

"No, Vincent," Tom Ardrahan said. "You'd better not." He cackled. "I knew her mother. She led me a dance, a fine dance, I can tell you. And a great many other young men. But I had my examinations to pass, and it took a great deal of struggle to send me to the university. There weren't any grants then."

"There weren't any for me," Vincent said.

"That was because your father earned a lot of money. In my day there weren't any grants."

"It was difficult for everyone." The red-haired woman turned and frankly stared at him, not smiling and not frowning, appraising him, he thought angrily, as if he were a stock animal. She turned back to the bar; there was a singing in his ears and a pain like cramp in the pit of his stomach. It wasn't the red-haired woman whom he desired, he realized; it was Laura. He saw her again in her white slip and felt a fierce contempt for himself. He had committed the sin, he had looked at her with adultery in his heart if ever man had, but he hadn't committed the sin: he had all the guilt and none of the pleasure.

"I couldn't get married when I was a young man," Tom Ardrahan said. "I had to do something to repay my parents. No one thinks like that today. No indeed. Sometimes they're hardly out of training college before they're married. And then, you see, when my parents died, my habits were fixed. My elder sister was a widow with two young children and she looked after me. You get into the habit of not being married, you see. And who was going to help my nephews but me?"

"Who indeed?" said Vincent. He stared at the red-haired woman, willing her to turn round and look at him again. "What's her name?"

"Who?"

"The woman you've warned me against." He mopped his forehead and ran his finger round his tight collar.

"I don't know, Vincent. I know her mother's name, though." He began to laugh. "I used to feel like you at your age. Oh yes, Vincent, there's been the time when I had something to confess. It passes though. You're better for it. Everyone hasn't the vocation."

His shirt-cuffs were grubby; Vincent began to feel an increasing disgust; remembering the time when the old man had the reputation of being something of a dandy and would as soon be seen without his trousers as in the same shirt two days running.

"I haven't any evil intentions," he said, "It's merely idle curiosity."

Tom Ardrahan took out a cigar, sniffed it, and scraped the unopened end with his thumbnail. "That was my excuse, too," he said. He lit the cigar. "When I was in the clutch of the wild beast. Who said that, Vincent?" He puffed vigorously; the end of the cigar in his mouth perceptibly dark-ended.

"Some Greek philosopher." The red-haired woman was laughing at something the barman had said; suddenly Vincent found himself pushed as if by some exterior force, to the bar, and he was smiling at the red-haired woman who wasn't Laura but who, now that he was standing next to her, did, without a shadow of a doubt, like it. "We've met already, haven't we?" he said.

"I've seen you somewhere," she said. "Wait a moment." She came a step nearer. "I should wear glasses, you know, my husband's always saying – " Then she looked at him with something like consternation. "Your name's Dungarvan, isn't it?"

"Vincent."

"The quiet one," she said. "You're a chip off the old block, aren't you, Vincent?"

"We've met then. Can I buy you a drink?"

"Have you a car, Vincent?"

"A gold-plated Rolls-Royce. A *sedanca de ville* with a footman beside the chauffeur."

"No joking, Vincent. Have you a car?" A flush had come to her face.

"An A 35."

"They're little ones aren't they?"

"You can't get them very much smaller."

"You're not a bad-looking young man, Vincent. But your car's too small."

"What's that got to do with it?"

His mouth was dry now and there was a hammering somewhere inside his head: he restrained an impulse to take her by the wrist and drag her out: he wanted nothing as much as to rip the tight green dress from neck to hem, to hear her scream, to see the fuchsia-pink mouth distorted with pain instead of a smile as of a mother whose baby had wet itself.

She looked behind her at Tom Ardrahan. "I generally go to the Golden Boy," she said. "In Sarnley. Most Saturdays."

"It's along way out" he said.

"Not if you have a car. Even a little one. Excuse me, Vincent." She moved away towards the TV room. As he went back to his seat he saw that Jack Herning was struggling hard to repress his laughter.

The look on the barman's face was the duplicate of Tom Ardrahan's; Vincent sat with him for ten minutes for appearance's sake then looked at his watch with a simulation of panic. "I must be away. There's someone calling tonight."

Tom Ardrahan's eyes had nearly closed. He opened them again and for a second they were the same eyes that once could see not only who had thrown the spitball in the back row, but straight through into your mind.

"It's all to no avail, Vincent," he said. "It isn't what you want and what you *think* you want you won't find here." The voice deepened; it wasn't what it once had been, but it still carried authority. "If I were you, I wouldn't try to either. Not here, Vincent, not here."

"I'm not a fool," Vincent said. "Good night – sir." No one seemed to look at him as he walked quickly out, but as he unlocked the car door he realized that it would have been less disturbing if they had. You weren't supposed to make pick-ups at the Hibernian Club. It was really a man's club which admitted women, not a mixed club. And that was what he had been trying to do, without even the excuse of being drunk. They would all have understood that, even if he had tried to rape her there and then. There wasn't any world to which he belonged, and all his friends had gone away: he had been part of the city once, part even of its meanest streets, but now, without notice, he was a stranger there, as much a stranger as any Pakistani or West Indian, as full of nostalgia as they surely must be. But the nostalgia was for no place he'd ever lived in. He put his foot down to the floorboards to pass a bus and found that another driver had attempted the same thing in the opposite direction; there was a second of fear as he and the other car were side by side with no more than half an inch to spare and then he was well into the left again and the fear was replaced by something quite different, something not very far removed from what he had felt when he was talking to the red-haired woman at the club: he had stopped sitting in the corner with the old men, he was driving away as fast as he could from the old men and the picture of the Pope and the darkened TV room where the watchers were silent. Dear St Joseph, pure and gentle, teach O teach us how to die. He laughed to himself: it was as if he were drunk, though he had had only two drinks that evening, and had left one of those half finished, another count against him in the indictment that was doubtless being drawn up at this very moment at the Hibernian. Son of Thermocles or whoever it was – you have danced your marriage away. And the young man answered, Hippocleides doesn't care. Vincent Dungarvan doesn't care either. He took the right-hand lane as soon as he entered the dual carriageway and kept on it to the roundabout, slowing down only at the last moment, the tyres squealing. He saw himself lying in the wrecked car, his head a mess of bones and blood and grey slime, and was astounded to find that the picture didn't greatly disturb him when compared with the picture of himself at Tom Ardrahan's age, an old man with grubby linen and two scarves, huddled in his corner seat at the Hibernian, waiting for death as he would wait for a bus to take him from one patch of waste ground to another. He put his foot down again and the road and the moonlight pulled him towards the horizon. As he came towards the Beckfield crossroads he said the Act of Contrition, speaking it aloud; when he had finished it he wondered if it counted.

He passed the War Memorial and took the Sarnley road, still mulling over the problem. To knowingly drive dangerously or, if one is drunk, even unknowingly to drive dangerously, is a grave sin. I have slowed down now and if I have an accident it won't be my fault, so if I'm killed I'll die in a state of grace. Now I'm out of the town and my foot is hard down on the accelerator; there's a wind springing up from the east and it's difficult to hold the car on a straight course. If I don't reduce my speed by half it's as good as suicide and you can't have a graver sin than that. Far ahead of him he saw the headlights of an oncoming car; as it came nearer he looked away from it to the left, frightened at the strength of the temptation to look straight into the light. He slowed down again when he came into Sarnley; the wind was carrying rain on it now and the thoughts which had been reasonable on the moors were now reduced to absurdity by the presence of people and noise and light.

By the time he reached Matthew's house cheerfulness was already returning: he even looked forward to the smell of washing and tobacco and children, the litter of toys and half-mended socks and unwashed crockery which he would find there: it was the irrefutable evidence that life was going on, that at least one set of people weren't simply waiting for death.

He rang the bell three times before Maureen answered it, her hair ruffled and the top button of her dress undone.

"Don't stand there catching your death," she said impatiently. "Come in out of the wind and rain, can't you?"

"I told Matt I'd be coming." There was an atmosphere about the house as if of cold, though he could see the thermostat light of the hall radiator glowing red and the reflections of the fire in the living-room were caught in the mirror in the hall.

"He didn't deign to tell me."

Vincent turned on his heel; she caught his hand and half pulled him into the house,

"It's not your fault, love. Come in and for God's sake shut the door, there's a draught like a stepmother's breath."

"Has he gone out?"

"To Bradford. On business. Oh God, Vincent, don't stand there fidgeting like a little boy frightened to ask if he can leave the room. Come into the lounge and be warm." She put her hand to her mouth. "Excuse me. I'd fallen off to sleep in front of the fire. Did you know the average housewife walks ten miles a day about the house? I heard so on the radio today."

Vincent sat on the armchair beside the fire. "I hadn't thought about it," he said. "When will Matthew be back, Maureen?" He pushed his chair back; the heat from the fire was tightening his skin uncomfortably.

"Whatever hour God sends," she said. She kicked off her slippers and drew up her feet under her on the sofa. "But it's a good forty minutes from Bradford and it's not closing time yet."

"I really had better be going." There was a wide space between the undone top button on her dress and the one underneath; when she shifted her position slightly he could see the division between her breasts.

127

"You must be scared," she said. "If you were married, Matt wouldn't be scared of his sister-in-law." The pink slip was slightly grubby: Vincent looked away.

"I'm not Matt," he said. His fingers began to drum upon the side of the chair.

"No, you're not. It's queer how two brothers can be so different. Matt boozes and you're nearly teetotal, Matt smokes and you never have smoked. And he's getting fat and there's little red broken veins on his face. You've a skin like a baby's and you've no belly at all."

"I haven't any responsibilities."

"You wouldn't think Matthew had the way he carries on. Ah, I don't mind a man having his little drink but there's no sense in the way he carries on – " The telephone rang. As she listened her face set itself into a frown. "I'll not wait up," she said finally, and slammed the receiver down.

Vincent raised his eyebrows inquiringly.

"You might have guessed it," she said. "He's ended up in Skipton of all places. Striking whilst the iron's hot, that's what he says he's doing. I know damn well what kind of iron he's striking."

"You don't know," Vincent said. "He wouldn't have phoned you if he'd been doing anything that he shouldn't."

She laughed. "Vincent, you're a child besides your brother. That's his latest trick. Once I never knew what time he was going to roll home. Now I do know. It's still the same time, which is the small hours, but he thinks it makes it all right if he tells me. He sends you his warmest regards, by the way, and says I have to give you a drink and make you at home. He's very sorry he forgot about your coming to see him. Isn't that nice?"

"He has a lot on his mind," Vincent said. He tried to fix his attention on the statuette of the Virgin Mary on the mantelpiece; he had brought it back from Andorra as a present three years ago and liked it so much that each time he looked at it he regretted not having kept it for himself. The body wasn't essentially much more than an elongated cone, but the face was acquainted with grief. It couldn't take any more, nothing could make it more sorrowful because everything that had been dreaded from the beginning had in fact happened: her expression couldn't make you cry because she'd reached the stage past that easy animal relief. What would make you cry would be the picture of her as Madonna; and as he thought of it he discovered his eyes moistening.

He felt Maureen's fingers on his eyes. "Vince. You're not to be upset just because of your damned fool of a brother. He's not as bad as all that, he's just weak."

She sat on the arm of his chair. "He's not bad at heart, isn't Matthew. He does his best." She squeezed Vincent's shoulder painfully hard. "With all his faults, he never left me in any doubt. He asked me to marry him the third time he took me out, he didn't play fast and loose. And he'll do anything for the children, anything at all. He's a very kind–" She stopped suddenly, breathing heavily. She took the handkerchief from his breast pocket and dabbed his eyes gently.

He drew her down into his lap and kissed her. "I wondered when you would," she said. "I've been wondering for a long time. Oh, Vince, you're stupid." She kissed his eyes gently, looking at them as if they were organs whose existence she had only at that moment discovered.

"Sometimes you put yourself in other people's shoes, don't you?"

He nodded. It wasn't any use now trying to explain why the tears had come to his eyes; Laura would have understood and Laura would not have been hurt, but Maureen would not only be hurt if he told her the truth, but shocked at what she would consider to be blasphemous. And now that she was in his arms pity was taking over: it was the first time that he'd ever had the chance to comfort a woman, it was the first time he'd not felt himself being put to the test.

He kissed her again; she relaxed in his arms, her eyes closed, then abruptly rose and stood over him smiling. "Don't go," he said.

"I won't be long." He leaned back in the chair and then, half-guiltily, went over to the mantelpiece and began to stroke the Virgin's face. It was wood, and it was something more than wood; but, he realized bemusedly, it wasn't the only object in the room that had, so as to speak, got above itself. The shabby slab-sided blue suite, the blank TV set with smeary handprints upon it, the faded grey carpet, were all putting on airs: the room would never be the same again.

When she returned she stood for a moment by the door with her hand on the light switch, then went over to the sofa and with an exaggerated slowness put the cushions on the floor.

"I daren't switch off the light," she said. "Vincent, aren't you ashamed?" She knelt down and held out her hands to the fire. "It's cold upstairs. Aren't you ashamed, Vincent?"

He pushed her down to the floor with a roughness that surprised him. As he knelt beside her she asked him the question again, but this time with a note of desperation as if not expecting an answer.

Nine

Waking up the next morning he stared for a long time at the Pissarro snow scene on the wall opposite, trying to find there a reason for his happiness. Then, as the sleep left his brain, he saw that the room was as it had always been since he'd come back from the Army – it was a student's room, with a large desk, office chair, arm-chair, two large bookcases, and a recently installed gas-fire which he saw someone had just switched on. The heavy green velvet curtains were drawn back a little; the sunlight was a pale yellow on the beige carpet.

He heard a knock at the door, and his mother came in with a cup of tea. She was fully dressed and smelled strongly of soap and eau de cologne; he sniffed and recognized the more expensive brand she generally used only on Sunday and festive occasions.

"Good morning, son," she said. "It's a lovely day, but there's a nip in the air. I've switched the gas-fire on to take the chill off the air."

"Thank you, Mother," he said.

"You'll feel better now," she said. "You know you've done the right thing."

He took a drink of tea. "Not first thing in the morning, Mother," he said sharply. "I don't want to talk about it again."

"Just as you like," she said, with a surprising mildness. "Drink your tea now whilst it's hot and come down for your breakfast. I got some beautiful eggs from the milkman. How would you like them?"

"Scrambled, please."

"You've ten minutes," she said. As she went out of the room he noticed that her step had regained its usual elasticity: she had got her own way or thought that she had. The tea on his empty stomach seemed to react almost exactly like alcohol: he wanted absurdly to laugh and sing and dance, he was seized by an enormous elation.

He lay back in bed, the memory now coming back to him. The stiff dark nipples, the white shoulders, the face distorted with satisfaction – this was what the rest of the world knew about, this was what the rest of the world enjoyed – or, if what she had implied about Matthew was true, sometimes didn't enjoy any longer. He had deliberately denied himself the one pleasure that had the power to transform his very notion of pleasure; he had committed all the other sins because of indolence or indifference, never stopping to calculate the price. He smiled; it was the same for the sin you enjoyed as the sin that you didn't.

To spend the day talking to schoolboys about James I was, he reflected over his scrambled eggs, an anticlimax; he could almost have wished that he was going to drive a lorry or build a bridge or go on a Commando course. He smiled to himself: if he had been a savage he'd have been entitled to wear some special insignia; he had left the women's compound for ever.

"I'm glad you're so cheerful," his mother said.

"It was something in the *Guardian*," he said.

"Don't bother to explain it to me," she said. "I'll stick with my paper, peasant that I am." Her tone was good-humoured; even the use of the expression *peasant*, which had just reached Charbury via Chelsea via New York, was a manifestation of her general desire to please.

"I'm surprised you read that vulgar rag, Mother. You know what Monsignor Carndonagh called it the other day? The Devil's Comic Cuts."

"He doesn't know everything, clever man though he is. You've not forgotten you've to see him today, have you?"

He folded up his napkin. "I dare say he's forgotten."

"No, he hasn't. He made that appointment three months ago, and he'll keep it if he knew the world was going to end the moment after. What are you going to tell him?"

"That's my business," he said. "I may not even see him. It's not really necessary."

"You're quite sure, are you, Vincent? You haven't the vocation?"

"Of course I haven't. I never did have. I never will have."

"That's between you and God," she said. "You'll not avoid it, though. It was the grace of God that saved you from that Protestant woman. You can't think of anything else now. Don't think I don't understand, Vincent. You're a man and she's a good-looking girl and she'll know how to please men. If you weren't a real man you'd be no good as a priest. You with all your cleverness should know that."

"I mustn't be late," he said. "I've got to take Assembly this morning."

They said the grace after meals, their heads bowed; he saw her looking at him surreptitiously and knew what her thoughts were. It was Father Dungarvan who was standing there: she never gave in.

It was not until he had confirmed his appointment with Monsignor Carndonagh that the euphoria began to leave him. It had persisted through morning prayers, it had persisted through the school hymn, it had persisted through a trying period with the Lower Third, whose brightest members seemed to have all acquired an awkward interest in James the First's favourites (What did they *do*, Sir? Sir, why were they despised? Sir, my dictionary says something different about minions, Sir, my big dictionary at home, Sir) – and it had even survived leathery rissoles and semolina at lunch-time; his body had been in charge, his pride had been in charge, he'd been able to see himself not as an ox turning a creaking mill but as a lion in a cage from which at any moment he chose he could break out.

He put the staff-room telephone down slowly as if it were of extreme fragility."

"Don't look so downcast, Vincent," Jack Millstreet said. Millstreet, a year the senior of Vincent, taught physics and chemistry to the Lower School. He was tall and pale and shabby and carried about with him a smell of pipe tobacco and coal gas and iodoform; he was married with four children and recently had been talking more and more often about the salaries offered to science graduates in industry.

"I'm not glum," Vincent said. "I just wondered if he'd forgotten, that's all."

"He never does," Millstreet said. "Miss Wicklow wouldn't let him." He yawned. "Another five minutes and I'll be explaining the law of gravity to another set of juvenile morons. I'll make the same old jokes, you know. They'll laugh at them in the same old way. There's just one who has any resemblance to a human being, and I bet he won't end up a schoolteacher. You know that young Smithson has just landed himself a very nice job at Porton?"

"He used to be very pious," Vincent said. "How does he square it with his conscience?"

"He'll find some formula," Millstreet said. "The Church has one to fit every situation. He's married with two children, anyway. Hasn't much option, has he?" He grinned. "Not that you have that problem, Vincent."

"You never know. I'm not dead yet." The bell began to ring in the distance, becoming louder and louder. Millstreet was a man too, Millstreet had as much right to think of himself as a lion; but Millstreet had been married at St Maurice's, there was a framed Papal blessing hanging over the mantelpiece in his drawing-room, there was no sin, he had betrayed no one, he had hurt and humiliated no one.

As he picked up his sheaf of notes and went out of the staff-room he found himself remembering Maureen again. At first there was no pleasure there, merely an almost impersonal appraisal of the facts. Millstreet's wife, whom he had once met at the St Theo's annual garden party, was not unlike Maureen; if he had seen Maureen naked he had seen Mrs Millstreet naked too. He should have been disillusioned: what he had always imagined to be convex was concave, what he had always imagined to be light was dark, what he had always imagined to be smooth was a thick soft bush. He had long known in theory what the reality would be and the reality was even less pretty; but it was even better, it was nothing but good, he still couldn't find any contrition for what he'd done. But intermittently he kept thinking of Matthew, rather as if Matthew had recently died; Matthew slipping a pound note into his hand when he was at the University. Matthew making a model of the Supermarine Spitfire for him, Matthew playing chess with him: he didn't seem to be able to remember Matthew losing his temper or being envious or mean or jealous.

What he couldn't do still was to find any link between Matthew and what had happened between Maureen and himself. I had no choice, he said to himself in the classroom. I had no choice. He heard his own voice, cool and controlled, expounding the weakness, the cunning, the extravagance of James the First, the hand that had touched Maureen scribbled dates and diagrams on the blackboard. I had no choice, he said to himself, explaining to the attentive fourteen-year-old faces why James had behaved as he did; I had no choice.

The bell took him by surprise in the middle of a sentence; he finished it, reminded the form of their homework, and walked stiffly out of the room. It was absurd he knew; but now that he had actually to keep the appointment, it was more as if he were to be judged than as if he were simply going to announce that he had changed his mind. His decision, he reminded himself firmly, had nothing to do with what had happened with Maureen; or even what had happened or what might have happened with Laura. It had never in any case been a firm decision; three months ago he'd talked with Monsignor Carndonagh about entering the priesthood and Monsignor Carndonagh had told him to think it over. He'd thought it over and it was time for him to come to a decision. He knocked at the door.

The headmaster was signing letters when Vincent came in. He looked up and smiled. "Sit down, Vincent, please. And do forgive me. It's a typical administrative trick. One appears terribly busy whilst in fact one isn't working at all."

He pressed a bell somewhere beneath the huge oak desk and Miss Wicklow appeared suddenly and picked up the letters. Miss Wicklow, now approaching sixty, was small and severely dressed always in variations of black and white; the rumour was that she had wanted to be a nun once but at the last moment had decided that she didn't have the vocation. She inclined her head at the headmaster and, briefly, smiled at Vincent, and was gone. She had, Vincent thought, the nun's trick of being apparently propelled on castors; there was no sound as she left the room.

The headmaster offered Vincent a small cheroot.

"No, thank you, Monsignor."

"I forgot." He lit one himself; the smell of Havana tobacco instantly gave the rather bare room a more comfortable atmosphere. "We blackbeetles tend to smoke like chimneys, Compensation, I expect." He gathered his gown around him as if to protect himself from the cold. "You've been thinking it over, have you, Vincent?"

"Yes." Apart from the large crucifix on the wall facing the headmaster, and the huge old oak desk with the leather top, the room might have been any business office: the walls were plain cream, the floor parquet, the books in the cream-painted steel bookshelves were for the most part glossy new. Only the desk and the crucifix were left from the days of his predecessor: even the two narrow sham-Gothic windows had been replaced by one large picture window with Venetian blinds. "I don't think that I have the vocation."

The headmaster took off his gold-rimmed spectacles and rubbed his eyes. "You remember what Campion said when one of his companions decided that he couldn't face going to England after all?"

"Better now than later."

"Just so." Despite the dark shadow round his mouth and chin – he was reputed to shave three times a day – and the almost entirely bald head, there was something about the face, Vincent thought, that was feminine. But that was the wrong word; the headmaster, now in his late fifties, had moved beyond sex.

"It would be better for the Church to have only one hundred true priests than to have ten million who were unhappy about their vocation. I sometimes think that we should make it even more difficult to enter our ranks. Mind you, I'm not entirely unhappy that St Theo's isn't going to lose you. I'd miss you, and so would the boys. You're fond of them, aren't you?"

"I enjoy teaching them!'

"They're very agreeable creatures if you get on the right side of them. They're monsters if you don't, and some men, men who really know their subject, never do. You'd do very well for the priesthood in any case; if you can manage adolescent boys, you can manage anyone. Of course, you must realize that things are changing. Clerical heads are on the way out. It's not fair to the lay teacher. If a lay man becomes a teacher in a Catholic grammar school he hasn't much chance of becoming a headmaster. It's rather discouraging. Why do you look so surprised?"

"I didn't know that you sympathized so strongly with the layman's point of view, Monsignor."

"If we didn't have any laity we wouldn't have any priests, my dear Vincent. Or any Church for that matter. The laity will do without us before we do without the laity."

"I wasn't thinking of my career, Monsignor."

"No, of course not." Miss Wicklow brought in a silver tray with a silver teapot, milk jug, sugar-bowl, and two Royal

Doulton cups and saucers. The headmaster picked up the teapot, wrapping his yellow silk handkerchief round the handle. "A present," he said. "The kind with the silver handle is, of course, more expensive. But I prefer them with handles that don't conduct heat myself. You're Irish like me and take it with milk, don't you?" He put out the cheroot and took out a cigarette. "They don't go with tea," he said. He smiled. "You needn't tell me if you don't want to but what made you change your mind?" He replaced the spectacles, the thin face, still smiling, was that of an inquisitor.

"I thought that I didn't really like women, I thought that I was above sex. I found myself attracted to a girl despite myself, then ran away when I discovered that she was married. I should have been happy at my escape but instead I was frustrated and savage and I let myself be seduced by my brother's wife. Now I can get neither her nor the other woman out of my head..."

He was surprised to discover that the expression on the headmaster's face hadn't changed, that he hadn't actually told him the truth: he put down his teacup. "I don't feel that I'm quite suitable for the celibate life," he said.

The headmaster laughed outright. "You mean that you've met a young lady," he said. "It isn't a crime, you know."

"I did meet a girl," Vincent said. "I thought I might want to marry her."

"A Catholic?"

"No. Anyway, I discovered she was divorced. She used her maiden name. Her friend told me."

"I wonder what her friend's motives were? Never mind. What did you do?"

"I stopped seeing her."

"At once?"

Vincent nodded.

"You behaved absolutely correctly, of course. But you mustn't blame the girl too much. Her marriage may well have been a complete disaster. You must pray for her."

"It was my own fault. I shouldn't have thought of marrying a non-Catholic."

"Nonsense. Are Catholics to live in a ghetto? As long as we're in the minority there are going to be mixed marriages."

"That's what my brother Paul said."

"I remember Paul. He married a Protestant, didn't he?"

"She became a Catholic."

"There you are then. Not that all this matters. You haven't the vocation, and that's all there is to it. Your liking the company of young women has nothing to do with it. The Church isn't against sex, Vincent. On the contrary; that's why She was so severe with the Manichaeans. I met your mamma recently, by the way." He hesitated, staring at the crucifix. "She's a very good woman. She showed great fortitude when your father died. It would mean a great deal to her if you took Holy Orders. But at all costs you must consider only your own wishes in this matter. Talk to someone else about it if you like. But, frankly, be selfish. Have no thought of pleasing anyone else. Don't be in the least guilty if your decision displeases anyone else. It's too important a matter to be squeamish about." He glanced at his wrist-watch. "If I were you," he said. "I should put myself in a marrying frame of mind. Look around for a nice Catholic girl." He stood up suddenly. "I have to be away," he said. "I have a very boring lecture to give in Bradford. I'm very glad to have had this talk with you, Vincent. God bless you, my son."

"Thank you, Monsignor," Vincent said.

He went out of the room feeling as if a burden had been taken from him; it was not until he was nearly home that he realized that the headmaster had not given him what he had needed. "*Absolvo te,*" he muttered to himself, "*absolvo te.*" But the words were not even blasphemous, only meaningless.

Ten

"You haven't been out for a week," his mother said.

"Five days." Vincent put down *Officers and Gentlemen*.

"You'll be taking root in that arm-chair. Your face is growing pastier every day."

"I'm not doing you any harm." He took up the book again; bearing in mind the difference in his and the hero's circumstances, he began to feel an enormous sympathy for him. "Have you read this?" he asked his mother.

"When it first came out. It's a very silly book and he's a very silly man. It's evident that he thinks we Irish are the lowest form of human life."

"I liked it better the second time." He was talking for the sake of talking; from the look of her face he knew that there would be no real interchange of ideas between them. He didn't like this middle-aged woman with the tight mouth; he wondered if he had ever liked her.

"I've Mrs Donavan coming in tonight," she said.

"I'll go to my room."

"We don't want you cluttering up the place. Besides you ought to get some fresh air. It's not good for a young man to be cooped inside all the time."

"It's raining," he said. "Can't you hear it?"

"Put on the goloshes I bought you."

"You know what you can do with your damned goloshes," he said.

"Why don't you go to see Matthew? Are you avoiding him?"

He flushed.

"That's caught you on the raw. You're well aware he needs your help."

"I'd forgotten."

"You wanted to forget. You know he's too proud to ask you, idiot that he is."

"You're not breaking your neck to help."

She raised her hands in a gesture of supplication. "Merciful God, I've a halfwit for a son. A half-wit without a heart. He doesn't know that I'm a widow, he doesn't know that I've only just paid off the mortgage; and he doesn't know that Matthew wouldn't dream of asking me."

"Or Paul? One's always hearing how well-off he is."

"Paul has three children. Paul has appearances to keep up. Paul's considering buying himself a partnership. You've only yourself to think about, and you're very careful with money. Though no doubt you weren't when you were gallivanting around with Madame Heycliff."

"I don't want to hear her name again."

"It isn't really her name either, is it? She has a lot to answer for, that one. It's a queer thing, but you've not been happy since you saw Monsignor Carndonagh last week. You've made up your mind not to be a priest, but it hasn't made you happier. You haven't been to confession lately, have you?"

"That's nothing to do with you."

"I wonder what secrets you have," she said softly. "I wonder what went on between you and that Laura. You never used to be so unhappy, you never used to sit around the house so much…"

He was already picking up the telephone and dialling Matthew's number; when Maureen answered he smiled despite himself. When he had finished he left the room without a word, afraid that his thoughts would show on his face. His mother caught him up at the garage door.

141

"Never leave the house like that again," she said. "Always say goodbye. You might never come back, and then what sort of a memory would I have of you?"

He started to laugh, almost hysterically. "You're absolutely right, Mother," he said. "Goodbye, God be with you."

"Goodbye," she said. "Take care, my son."

Maureen was wearing bright red slacks and a blue sweater; the bright colours made her face seem paler. He had imagined that there would be a sense of constraint between them; but the evening began as all the other evenings at Matthew's house had begun. There was only one difference, he realized after half an hour of desultory conversation by the television: she wasn't flirting with him any longer.

The telephone rang; Matthew with an unusual alacrity leapt to answer it.

"Not tonight, surely?" he said. "I've visitors. Don't be like that – " His grip on the telephone tightened. "All right. Godammit, I've told you if I could I would. I'll see you, then." He hung up, failing to put the telephone in its proper place at the first attempt. He rubbed his hands together nervously. "Business," he said. "I won't be long."

"I'd better come with you," Vincent said.

"Why the hell should you? It's business. You heard me. Look after Maureen whilst I'm gone. If I'm late I'll bring back some fish and chips. I'll bring some back anyway and some beer. I've drunk the place dry."

"You're the end, you really are," Maureen said. "Let your damned business wait – "

The door had already slammed behind him; there was the sound of a car being started.

"He'll not do the engine any good, revving it like that," Vincent said. The mirror was behind him; but he knew that his face was assuming an expression which was both furtive and greedy. He sat down beside Maureen. "I'm sorry," he said. He began to stroke her forearm.

She pulled it away and stood up.

"You're not the one who's committed the real sin," she said. "I could have stopped you. One word and you'd have stopped. I could have stopped you from coming tonight; there's always an excuse. And I could have stopped Matthew from going out. You know what sort of business took him out in such a hurry. You could have stopped him too." She sat down beside him. "Put your arm around me," she said. "If I'd known you were coming I'd have put a dress on. I know what a fright I look in this outfit."

He kissed her; she returned the kiss, her tongue forcing his lips open, but when he touched her breast she moved away from him. "No," she said. "I won't be able to stop myself. They say in all these marriage manuals that the woman's always in control, but it's a damned lie. I've never done it with anyone before, though God knows I've had plenty of offers. It hasn't got to happen again."

"I want you," he said. "I've had nothing else on my mind. We can meet somehow – "

"Me with three young children? I wouldn't know how to begin. It's easy on the films – not that people in films seem to have any children."

"We can do it. Don't you love me?" He found it easy to use the word and was aware, at the moment he used it of its effect upon her. Her face softened, she came closer towards him; her whole body seemed to relax. "Don't I love you? Don't I love you? Do you think I'd have let you do it if I didn't love you?"

"Listen. There's a place near Honiston Woods – "

Her face hardened. "You're worse than Matthew," she said. "He's just clumsy and stupid but you're cold, cold right through. Don't look so hurt, Vincent. I know it's no fun being cold, I know you must be lonely, but you can't expect me to like it. Perhaps you should have been a priest after all. You could have had me a long time ago, before I married Matthew. But I'm not good enough for you and that's the truth of it."

"It's not true. I've always liked you – "

"Like. Not love. You're not very good at telling lies, are you? And you're not very good with people. I bet you're the bee's-knees with the boys at school because you're in charge and you're in charge all the time – " Suddenly she clutched his hand as if to help her to bear some huge pain. "I cried myself to sleep last Thursday night and longed for nothing so much as for you to be beside me. If you asked me to go away with you now, I would. I would even at this very moment. I'd leave the children and I'd risk my immortal soul. Because I'm not dead yet and you're here now and we can't make love in the grave. But you won't ask that of me. It's not even your religion that holds you back. It's because you won't give all of yourself. You couldn't be a priest, not in a thousand years."

"Shut up," he said. "Stop telling me how bad I am. I hear it all the time – "

"If you don't like it, why do you put up with it?" Her voice was cold.

"I haven't any choice." He kissed her again; this time she did not resist but became a dead weight in his arms, her eyes staring at him without expression. He released her. "What's wrong?"

"If you don't know, I'll not waste my breath telling you." She went over to the cocktail cabinet. "A miracle has occurred," she said. "There's some whisky. Matthew doesn't generally leave a full bottle there for longer than a day." She poured out drinks, spilling some on the top off the cabinet. "I remember buying that cabinet," she said. "That was in the days when I was going to be a hostess and entertain my husband's business friends. You pull the little lever and it becomes a well-equipped bar. But I don't bother with it now."

"It's very nice," he said.

She found the lever and the top part of the cabinet opened out. "Glass, so it'll look bigger," she said. "There's holders for glasses and cocktail sticks and all the other things that hostesses need. The light comes on when you open it, but naturally it doesn't work. It's not nice at all, is it? Just a deal cupboard with a funny top. Real hostesses put the drinks on a long table. Did you know that?"

"I don't think it matters."

"Who knows what you think?" She lit a cigarette and took a mouthful of whisky. "I generally tidy up before you come," she said. "I haven't bothered this time." She sat down opposite him, arranging her legs with an unusual primness. "What sort of a place has Laura?"

"I didn't notice. I shan't be seeing her again in any case."

"Yes, I heard. She's divorced, isn't she? You couldn't have anything to do with a bad woman. They'll give you a medal for chastity, I shouldn't wonder."

"I'd better be off."

"It'll look very strange. Besides, if you go now, you might miss a chance of a – ". She grinned and repeated the word more loudly.

"Don't talk like that," he said sharply.

"It's true, isn't it?" She repeated the word in a more ordinary tone. "That's what you've done to *me*. Did you with Laura? But you haven't, of course. I bet you thought of marrying her. I used to think that you couldn't; there are some men like that. There was a boy who lived near us who gassed himself the night before his wedding. But that isn't what's wrong with you. Oh no. You're all there, Vincent, you're a chip off the old block." She smiled. "He was a man," she said. "There's more to being a man than the one thing, though."

"You've been drinking," he said. He should have been shocked, he should have been angry; but in an odd way he was enjoying himself. He was even glad that he couldn't fully comprehend why Maureen was talking so strangely; he was grateful for being obtuse because to be obtuse about women's moods was to be masculine. If I never have another woman

145

again, he thought, I've been issued with my certificate of virility; he finished his whisky and went to the cabinet to pour himself another. He didn't need to drink, but there was a meretricious pleasure in the action, he was a bad actor in a bad play who nevertheless was going to be paid a huge salary. He could never be alone again, he could never again be entirely disregarded as a human being.

"I'm quite sober," she said. "I don't often have a drink. God help the children and God help Matthew if I did. You won't ever drink, of course. You're too scared of your mother. That's why you gave Laura up."

"She had nothing to do with it." At the mention of his mother, suddenly he was invaded by a sense of strong physical shame. It was as if his body were a set of dirty clothes, clothes which didn't even belong to him, and as if, dirty though they were, they covered something which was not to be revealed. "I did what was right," he said with an effort. "I didn't enjoy doing it."

"You didn't enjoy doing it. You're actually sorry for yourself. Not one word of pity for Laura. All men are the same, and that's a fact. It serves me right; all these years I've been dreaming about you like some silly schoolgirl."

"She shouldn't have lied to me."

"She ought to be perfect, oughtn't she, like your damned mother?"

"I've told you that has nothing to do with it."

"Matt and I had the devil of a tussle with her when we first married. She wanted to take over our whole lives. She doesn't like me, you see. Not that she'd like any woman who married one of her precious sons."

"She only means it for the best," Vincent said. "She only wants to help." He was aware that his words lacked conviction; at the moment he disliked all women, his mother most of all.

"We'll help ourselves," Maureen said. "I know Matt's struck a bad patch just now but we'll get out of it in our own way –" her face convulsed and she began to weep noisily. "Give me your hanky," she said. "I'm helping him, aren't I, the poor bumbling fool? Making love to his own brother. He'd be better off without me. It's only the children that keep me going. I swear to God it is. He's not a bad father with all his faults, he wouldn't even know how to begin being unkind. He thinks the world of you, Vincent. When he heard you were coming here tonight, he was delighted. If only I could put some badness into him, if only I could make him harder and stronger and not so damned ready to please – " Her tears had ceased, she was hitting the arm of the chair with her fist as if it were animate. "He'll not fix things, he doesn't care, he won't look ahead, he doesn't want to make anything of himself."

"He needs some money," Vincent said. "It's very simple."

"I'm not asking you to lend him it," Maureen said. She sat down beside him. "It won't ease your conscience, Vincent." She stroked his hair. "How thick it is," she said. "It's plain to see you don't worry. At this moment you're longing to be back in your own cosy little room listening to your records. Wouldn't it be marvellous if you could just pay me off and have done with me? They used to sell indulgences, didn't they? You could even buy them for sins you were going to commit. A few shillings for swearing, a bit more for eating meat on a Friday, and about a hundred pounds for adultery. You're thinking now that if you lend Matthew fifty quid that lets you off." She kissed him, holding him by his hair, and then pushed him away suddenly. "That'll be extra," she said. She turned up the sound on the television. "He'll be back in a moment. Have you a comb?"

He took a comb from his pocket; with an impersonal deftness she straightened his hair. She burst out laughing. "No one would know," she said. "Not that we've done anything."

"I'll lend him the money," Vincent said. He had the feeling of being directed by an intelligence superior to his own; he would do whatever Maureen asked him to do or, rather, wished him to do. There would be no question of being asked; she was in charge of the whole situation.

"He'll ask you for about half of what he needs," Maureen said briskly. "He'll want the cheque payable to himself. Find out who he owes it to and send it to them direct." She leaned back and lit a cigarette. "I'll make us some tea."

"Don't bother for me," he said. He looked at her coldly; the matter-of-fact way in which she had told him to lend Matthew the money to pay what he suspected to be his gambling debts had made it as if nothing had passed between them. It was almost as if he'd paid in cash for those ten minutes with her. When he signed the cheque he would have settled his account with the world; God was a different matter. His cheque would be honoured, but God would know how much his repentance was worth. It seemed incredible now that he had ever desired the woman sitting opposite him, her blonde hair streaky, her fingernails not over-clean, her face untouched by thought about anything that couldn't be seen or felt or heard or touched or smelled; and yet one of the reasons why he hadn't yet been to confession was that he'd gone there tonight with the intention of making love to her again.

"I want some tea even if you don't," she said. She took her glass of whisky to the cocktail cabinet and poured it back into the bottle. "Waste not, want not."

When she had left the room Vincent lifted his own glass to his lips and then put it down again. He didn't want it, he was tired of putting things into his mouth, tired of his own body, tired not of living but of living among strangers. Pride, a voice said, lust, despair; he fixed his eyes on the Madonna on the mantelpiece and tried to pray.

PART TWO

Eleven

Vincent fidgeted uneasily as the kneeler cut into his flesh. His mother's face was impassive as she listened to his cousin Delia's responses; his Aunt Edith's eyes were wet, and as Delia loudly and clearly and even theatrically said *Until death us do part*, the tears began to trickle down her cheeks. Briefly his mother's face wore an expression of contempt; Vincent would hear what she thought about such lack of dignity later, just as he would hear about the too deeply cut wedding-dress, the men's morning suits, but how, despite it all, nothing could mar the beauty of the Nuptial Mass, the true Catholic marriage with the Papal blessing.

St Maurice's, one of the first Catholic churches to be built in Charbury, was the one he liked the best; there had always, until today, been something there for him. There was nothing today; its cool darkness – did the architect have a siege in mind when he made the windows so small and so high? – seemed dank and gloomy.

As he joined the wedding party in the vestry afterwards he felt both an immense boredom at the prospect of the reception and, naggingly, a sensation of having been passed by. He had missed something the others had not missed. All of them – his Uncle Peter, his lack of inches emphasized by the length of his morning coat, his Aunt Edith, her tears dry now, in her purple coat and grey fur hat and her blue-rinsed hair that was set in waves too regular and elaborate to match her faded fairness, her air of abstracted kindliness, her daughter the bride with the Dresden doll's face a shade too delicate for the large-limbed body, an Amazon's with nothing missing, the bridegroom Harry Bandon scarcely as tall as Delia with narrow shoulders and a narrow worried face, Harry Bandon Senior who had wanted to marry his Uncle Matthew's girl, small and wizened, but sure of himself, leaning on a silver-topped stick, his eyes bright and watchful behind gold-rimmed glasses – all of them, he thought, belong in a way I do not, all the vestments hanging in the cupboards here are for their benefit, they are the Church and they are the world too, the spirit and the flesh. He kissed Delia on her cheek, his eyes wandering downwards to confirm that her dress would certainly not escape comment from his mother. He grinned at Delia, holding her hand a little longer than was strictly necessary. "Harry's a lucky man," he said, and saw from her smile that she knew what was in his mind.

As he went out into the street he put his hand over his eyes. He heard his mother's voice: it had that malicious edge to it which he had always hated. "You should have hidden your eyes in the vestry," she said. "It's too late for hiding them now." She lowered her voice. "She looks more like a nursing mother than a bride."

"The sun's very strong for October," he said, pretending that he had not heard her. There would be the photographs now, he thought, the wedding breakfast, the speeches, the drinking after the bride and groom had been seen off; and after that he'd be alone unless he wanted to continue drinking with his uncle and his cousins. They were all here – Oswald the bus-driver, Dennis the plasterer, Tom the plumber, Stephen the TV dealer, Alfred the wages clerk – and in a while he would remember them all and he would pretend that only pressure of work kept them from seeing each other except at weddings and funerals; and they would all be both painfully polite and ostentatiously familiar with the groom's family who couldn't, to be absolutely fair, help being lousy rich.

"See you don't get edged out of the photo," his mother said.

"It's not me who's getting married. There's not many of your lot here, is there?"

"It's all Dungarvans," his mother said. "And Bandons." She lowered her voice. "Look at his father, more wizened-up than ever. He's a poor weak-looking object, isn't he?"

"You seem to measure men by the pound like meat," he said crossly,

"Then there's none here worth much," she said.

He saw his Uncle Hubert, bulky in green thornproof tweed, his face brown with a tan he could not have acquired in England that summer, striding over towards him.

"Hello, Uncle," he said. "This is an unexpected pleasure."

His uncle's heavy face gave him a careful smile, a thin man's smile, and then awarded Vincent's mother a wider and warmer one. "I'm *en route* to a conference in Newcastle. Thought I'd pop in to see you, Bea. Might as well see Delia married. Wed" – he exaggeratedly deepened his voice – "as they doubtless still put it in this region." He shook Vincent's hand and kissed Vincent's mother almost simultaneously, then lit a small cheroot with a flourish as if rewarding himself for his act of skill. "You're looking younger every time I see you, Bea. You look absolutely, splendid too, Vincent. Wish I were a teacher instead of a poor harried GP. Or, I should say, a National Health clerk…"

His mother was happy now; he left her talking with his uncle and joined his grandmother who was standing at a distance smiling sardonically in the lilac toque and silver fox which had been her wedding attire for the past twenty years.

"It's a wonder he could get away," his grandmother said.

"He's travelling north to some conference," Vincent said.

"It's made your mother's day. Hubert was always her great favourite. Couldn't your Uncle Cyril and Aunt Sophie come?"

"It's a long way. Cyril's up to his eyes at the Ministry and Sophie's not been very well. Or so one hears."

"It'd be a different matter if it were a Rosslea getting married," she said. "Or you perhaps."

The photographer was already posing Delia and Harry: suddenly everyone fell silent as if their voices would somehow over-expose the film. Harry was sweating a little; he ran his finger round his collar, and then his hand jerked down in obedience to the photographer's gesture. A wind sprang up, pressing Delia's gown between her long legs; automatically there was induced in him a shamefaced stirring of desire. He was not going to enjoy this wedding any more than he ever enjoyed any wedding, he was not going to be released from lust and envy, he could not live on the memory of his one real encounter like a camel on its hump. His grandmother looked at him and drew in her breath sharply. "Vincent."

"Yes, Grandmother?"

"I want to see you married."

"It's supposed to be catching," he said.

"Your father was my son," she said. "I'm an old woman, Vincent, but I'm not stupid. I might even be cleverer than your mother, for all her education."

"Grandma," Delia called. "Come, here, Grandma. And Vincent."

Her voice was almost petulant. "Come and have your photo taken."

His grandmother straightened her back. "We're coming child."

"Leave me out," he said. "There'll be too many people in the picture as it is."

"You're waiting to be coaxed," Delia said. "Come on, and I'll give you another kiss. Not now, though, or the marriage'll end before it begins." Her face was now alive with sexual provocation but even as she smiled at him he realized that it wasn't for him, that he had only, so as to speak, been thrown a copper; the bridegroom would get the gold.

The wedding breakfast was the standard Bandon Restaurant meal of tomato soup, ham, chicken, potatoes, peas, and a trifle of which the chief ingredient was a bone-white synthetic cream. Vincent put his aside after one spoonful and listened in a haze of boredom to the speeches. The colour scheme – dark brown and beige and off-white – depressed him intensely; he had been here at least a dozen times since childhood and it had never changed, just as the food never changed. Bandon's was a habit; it was inexpensive, clean, and, due more to luck than foresight, it was the only large restaurant in Charbury which had a car-park. Delia, like the bridegroom, was looking tired now, the bright smile becoming less frequent. The envy persisted; he wanted to be in the bridegroom's place, assured after the speeches and the cutting of the cake and the confetti of a freedom which, however circumscribed, was infinitely greater than a bachelor living with his mother ever would have. Harry Bandon was only half an inch taller than Delia, his face was utterly lacking in distinction and in another five years he would be completely bald, but he was a man who had a home of his own: he had, whether he realized it or not, broken out of prison. He would in the years to come perhaps be bored, discontented, frustrated, weighed down by responsibilities; he might even betray or be betrayed. But he wouldn't be lonely; and tonight – which was after all the reason for the wedding – he'd be sleeping with Delia.

The best man, a brasher version of the bridegroom, was toasting the bridesmaids; the speech seemed to continue interminably. There was now a smell of frying fish from downstairs; the best man sniffed and made a limp joke about newlyweds' cooking; Vincent looked across at his Uncle Hubert and saw him stifle a yawn. The moment when he felt at one with the family was over: he was now alone again, the weekend stretching before him like a desert.

As the bride and groom left he saw with a twinge of apprehension that the father of the bride, his Uncle Peter, was strutting towards him, blowing out clouds of cigar smoke. "How about some ale, Vince?"

"It's too soon after lunch, Uncle. I've got some papers to correct – "

"Nonsense. You've plenty of time for work. I never thought you were toffee-nosed, Vincent." He jerked his thumb at Uncle Hubert. "No use asking him, of course. But Harry's left some money behind with the best man. No point in wasting it. We're going to the Green Goose, it's not very far from here."

"I'd better take mother home."

"Hubert'll do that." His uncle's face was very red; Vincent realized, with amused affection, that he had embarked upon one of his twice-yearly binges. "Bert," he yelled, "are you coming with us for a jar?"

Uncle Hubert turned his head slowly. "Thank you, Peter, but no. I've two hundred miles to drive today. I'm going to have a cup of tea with Bea." He walked over slowly to Uncle Peter. "How are you, Peter? We only seem to meet at weddings and funerals. One's so busy and Berkshire's a great distance away. I break my journey at Sophie's, you know. She was sorry she couldn't come."

His Uncle Peter began for the first time to look vaguely embarrassed; Uncle Hubert, with his hair beginning to silver about the temples and his deep comforting voice which by now hadn't the faintest trace of Yorkshire about it, was, without really trying, putting Uncle Peter in his place; it was obvious that he was not only not going to meet him except at weddings and funerals but also that he wouldn't under any circumstances drink beer with him. He was looking rather coldly at Vincent now. "I hope I'll see you before I depart, Vincent."

"I shan't be long," Vincent said. He put his hand on Uncle Peter's shoulder. "We always have a jar at weddings, Uncle Peter and me. I keep him out of trouble, you see."

"Admirable, admirable," Uncle Hubert said. "I'll see you then, Vincent." He took Uncle Peter's hand. "It's a lovely daughter you have, Peter. Tell her and her young man to come and see us. Una and I would love to see them." He walked away, his hands clasped behind his back, to talk to Matthew.

"A clever man, that," Uncle Peter said. "Mind you, those Rossleas think they're first cousins to God Almighty. He'd be taken aback if Delia and Harry did drop in. Even if Harry's old man could buy and sell him twice over." He rubbed his hands. "Let's find that bloody best man or else it'll be closing-time before we know where we are."

After an hour in the Green Goose Vincent began to wish that he had gone home with his mother and Uncle Hubert: the Green Goose was uncomfortably full and uncomfortably smoky, and the beer seemed to lack taste. Their group was rapidly augmented with drinkers who hadn't been at the wedding; the best man was muttering that Harry hadn't left enough money for all this lot and he wasn't going to pay out for drinks for people he didn't know.

Vincent quietly bought himself a gin and tonic and left his pint standing on the bar, knowing as he did so that there was nothing wrong with the beer. It was simply that he had changed; he didn't belong to his father's side of the family, he didn't belong to his mother's side of the family, he didn't, most emphatically, belong to the world represented by Delia's husband.

Uncle Peter hit him on the back. "Cheer up, Vincent. Have a cigar."

"You know I don't smoke, Uncle."

"A saint, this lad," Uncle Peter said. "He won't sup his ale neither."

"He's better things to do," the best man said.

"No, he hasn't. He reads, does Vincent. And listens to music."

"Nothing wrong with that," the best man said, swaying slightly. His mouth was half-open, his eyes not focusing properly.

"Keeps him out of trouble," his uncle said. "Old Vincent'll never get married. It's a high price we pay for a few moments' pleasure, by God it is. Aye, your brother's troubles are just beginning, Kenneth."

"I'd say the pleasure was just beginning," the best man said. He winked at Vincent. "They'll be in Tenerife tonight."

"Tenerife," Vincent's uncle said. "Tenerife. Me and her mother were damned lucky to have a couple of days in Blackpool."

"There's nothing you can do in Tenerife that you can't do in Blackpool," Stephen Dungarvan said. He poked Vincent in the ribs with a thick forefinger. "I always thought you fancied Delia yourself, Vincent. You could have got a dispensation." He laughed loudly, showing square white teeth. Since Vincent had seen him last he had grown even fatter; his bright blue window-pane check suit did nothing to reduce the illusion of his being literally as broad as he was long.

"Less of that talk," his father said. "Cousins shouldn't marry."

"It's all right if you breed from good stock," Stephen said. "I've bred from Airedales that were a damned sight closer kin than cousins."

"I'm not a dog," Vincent said. Stephen was the most successful of his Uncle Peter's children: between him and Vincent there had always been an intense rivalry. Stephen had left school at sixteen, had worked in the radio department of Thompson and Cavendish until he was twenty-three and now ran two shops of his own. There had been trouble in the early days when he had ordered too many sets from a manufacturer now long since out of business; but Stephen had bounced back, as he always would. The Green Goose, a cut above the run of pubs in this district, several cuts below the Country Club, was his environment, always apparently freshly painted in dashing shades of green and red, always noisy and cheerful, always respectable. Gatecrashers in a wedding party would have certainly been the cause of a ferocious brawl at any of the other pubs nearby; here it would all be sorted out amicably.

"Your father used to come here a lot," Stephen said, not seeming to hear Vincent's reply. "There was a man for you; they broke the mould when he was made. Never drunk, mind you, but always full of fun. He'd come in here of an evening with his hat on the back of his head and he'd say 'They're too quiet here, they need livening up,' and he'd have them all singing and if there'd only been more room he'd have had them dancing too..."

"Vincent wouldn't have been there," his father said. "Vincent would have been studying and that's why he's a teacher now, you ignorant lout."

"Stephen can buy and sell me," Vincent said. His head was beginning to ache and his eyes to run; the Green Goose, despite its determinedly twentieth century interior was an eighteenth century building with low ceilings and inadequate ventilation; the tobacco smoke and the smell of beer seemed as if pressing him down by sheer weight.

The bride's and the bridegroom's families had now drifted apart; they would make brief attempts at communication whilst the pub was open and then would not meet again until the next wedding or funeral: the gap was too great to be bridged. The Bandons were the smaller; they wouldn't be at home here, Vincent thought, because they had more money than the Dungarvans; and they wouldn't be at home among the Charbury businessmen because they were Catholics – and Irish to make it worse... He yawned.

"Your father would have gingered them all up," his Uncle Peter said. "This is a bloody poor wedding party, I've been to better wakes. Can't you give us a song, Vincent?"

"Not in my line," Vincent said. "I must be away in a minute in any case."

Uncle Peter grunted. "You're always bloody well going off in a minute," he said.

There was no answer to that: these were his father's brothers and their children, in each of their faces he could see, however dimly, his father's thin quizzical face, and yet he had nothing to say to them. His father had known the right things to say to them all, his father had even remembered, as his son did not, their wives' names and their children's names and even their birthdays; But his son didn't remember because he didn't care.

"There's time for a drink, Uncle," he said. "It's a long time, you're quite right – " He searched his memory for the names of his uncle's children and as he made his way to the bar the names came back to him. He would have to talk about them, he would have to talk about his mother and his brothers, he would have to talk with his cousin Stephen and his cousin Dennis and his cousin Alfred, he would even have to talk to Harry Bandon about his mother and father and friends and relations, he would have to resist the temptation to stand apart, he would have to, as far as he was able, give something of himself. His father would have gingered them up, his father would have had them all singing; but his father had gone on ahead, he had served his sentence and been given remission for good conduct. He glanced at the Dungarvan group; their glasses were nearly empty. "Eight pints of bitter, please," he said to the barmaid. He looked at the bridegroom's party. "No, make it twelve." He waved at Harry Bandon's brother. "Give me a hand," he said.

"You needn't do that, Mr Dungarvan. Harry's left the money – "

"Vincent. We're all friends here."

"Kenneth. I was a bit worried, you see, Vincent, there's been some interlopers. Interlopers. They're not with us really – "

"Never mind, Kenneth," Vincent said. I interlope myself, I interlope all the time."

There had to be something more, he thought. There was Laura, and he knew now, as he had not known at the beginning of the day, that he was going to see her again: but there had to be something more.

"I never thought our Harry'd get married so soon," Kenneth said. "Now, I was wed when I was twenty-two, but Harry's different. Bit of a lad, is Harry. I dare say he'll cut down on the rally-driving now. It scares the old man stiff."

"Delia's a lovely girl," Vincent said.

"You're not married yourself, are you, Vincent?"

"I run too fast."

"You've got to come to it in the end. I'm surprised a chap like you hasn't got hitched."

"I'll keep on running," Vincent said.

"The bloody women can always run faster than you," Kenneth said.

"No, we get tired. Down the arches of the years –" He stopped, seeing the puzzled expression on the other's face. "It's a poem, Kenneth," he said. "A very bad poem really. It's supposed to be about God, but actually it's about sex."

"You're having me on," Kenneth said.

"It doesn't matter," Vincent said. "I told you, it's a very bad poem."

But the barriers were up again; the thin face was puzzled and resentful. He wondered what precisely he should say to Laura when he met her again and then ceased to wonder. There would be no trouble to find something to say, meeting in this foreign city so many miles away from home.

Twelve

When he opened the door of the Reference Department his teeth began to chatter; the trembling communicated itself to his whole body, forcing him to sit down in the first chair available, opposite an old man who was surreptitiously eating chocolate under cover of a pile of books. The old man, though respectably dressed, smelled of eucalyptus and urine; Vincent put his handkerchief to his nose and moved to the open shelves. The trembling had stopped now; it was warm and quiet in the Reference Department and the smell, once one was out of the old man's way, was of books and, inexplicably, freshly-laundered cotton.

Laura, at the far end of the counter, had not seen him yet; he took Hitler's *Table Talk* from the shelf and sat down to read. Looking at the dark head bent over a pile of catalogue cards, he felt no excitement but only a sense of inevitability; there is no one else in the city, he thought. There is no one else to whom I can talk; there is no one else to whom she can talk. After five minutes had passed she lifted up her head and said something to the girl beside her, then glanced idly round the room. The green smock. she was wearing made her look unexpectedly young and demure; her face was smooth and a little bored. He wondered for a moment whether or not he had made a mistake; her face was not the face of one who knew his language. Then she saw him, and her face suddenly was broken up, almost ugly, and she was blushing: it was Laura after all, and he smiled at her. It was all extraordinarily easy, he thought: at two o'clock you were bored and absolutely alone, at six o'clock you were in the presence of the only person with whom you wanted to be. There was an hour to wait, the room was warm, he could read and from time to time look at Laura. She hadn't returned his smile but had returned to whatever she was doing with the catalogue cards. He wasn't thinking of Maureen any longer, he had given himself absolution; nor was he thinking of Laura as a body. He knew now what physical love was; the whole ugly world shared that knowledge with him, Delia and Harry Bandon would have that knowledge tonight if they hadn't had it before; it wasn't, he decided, good enough for him.

When closing-time came, he was half asleep: Laura had left the counter ten minutes after his entry. He had not allowed this to disturb him; he was contented by the fact of her being there, more contented, he thought drowsily, than ever he had been in his whole life. He looked up and saw her standing over him in a white trench-coat, her face unsmiling: the smell of the trench-coat – rubber and pear drops – as much as her own scent, jerked him awake. He tried to put a name to the scent – violet, lily-of-the-valley, rose – and came to the conclusion that it wasn't a scent that he could name except by her own name; for the first time he was smelling her as a person.

"We'll go to your place," he said as he started the car.

"I couldn't bear waiting," she said. "I'd have run away with you, and I need the job. I was so excited when I saw you that I was nearly sick."

He laughed. "At least your feelings towards me aren't lukewarm," he said.

"What made you come to the library?"

"I was lonely. I couldn't manage any longer by myself. There wasn't anyone else who would do."

"Have you been with anyone else?"

"No. I thought of it, but it wouldn't have been fair."

"Your mother won't be pleased."

"To hell with my mother."

She grabbed his wrist so suddenly that the car veered to the left, the brakes shrieking. "Vincent, don't forget that you said that. Once you've said that, you're free. I knew someone once who couldn't say that to save his life. He couldn't say it to save his marriage."

"It shouldn't be necessary to say it," Vincent said. The road to Marlcliffe was steep and narrow and winding with a high stone wall to the left, massive and smoke-blackened, and to the right a precipitous hillside with the chimneys of Charbury below. Under the moonlight it was as if the grass were dark green stone, harder even than the stone wall; and now that the sun had gone in, the cold was seeping into the car, exhaled from that dark green stone. Human beings were made from the wrong material for this landscape, he thought: one needed to be of stone too.

"Are you regretting it already?" Laura asked. "Do you think a boy's best friend is his mother? Do you want to be like everyone else? Are you still fighting with your conscience?"

"The decision's taken," he said. "I don't feel that it matters any longer what my mother thinks."

"We'll go away," she said. "Haven't you realized, Vincent, we're absolutely free?"

"I hadn't thought of it before," he said.

"We never do. We soldier on, we say we can't do this, we can't do that, and we never ask ourselves why."

Suddenly he saw himself from outside and was almost frightened. He opened his mouth to answer her but could not find the words; instead he touched her hand briefly and they rode on in silence. Here he was, Vincent Kevin Dungarvan, alone with a married woman, driving to her flat; there would be no one else in the flat and he was well aware that there would be no one else in the flat. He was not being led into sin, he was not being tempted; with his eyes wide open he was rushing into sin. He had not stumbled into the occasion of sin; he had created the occasion of sin. There was a hell and he was a hairsbreadth from it, even if he never committed the sin; over and over again he recapitulated the definitions learned so many times, learned ever since he could remember, over and over again he tried to make the one word bigger and blacker and more terrible, over and over again he tried to conjure up the suffering face, the crown of thorns, the spear in the side, and his own hand on the spear. It worked in the stories in the Catholic magazines, it worked for the mystics and the saints; but he could only see Laura, could only see sin as a word, an abstraction; Laura's face was real, the suffering face had suffered two thousand years ago.

When they were at last inside the flat he felt a sense of anti-climax. They stood for a moment looking at each other; there was a smell of stale tobacco and disinfectant about the room which he had not noticed before. It had been her undeniable reality as a person which had prevented him from thinking until now; but now the room seemed to be deciding his actions for him, it was as if somewhere there were a huge key that would wind him up: she was a stranger, she was the bad woman who would ask him to cut out his mother's heart, and she was worse than bad, because she didn't know that she was about to commit a sin, because she didn't believe in hell, because she chose her actions as she had chosen the new gold and scarlet curtains, because one action gave her more pleasure than the rest. Maureen was not a stranger, Maureen had been compelled into sin by the violence of her desires; but Laura would get him cheap, and if him, why not another? There was a choice after all; he could leave now, and when he left there was still the choice of returning to his home or if not returning, of driving on alone. There was no curiosity left to hold him; what he would see and touch he had seen and touched before.

This was where it had all begun; he had come here knowing that he was wrong in doing so, he had, too late, come to his senses, and then he had made love to Maureen. It all built up; he had put himself in a new prison. Already he had ceased to notice the smell of stale tobacco and disinfectant; or was it that he had grown to like it?

"I love you," she said. "You and your conscience." She was still standing apart from him; she turned away from him and went over to the fireplace and took down a box of matches from the mantelpiece. "I clean it out in the morning and lay it for when I come home," she said. "It's very good; I sprinkle it with paraffin so it lights straight away." She lit the fire; immediately it flared up. Kneeling on the hearthrug, she stared at the flames for a moment, then burst into tears.

He knelt down beside her. "I love you too," he said. "Why are you crying?" But the question was superfluous; he could in his mind's eye see her coming home night after night to the cold room with everything there just as she had left it: he put his arm round her and stroked her hair, his detachment gone.

"I'm all right now," she said. "I've never disliked living on my own so much before. I've almost felt like going to live at the YWCA, where there'd be people around me." She sniffed. "I can't leave the windows open when I'm out, you see. I could see you wrinkling up your nose, and I was ashamed."

"It's nothing," he said. Her face was very hot against his; he could no longer smell her scent and no longer see her as a female body. Compassion had driven all else out; he kissed her gently and gently rocked her in his arms.

She pulled herself away from him gently and stood up. "I must wash my face," she said.

When she had left the room he drew up a basket chair to the fire and composed himself to wait, his hands folded in his lap. It was as if he had lived here with her for a long time, had chosen with her the furniture and the books and the curtains and the pictures; he was surprised to find how his taste coincided with hers.

He was staring into the fire when he felt her hands over his eyes. "Don't look," she said. He closed his eyes; he heard her move away, stepping very softly, and then heard the click of an electric light switch.

"You can look now, darling."

He went over to the studio couch, his mouth dry. "I'm cold," she said. "Make me warm."

For a second after he had undressed, there was a feeling of panic, of prohibitions descending upon him like weighted nets; and then, with a force which astounded him, she drew him on top of her.

For a long time afterwards they lay absolutely still in the silent room. He waited for the sadness to begin but instead he was swallowed up by a huge contentment. He had at last been rid of his identity, and with it the sense of sin, he told himself, feeling her stir underneath him; he would stay here all evening and all night and if he put his hand in the fire it wouldn't hurt him. They had told him the body didn't matter, that it was merely an awkwardly shaped piece of luggage one was chained to for one's brief journey through life, to be cast aside joyfully at the terminus; one hadn't to deliberately damage it or throw it away but it wasn't of any value, it was an ugly necessity. They had lied, they had spoken as if the trunk were full of corruption; but he had opened it and now he was free. "I love you," he whispered to Laura. "I've never been so happy."

Suddenly his left leg was seized by cramp; it was as if the pain were expanding from under the flesh. He rolled off the couch and started to rub his leg; Laura looked at him in bewilderment then ran into the kitchen and came back with a glass of water. He drank it then retched; it tasted of salt.

"That always does the trick," she said. She laughed. "It's just as well it didn't happen before."

"Perhaps it was my guardian angel," he said. "Intervening to protect my virtue."

"He's left it a bit late," she said.

"We took him by surprise. He didn't expect such behaviour from me." The pain had gone now; he stood up and looked round for his clothes.

"You're not cold, are you?" She had lit a cigarette and was sitting on the couch, her knees firmly together, her back upright, in a posture that would have been ridiculously prim except for her nakedness.

"Not any more," he said.

"Sit here. It's a long time since I talked to a man. But you've been talking to a woman very recently, haven't you? It doesn't matter, I won't cross-examine you. You're not going with her again, though. I'll scratch her eyes out."

"There hasn't been anyone," he said, stroking her back.

"There has. The bitch. It'd be so easy with an innocent like you. Some women are always on the look-out for an unattached male. They eat them up – " she bit his finger. "But I won't let her. Is she married?"

"You said you wouldn't cross-examine me."

"I don't believe you know anything about women at all." Suddenly she knelt before him, her hands on his thighs. "Will you have to confess going with me, Vincent?"

"Don't talk about it now."

"Will you? I've never been with a Catholic before. I've only read about them. Will you?"

He tried half-heartedly to move away but the soft hands held him tightly. Now nakedness was no longer simply a condition of pleasure but a sort of punishment, the shaving of the head, the whipping at the cart-tail; once again he had lost himself but this time there was no happiness in it: it was in its own way as painful as the cramp but instead of begging her to stop he was begging her to go on; and now, beside her in a struggling heap on the floor, there was only a greedy haste and a desire to hurt; when finally he pulled himself away from her he expected her to be in tears. Instead she stretched out her hand to be helped to her feet and calmly, gently, almost maternally, kissed him on the fore-head. "You animal," she said. "You crude animal," making the abuse an endearment. "You'd better dress now. Or put some coal on the fire. Or both." Her face was very red, her eyes were dull: there was no smell of alcohol about her but it was as if she were drunk.

"I don't want to go," he said.

"There's a very nosy old couple in the flat above. I don't want you to go, either; but if we don't get dressed, you know what will happen. You'll stay all night. And then you'll have to leave home. And your job. I've an idea that the nosy old couple are Papists. Just my luck, isn't it?" She laughed harshly: he tried to take her into his arms but she ran out of room. He dressed quickly and for a moment stood hesitating by the hall door; from behind the door through which she had left he could hear running water. After the act of love, he thought, Maureen had been more herself; he hadn't found himself any nearer to loving her but at least he had known her identity. He had known Laura before; he didn't know her now, he was, in fact, afraid of who would emerge. He switched on the table light that stood on the radiogram and sat down to wait.

When she came back she was wearing a high-necked black dress with a white collar. She had put on her makeup again and brushed her hair; it was the librarian who stood before him, smiling faintly, even a little shyly.

"Can I give you a drink, Vincent?"

He shook his head. "I had too much at the wedding."

"Whose wedding?" The librarian vanished. The maenad knelt beside his chair. "Whose wedding? Is that why you're here?"

"My cousin Delia's." He kissed her, half-expecting a blow. This, he thought dazedly, was the Laura he wanted; he stroked her hair, only to have her jerk her head away savagely. He stroked her hair again; it was like trying to gain the confidence of an animal or a child. "There's nothing in it," he said. "She's my first cousin."

"What difference does that make? How old is she?"

"Twenty."

"She's still in business then, isn't she? You're horrible. Absolutely horrible. And a bloody hypocrite, too."

He continued stroking her head, wondering dreamily whether the parting was so snowy white because of the contrasting

169

blackness of her hair or merely because she washed it so often. "Make me some coffee," he said.

"You're horrible. All the girls at the library say what a nice young man you are, so quiet, so clever, so religious. But I know you're horrible. One girl said you were queer, but probably hadn't the guts to get down to it seriously. But I didn't think you were queer. I just thought you were shy. But nice with it. Gentle and decent. You're as bad as the rest, though. Why aren't you angry with me?"

"Because I love you."

"You've said that before."

"I mean it now. Will you marry me?" As he spoke he saw her face soften, all defences down.

"It's impossible. You'd never forgive me if I said yes. Your religion – "

"To hell with my religion. I didn't ask to be a Catholic."

"I didn't ask not to be one either," she said. "Don't talk about marriage again, darling. Enjoy what you have now, and don't yearn after what you'll never have."

Her tone was brisk and matter of fact; but her words seemed to reverberate inside his skull. It was the one word which, deafeningly, proclaimed the difference between them; she would never understand that what had just happened between them wasn't something which one enjoyed, any more than one enjoyed being born. It wasn't sacred, but it was too shattering to be enjoyed as one would enjoy a drink or a meal or a hot bath. He thought: we mean different things by love and always will.

"We can have whatever we want," he said. "You've just uttered a very grave heresy. It's a variation of predestination. We have free will, you see. Otherwise our souls wouldn't be worth much. I'm not so sure that I shouldn't excommunicate you. Otherwise the heresy spreads. It is sometimes necessary, for the good of the greatest number, that the Church should be ruthless. But even at the eleventh hour, even for a sinner like you, there may be mercy." He took hold of her wrists and pressed both her hands together. "We can have anything we want, we can do anything we want. We can rule the whole damned earth, we can flap our arms and fly away like birds. Whatever did they teach you at school?"

To his surprise he saw that she was crying. "I spoil everything," she said. "I'm spoiling you, I'm making you savage, I'm making you say things you'll hate yourself for afterwards – "

"Shut up," he said. "Make your act of contrition. Do your penance. Then perhaps I won't excommunicate you."

Once, and only once, in his second year at St Theo's he had caned a boy, an overgrown twelve-year-old whose face never lost its dumbly insolent grin. At the fifth stroke the grin had disappeared, the face had become a mask of animal suffering; when he saw the tears come to the boy's eyes, Vincent had stopped, disgusted with himself. He couldn't help being reminded of the incident now; what had disgusted him was his own enjoyment not so much in the infliction of pain as in the possession of power over another human being. He had absolute power over Laura now; almost casually he unhooked the top of her dress and pulled down the zipper. She did not move, but when the dress had fallen to her waist she shivered convulsively. The tears stopped; the expression on her face was of complete submission.

Thirteen

"I hope to God you'll bring me some better books this time," his grandmother said. "Those two are disgraceful. And him with a good Irish name too; you'd think God would strike him dead." She pointed at the book case. "There they are. I nearly threw them in the fire. I swear I did."

"You asked for them specially," Vincent said. He grinned as he looked at the bookcase. "I see you've given them brown paper wrappers," he said. "Lend me the fire-tongs so I won't have to touch them. You've not read them right through, of course."

"How would I know how disgraceful they were if I hadn't read them?" she snapped. "Father Duncombe was in this morning, and he's a very nosy man. I don't want him to know I have dirty books in the house. He was asking after you, by the way."

"I'm very popular," Vincent said. He put the books in his briefcase. "I'd better change these before the library closes."

"You're always in a great hurry these days." The bright blue eyes seemed to dim for a moment. "I'll not be with you that much longer."

"You'll live to bury me," Vincent said.

"Ah, God, don't say that. Isn't it enough that I've outlived two of my sons?"

He sat down in the wing chair. The fire was blazing, there was a smell of new bread from the kitchen, outside it was raw and cold; all the circumstances conspired to make staying with her a pleasure. But, still shell-shocked from his mother's reproaches

172

two days since, he wanted no further contact with his family than was necessary. To shout his mother down was one thing; to shout his grandmother down another. It was true enough, he thought, she wouldn't be with him very much longer; her eyes were still bright, her mind sharp, but it was – why hadn't he noticed it before? – beginning to be an effort for her to hold her back straight. "I've been in trouble," he said. "I expect you've heard?"

"I heard you went to the Green Goose with your uncles and your cousins," she said. "And you missed seeing your Uncle Hubert." She was smiling. "And you didn't come home until the small hours."

"You haven't heard it all," Vincent said. "I went to see Laura. You know about Laura, don't you?" The relief was almost ecstatic; it was in its own way as good as going to confession. "I went to see this divorced woman I'm not supposed to see any more. I'm as bad as a John O'Hara character, aren't I?"

"He's very true to life," she said calmly. "He seems to have lost the grace of God, but he knows what men are like."

Her face for a moment seemed to lose all traces of femininity, and yet not to become masculine. The heavy dark furniture, the red carpet, the big wooden crucifix on the wall, belonged to a priest's study, her long black dress could have been a cassock. The sound of traffic from outside seemed to accentuate the silence of the room; when he spoke his voice was almost a whisper.

"You're going to play the devil with me," he said. "You're going to tell me I'm in a state of mortal sin, aren't you, Grandma?"

"I've enough to do looking after my own soul," she said. "Do you think an old woman can't have any sins."

"Not any grave ones," he said.

"That's just where you're wrong, for all your cleverness. There's a few sins I can't commit any more because I'm too old and feeble." She smiled, the femininity returning to her face. "But I wish I could sometimes, and that's a sin. And there's many

173

a time when I just want to be off and away, just to rest, and that's a sin, too. Ah, sometimes you get tired of waiting, and that's a fact." Her voice had become so low that he had to strain to hear her.

"I think I'll have to leave St Theo's," he said.

"You've been there long enough. But there isn't a Catholic grammar school nearer than Bradford."

"I wasn't particularly thinking of a Catholic grammar school. Or even of a school."

"You'll have to make sure that this girl wants to go with you," she said. "She might patch things up with her husband."

"Not after two years," he said. "It's hopeless. She told me so." He felt a curious sadness, not for Robert, not even for Laura, but for marriage itself, as if the sacrament were animate, endearing, and helpless.

"Why did she divorce him?"

"We haven't talked about it very much. He was unfaithful to her. That's all I know."

"There'd be more to it than that," his grandmother said. "From what I've heard, she's a sensible girl. If every wife had to leave her husband for that reason, there wouldn't be many that weren't divorced. Not that Protestants see things as we do, poor creatures."

"I sometimes wish I'd been one," he said. "I wouldn't have any problems then, would I?"

"There's many a good Catholic wished that before you, child. It won't help you to wish for what you can't have."

He recognized Laura's words; he had run down the dark passage with the damp stone walls out into the sunlight and across the border and now, still running hard, he was back where he came from and the black tunnel-mouth was ahead of him. With an effort he rejected the image. "I can have anything I want," he said firmly. "I'm going to marry Laura."

"No one can stop you," she said calmly. "There was a man from this parish married a divorced woman, John Flanagan, I remember him well. She was a good woman, a decent-living woman who'd had a hard life of it with her first husband. She got a divorce for desertion; he'd gone off with another woman and wouldn't come back to her, and what else could she do?" She walked stiffly over to the Welsh dresser and began to rummage in one of the drawers.

"They were married in the registry office; I remember it nearly broke his mother's heart. Every Sunday and every holy day you'd see them there at Mass – in the back, of course, they couldn't take the sacraments. They had three grand children, all of them baptized and those children, the Canon said, were shining examples of Catholic children. There were some who wanted to cold-shoulder the Flanagans, mind you, for she wasn't a Catholic, but the Canon soon put his foot down. 'Turn the parents away' he said, 'and you turn the children away.' And John Flanagan died suddenly – he'd not be much more than fifty – but before he died he made his confession and he was received back into the Church. And Edie became a Catholic, which she couldn't before very well because she'd have had to stop being a wife to him." She held out a photograph to Vincent; he took it without looking at it.

"You aren't cheering me up very much, Grandma," he said. "You have poor Laura widowed already." The photo was faded but he could see that it was his father as a young man. The hair was black and thick, the face smooth; although the full mouth was unsmiling it was, he felt, held straight only with difficulty. It was the face of someone who was quite certain of himself and pleased with the world he lived in; he remembered now thinking as a child that his father would never die. The bold eyes under the thick eyebrows hadn't ever been afraid; he wondered what expression had come over them that night ten years ago when he'd died alone on the moors near Beckthorpe. His father had fought all his life, he'd often said that he'd fight until his last breath; but no one can fight a heart attack; he'd had time to stop

175

his car, time perhaps to say an Act of Contrition, but he'd died alone, taken by surprise, shot by the soldiers of God.

"It's a good likeness," he said.

"He never was a man for having his picture taken," she said. "He wouldn't keep still for long enough. Better wear out than rust out, was his great saying, and he wore himself out in the end, one way and another. One way and another." She frowned. "You're more like your mother's side of the family, the Rossleas are heavy thinkers, they like to work things out. But you're his son just the same. You'll not be driven." The frown deepened: it was as if he were being taken to task for some grave breach of morality. "And you'll not make a priest, Vincent. Some men can live without women, but you can't. And if you don't marry the right woman then it's a bitter life you'll have of it because you're not one for the pub and the club and you don't care very much about money either." She seemed to check herself on the verge of saying something more; they sat in silence for a moment, then Vincent handed back the photograph to her.

"Keep it," she said. "It'll remind you whose son you are."

He stood up. "I'll take good care of it."

"Are you seeing your young woman tonight?" she asked.

"I'm meeting her after I've brought you your books."

"Where are you meeting her?"

He glanced at his wristwatch. "The Espresso Nevada."

"That's an awkward arrangement. Bring her here. Or are you ashamed of her?"

"I don't think it'd be a good idea, Grandma. She might be embarrassed – "

"Muyah! It's a sight more embarrassing for a girl to be sitting alone in a snack-bar as if she belonged to no one. Or is it me you're ashamed of? Wouldn't I come up to her high standards?"

"You know that's not true, Grandma," he said. "She's not that sort of girl. I merely thought that you – "

She stood up and, surprisingly, instead of offering her cheek to be kissed, kissed him first. "Be off with you before the library closes. There's no need for you to tell me what you think. I know almost before you've thought it." She gave him a little push. "I'll expect to see you both. Without fail."

It was as if at the eleventh hour reinforcements had arrived; he had come to his grandmother's house expecting an intensification of his loneliness, expecting at the best not to have Laura's name mentioned; now it was plain that his grandmother was on his side, that the house he had known for thirty years was on his side too. When he went out into the street he found himself looking around him with almost a sense of affection; black and broken down though the district might be, it wasn't enemy territory.

But when, an hour later, he introduced Laura to his grandmother, he was, inexplicably, overwhelmed by a sense of physical shame. The shame was connected with Laura; it seemed impossible that his grandmother's bright blue eyes shouldn't have discovered that the body under the blouse and skirt was as well known to him as his own; and, hating himself for it, he couldn't help hearing his mother's reproaches. You take advantage of an old woman, his mother would say. You flaunt your mistress in front of your grandmother, you treat your grandmother's house like a brothel; and his grandmother at first did nothing to ease the atmosphere of constraint, holding herself with more than her usual stiffness and being a shade too profuse in her small talk and a shade too pressing in her hospitality, filling Laura's teacup almost as soon as she had drunk from it and offering her fresh cakes and biscuits almost as soon as she had begun to eat what was on her plate.

But after a while he looked at Laura and his grandmother and realized that somehow a barrier had been penetrated. Laura hadn't asked for approval but she had been given it; and given it to a degree that he hadn't seen given to Maureen or even to Jenny. They were talking about clothes now, their faces animated and frivolous, his grandmother showing a surprising grasp of fashion trends; he took little part in the conversation but leaned back in the wing chair, grateful for ordinariness, for the absence of high drama. It was exactly what he needed; when he heard his grandmother speak his name he paid no attention at first and then Laura put her hand on his knee. "Vincent. Your grand-mother's talking to you."

"I'm sorry," he said. "I was dreaming. What was it, Grandma?"

"It was nothing, nothing at all. Laura won't believe that she's the first young woman you've brought to see me."

"It's perfectly true," he said. "I'm hard to please. I didn't think I really wanted to get married until I met Laura." It was in the worst of taste for him to speak like that, he thought; and then, seeing the expression on her face, realized that good taste wasn't ever going to be an important issue between them. What would matter would be whether he spoke the truth or not; and there was a long time for them to discover the truth about themselves. There wasn't going to be another woman for him: he had made the decision now.

"I hope I'll always please you,' Laura said.

"It may not be easy," his grandmother said. "He's not always in this world, Laura. There's many a time he passes his own mother and family by in the street. He doesn't mean any harm, it's just that his mind is on other things. Once he went to school with one black and one brown shoe."

"That was a long time ago," Vincent said.

"Oh, you've reformed a little since then. But you'll have all your work cut out looking after him, Laura."

"I expect I shall manage," Laura said. The red and brown blouse was high-necked, the skirt comfortably covered her knees; she was sitting, he noticed with a shock, much as his grandmother sat, her back straight, her hands folded. The cuckoo clock above the fireplace chirped the hour; he rose and picked up his coat. He and Laura were inextricably together, this was a fact, and there was no need to be frightened of losing her; the certainty was almost an ecstasy, and then as they said their goodbyes and went out into the street it had gone and the girl with the black hair and green eyes was Laura Heycliff, who was his mistress and might be his wife if only he could break loose not only from his mother and his family and his job but all he'd ever lived by; he couldn't see himself sitting in the back of the church any more than he could see himself teaching in a Protestant school, among people who behaved as if they would never die.

"I liked your grandmother," Laura said.

"She liked you. She'd have made it pretty clear if she hadn't."

"She doesn't get on with your mother, does she?"

"Not really. But they keep up appearances. My mother's family don't mix very well."

"Did your mother and father?"

"They came to some kind of agreement." He changed down for the long climb to Marlcliffe. "Why do you ask?"

"I don't know much about you. I know much more than I did, but I still don't know enough."

"You will before you die."

"Death," she said, looking at the high black wall on her left, "always death. Do you ever think of anything else?"

"I was brought up on it," he said. "We always have to live as if we were going to die the next moment. Once you realize that, you're free, you're more than an animal walking upright, you're a human being." He was silent for a while; the night was so cold, the landscape so bleak, the road so empty, that only the evidence of his senses persuaded him that he was in fact alive.

"Go on," she said.

"It's too depressing. You can't be expected to see it my way. I wish sometimes I couldn't myself."

"That's why I think I love you," she said. "It's like gambling for high stakes. I knew a man once who gambled, really gambled, and he said that there was no point in playing unless you were hurt if you lost and could buy a Bentley if you won. If you marry me, you may lose your immortal soul. That's it, isn't it? All the blame's on you because I don't know any better and I can't be expected to. You're in a state of mortal sin now, aren't you?"

The tranquillity had gone from her voice; there was a high hysterical note about it. She was breathing quickly, her mouth parted; as the car reached the top of the hill he put his foot down on the accelerator.

"Steady," she said. "We want to get there alive."

"I was increasing the stakes," he said.

"But you've already won, Vincent. Don't break the bank." She started to laugh uncontrollably.

Fourteen

Laura had fallen asleep, one arm flung up over her eyes, the other around Vincent's neck; he lay beside her his eyes wide open, trying to re-orientate himself. This time there had been no hurry, this time she hadn't been as it were testing him; it had been quiet, it had been slow, it had been as if they were married. He wanted to join her in sleep, to slip beside her into whatever dream she was having, good or bad; but even that, he thought contentedly, was wrong, He wanted nothing, he needed nothing; it was like taking the vows of poverty and chastity.

Laura's eyes opened; for a moment she did not seem to recognize him. "Darling," she said. "Where are you?"

"I'm here," he said.

"I was dreaming. It was a marvellous dream, but I can't remember already. The sun was shining and we were by the river. We were going to swim." She switched on the table lamp by the bedside and lit a cigarette.

"That's a good dream."

"But I don't even know whether you can swim. I could easily have drowned you."

"I can swim. Everyone gets taught how to swim in Charbury. That and how to read music."

"I'm happy," she said. "You've made me happy. You're the first one, the first man I've met."

"The first?"

181

"The first who counted. There haven't been many. I'm not a tart, you know." Her voice had become sharp.

"You don't have to say anything about it. And then I won't say anything about my girl friends."

"We'll make a pact. We'll start from scratch." She looked at the clock on the dressing-table and in one movement got out of bed. "You'll have to go soon, my treasure."

"I'll stay here. We'll run away together in the morning. We'll easily get jobs in London – " His voice trailed away.

She sat down beside him on the edge of the bed. "I had a friend who did that once. Only he was married. It didn't work out. You can't run very far in this country, when you come to think of it." She put her head on his chest for a moment. "You smell so beautiful," she said. "All sweaty. Clean but sweaty. Once men realize what women really like the makers of cologne and aftershave lotion will all be out of business." She sat up again; her skin in the red glow from the electric fire and the paler light of the bedside lamp seemed gold rather than olive. He stroked her back gently.

"I'm happy too," he said. There was nothing else to say; the poems, he thought, are all written before the act and not after.

"You're not guilty? You don't see the flames of hell around you?"

"I see a new electric fire. What's the use of feeling guilty?"

"You're a strange man. Lots of men are guilty. Will you confess all this to the priest?"

"It's a long time till Easter," he said.

"Do you only have to go once a year?"

"That's the minimum. You're supposed to go more often."

"I had a friend once who was terribly devout. She had an affair with a married man. So she stopped going to confession because she said she couldn't sincerely promise not to go with him again. So what will you do when Easter comes, Vincent?"

"I'll worry when the time comes," he said, feeling for the first time a consciousness of betrayal.

"I'm a married woman," she said. "I know you don't believe in divorce. Even this furniture was bought by my husband. He was very good at buying things for me. It's a lovely bedroom suite – " She rose and walked round the bedroom, touching in turn the dressing-table, the linen chest, the wardrobe, the bedside table, the two chairs, as if she were trying to sell him them. "All in the best walnut. We had a great many discussions about the best kind. He was an expert on interior decoration. And music. And of course plastics, because that was his job. I sometimes think he was bloody well made from a plastic kit, the kind you get in a polythene bag at Woolworth's." Her voice changed. "What are you looking at, darling?"

"You know."

"Tell me."

He whispered into her ear.

"Yes" she said, "it is. It is beautiful. You said the right thing, because you couldn't help it. I don't care if you hit me, I don't care if you go with other women, though I'll kill them if I catch them at it. But you think that's beautiful, you don't think it's ugly, you know it's as much a part of me as my eyes or my nose or my mouth or my hands." She picked up a white towelling dressing-gown from one of the chairs. "Let's have some coffee. Or are you hungry?"

He shook his head.

"You don't think I'm disgusting, do you, Vincent?"

"I love you." He started to dress.

"I'm going to get rid of all this damned furniture. He would give me it – his damned guilt complex. I'd rather have had whitewood furniture and a baby. Or two or three or four. I bet I'd make a better Papist than you, Vincent."

"Why didn't you have children?"

"Can't you guess?" She looked around her wildly. "If you asked that damned wardrobe nicely, it would tell you. Or the linen chest. Or the bedside table." She was laughing hysterically.

"Didn't he want any?" He followed her out into the lounge.

"Don't ask me now," she said. "It's not something I like to think about."

"I'm sorry."

"Never mind. Do you really want coffee?"

"If it isn't too much trouble."

"It isn't any trouble at all and you've no need to be so damned polite. But if I make coffee I'll have to go into the kitchen and then you may run away again."

He fastened his tie. "I'll come in the kitchen with you."

"It's not tidy enough. I want everything to be right for you."

"Make the coffee and stop talking about it. I won't run way." He took off his shoes and handed them to her. "Keep those with you and then you'll be sure. Do you want my trousers too?" He kept his tone light and amused; her troubled face and the way in which she clutched the shoes suddenly evoked a compassion that was almost painful. He loved her, he thought with surprise, as he might have loved a child, or occasionally he might have loved his brothers; if he hadn't liked her it would still have been the same. She had opened her mind to him, she had offered herself without reservations; there need be no consequences after the act of love that had taken place in the bedroom, but there was no avoiding the consequences of the confession she had just made.

When she returned with the coffee he looked at her, half afraid that she might have changed. But her face was still open, troubled, trusting; he hadn't been used, he hadn't used her, it was more than their bodies which had come together. She poured him a cup of coffee and sat on the floor by the fire her eyes fixed on his face. "I couldn't be sure," she said in a low voice. "I couldn't be sure you didn't despise me. One way or the other."

"I want to marry you."

"Once is enough," she said. "Not that you will. But if you only knew – "

"Only knew what?"

"What my marriage was really like." She stood up and said in a different tone, hard and flippant: "You haven't said anything about my new carpet. Intellectual yellow, I got it cheap. Or the curtains. Robert would have done."

"They're very pretty," he said, glancing down at the floor and behind him at the window, registering nothing more than circular blurs of yellow and scarlet.

"I'm going to get rid of everything in the bedroom. I won't be paid what it's worth, but it doesn't matter."

"They're only bits of wood," he said.

"Do you mind if I have some gin?" She poured herself a large gin and opened a bottle of tonic.

"If you must," he said coldly.

"One day when you say *If you must* in that tone, I won't. Because I do want to please you. But I ought to tell you about Robert and I can't without a drink."

"It's your business," he said.

She took a swallow of her drink and put it down on the coffee-table. "It's your business too. I haven't told anyone about it before, not even Mummy and Daddy. Not even the solicitor. Though he might have guessed. I think he did guess, because he kept asking me if there wasn't something more."

"Your husband didn't want children then?" He was losing his bearings again, the room that was beginning to seem so familiar and warm, was becoming garish and alien, alternately too large and too small, too cold and too stuffy.

"Oh, God, Vincent, it wasn't just that. I mean, he didn't: I found that out pretty soon and that was bad enough, because I did want children, every woman wants children. But there was more than that. He didn't want them, he'd go into hysterics at the mere idea, but he couldn't give me one anyway."

"I see. He wasn't able – "

"Oh yes, he was. Before we were married he was. I remember thinking he wasn't terribly good at it, but then I wasn't either. Not that I know what being good at it is. But he was all right. It was when we'd been married for a month that I found out what was wrong."

185

Irrelevantly Vincent thought of himself going down the white-tiled corridor to the mortuary, the attendant was pulling out the big steel drawer, with the suspicion of a smile on his face. He dissolved the picture. "He was queer," he said. "Stop hurting yourself."

She looked away from him. "He was – well, sexually deformed. That's all. I just couldn't change him."

"Deformed?"

"That's the wrong word." She ripped open her dressing-gown. "Look. I know you like looking, even now. You're a man, you see. You might be absolutely awful. I don't know you well enough yet, but you are a man. Once Robert came into the bathroom when I'd just got out of the bath. That was early in our marriage, when we had our nice little house in a nice little suburb of Birmingham. He's an only child, and his father's quite well off. I thought he'd like looking at me, I didn't mind a bit, but then I saw a look on his face and he closed his eyes, so he didn't have to look at it. I don't think he minded the rest of me, because I'm not terribly big upstairs; it was just that one part of me he couldn't bear. You are shocked, aren't you, Vincent? I don't expect you've heard anything like this before." She pulled her dressing-gown together and began to cry; gently he parted it again and put his face on her lap. She pressed his head tightly to her. "He used to drink," she said. "Rum; he acquired a taste for it during the war. I still can't bear the smell of the stuff. That's how he managed at first. And he'd say, we don't want children yet, let's get the house furnished first... And there were parties, always parties, he had a good job in this plastics firm and he entertained a lot; and then he stopped drinking and I found out what he really liked. He shouldn't have got married at all, but I expect all his friends were, and his mother and father thought I was just the girl for him. I used to be thinner then, a real tomboy. Oh God, that bloody bloody expression, he used to love it, and before we were married, it was a great joke between us." She stroked his hair. "Now I'm a woman. You can do what you like with me, you can ask me to keep you and I'll keep you, you can make me pregnant every year and I'll never grumble. You'll never ask me to pretend – "

"Pretend what?"

"I can't tell you," she said. "There were other things he asked which I didn't mind so much because they were all right if they were part of the real thing. But he wanted always just what I wouldn't give." She put her hand on her breast as if in pain. "If only he'd given me a child. But the idea of me being pregnant made him sick. Do you understand? Physically sick."

"I think I see now," he said. "But the divorce – "

"It was arranged. He had to go on living, after all. The co-respondent was a professional. I didn't want the scandal either. The fire's going out, Vincent. Put some coal on."

"I'd better be going soon."

"I've got your shoes," she said. "Put some coal on the fire, Vincent."

When he went over to the coal scuttle he heard a rustle behind him but did not turn until he had built up the fire. Standing over the studio couch he took off his jacket and began to unloosen his tie. She reached up and struck away his hand. "You fool," she said, "there's no time." Looking down at her it was as if they were both someone else; he thought of her in the bathroom, her husband's eyes averted from her, he thought of what the whispered drunken demands must have been, and he was seized by an ugly excitement and an ugly sense of triumph not only over her husband but over her; he continued to undress and then walked slowly over and stood for a moment looking down at her. "We'll make the time," he said.

Fifteen

As they went out of the cinema Vincent was oppressed by the sense of the past. The cinema had been one of the first to be built in Charbury, he had gone there as a child when the scarlet plush seats and the gilt Egyptian pillars and the thick blue carpeting were glossy new; and now it was growing shabbier, and, no matter what the film, its audiences were growing smaller. Once, one had escaped from the cold empty street into the warm crowded darkness, but now there seemed to be little difference between one darkness and another. He glanced at the shop windows in the cinema block; three were empty. Development had moved away from this quarter of the city; even St Theo's, its main public building, would soon move away too. Nothing remained the same, even the coldness tonight was not the same coldness that it had been once, but had a closed-in, musty quality about it: it wasn't wild December but dank December; he had the sensation, despite the warmth of Laura's arm in his, of being imprisoned in a cellar.

"I'll take you home," he said to Laura.

"It's early yet," she said. She stopped. "What's the matter, Vincent?"

"Nothing."

"You haven't had a good word to say to me all evening. Has your mother been at you again?"

When he had first met her the clarity of her speech had been what had chiefly attracted him; now, as they stood in the light of a shop window in full view of the people leaving the cinema, he could have wished her to have spoken less distinctly. The bus stop was almost opposite the main entrance of the cinema and already people were looking in their direction.

"Come on," he said. "It's terribly cold."

"She has been at you, hasn't she? I was looking forward to this evening. You've hardly spoken since we met, there's been a scowl on your face all evening, you played hell at coming to this film because you didn't want to see it and now you just want to shunt me off home – "

It was the first time he had seen her lose her temper; it seemed the finishing touch to the congealed spaghetti and greasy chips in the cafe, the three hours in the draughty cinema, the bitter cold of the evening.

"Forget it, love," he said. "Let's have a drink."

"I don't want a bloody drink!" she said loudly. "I just want you to be kind to me, that's all." Her face was puckered up as if, he realized disquietingly, she were going to burst into tears.

"I thought you were kind, I thought you were a real man, and now I see you're just as obtuse as the rest of them."

"Yes, dear," he said. "You're absolutely right. I am obtuse and cruel and callous – " He patted her head cautiously; she jerked it away.

"I'm not a dog," she said.

"I'm sorry," he said and drew away from her. "Are we going to stand here all evening?"

"I'm looking at houses," she said, peering at the cards in the estate agent's window. "I'd forgotten how cheap property is here."

"Everyone's moving out, that's why." The journey to her flat then to his home in the opposite direction seemed in prospect an undeniably dreary distance; he had a sudden passionate longing for a softer landscape, for a city of boulevards and new white buildings untouched by smoke.

"Beckfield, three thousand," she said. "Three full-sized bedrooms, separate toilet, garage, large garden – that'd be about three hundred deposit, wouldn't it? What's Beckfield like, Vincent?"

"I live there," he said.

"I know. You forget that I've never seen it."

"Undistinguished," he said, taking her arm. "An over-grown village five miles out. Respectable, but not fashionable. The best people live in Burley or Skipton or Harrogate or Bingley or Warley."

Her cheeks pinched by the cold, her slenderness disguised by a rather shabby camel-hair coat, she didn't, he reflected, look at her best. He didn't admire himself for feeling it, but he wasn't pleased at being seen with her, there wasn't any pleasure in her company, he wanted his life to continue as it had been before.

"I'd like to see it just the same," she said as they walked towards the car park at the rear of the cinema where the building gave up all attempt to impress and displayed shamelessly its blackened brick and drainpipes and peeling posters and fire-escapes.

"I'll take you there. It's not worth seeing, believe me."

"Are you frightened that – " she began, but he had turned away to speak to a fair-haired girl who, together with a man obviously her husband and, she could see in the light of a car's headlamps, obviously Vincent's brother, was running towards them.

"Vincent! Won't you speak to us, or are you too proud?"

"My sister-in-law, Maureen," Vincent said. "And my big brother Matthew. He'll say how do you do when he gets his breath back. Laura Heycliff." He waved his hand vaguely at the three of them. "We were going for a drink, Matthew."

"Come to our place," Maureen said quickly.

"It's late," Vincent said.

"We're not going to have a party, just a drink of something hot."

"We'd better not," Vincent said. "The Deauville Arms – " His voice trailed away; he was not in charge of the situation, he realized: Maureen and Laura, each for reasons of their own he couldn't guess at, had already made up their minds. Then he remembered something. "My mother – " he said, but Maureen and Matthew were already walking away to their car. "We really shouldn't," he said.

Laura laughed. "Shouldn't what, Vincent?"

"Never mind," he said, opening the car door.

"Your mother's baby-sitting for them, isn't she?"

"I expect so."

"I wonder if your sister-in-law remembered that. Or perhaps she did."

He slowed down to avoid a man who was staggering about the middle of the road singing to himself in a high querulous whine. "I don't think she's capable of that much calculation," he said. "Or Matthew either. They act first and think, if at all, a long time afterwards."

"Don't you like people who act first, then?"

"I didn't mean that."

"It's just *people*, isn't it, Vincent? Sometimes you can't bear people, can you?"

"I can't bear being alive," he said. "I don't want to die but sometimes I hate the notion that I'm a human being. It isn't good enough for me. There's something else I want and can't have… I don't know why I'm telling you all this."

"Who else should you tell it to?"

"Yes, that's absolutely true," he said in a wondering voice. "I hadn't thought of it before." He stopped the car and kissed her gently.

"I do love you," she said. "I know I've been edgy this evening. Women do get edgy, you know. Every month regular as clockwork. And sometimes not so regular, which is worse. I shouldn't grumble, really, I'd be a damned sight more edgy if nothing had happened." She laughed. "Roll on the menopause."

191

"There's nothing to worry about then?" he asked.

"No, haven't I just explained?" Her voice became irritated. "I wish I could fathom the way your conscience works. I always remember when I was at the library in London one of the girls there had an affair with a Catholic. He wasn't nearly as bright as her, but they got on like a house on fire. They couldn't keep off each other, it was a real *folie à deux*, they were together every chance they could get. She told me once she was terribly worried every month. He wouldn't use contraceptives, you see. Said it was immoral."

"It's different for us," he said, laughing. "For God's sake, stop examining everything. You worry far more about these things than I do. Are you absolutely sure you want to go to Matthew's? I can easily phone them and say you don't feel well. It wouldn't really be a lie."

"You're being Jesuitical," she said. "I want to go, and if you won't take me I'll get a taxi and go by myself. How many children has your brother?"

"Three," he said. "Kevin's two, Michael's six, Eileen's eight. They're nice kids"

"She's only two or three years older than me. It's difficult to tell with that hair, of course. I shouldn't have said that, should I?"

"You'll always say exactly what you like, especially to me."

"Your mother won't like that."

They had reached the Roman road; the cold that had seemed stuffy and oppressive in the city was clean and stimulating now; he was, he realized, happy, however briefly. He had finished hiding; the legion, so as to speak, was on the march.

"She'll have to lump it, then. We can't just drift on. It isn't fair to you."

"Don't be too noble," she said. "Sometimes it is better to drift, just to let things happen. We can still phone. We might even catch your brother up, he can't be very far ahead."

"We'll do what we set out to do," he said. "Or rather I agree that what you intended to do from the beginning is the right thing to do. You're very clever, aren't you, darling?"

He was coming into the town now and a car was approaching at high speed from the opposite direction; he could not risk a glance in her direction but he knew that she was smiling.

When he introduced her to his mother there was a long silence. It was, he thought, incongruously like the stock Western scene where the sheriff meets the stranger from Texas; they were measuring each other up, ready if necessary to shoot to kill. His mother put out her hand and smiled, not very warmly but not with less warmth than she was accustomed to display on such occasions. The Dungarvans, she often said, were the great charmers to all and sundry, particularly when they thought there might be something to be gained from it; the Rossleas were temperate and polite, the same with a charwoman or a duchess.

"It was fortunate that you ran across Matthew and Maureen," she said to Laura. "I don't really know why Vincent has hidden you away so long."

There wasn't really any reply possible to that, Vincent thought, and was glad to see that Laura didn't make the attempt. Instead Matthew, who had been eyeing Laura with an undisguised curiosity, crashed into the conversation on both feet. "Vince still feels he ought to be a priest," he said. "He's scared of bringing girls home."

"Vincent will please himself," his mother said sharply. "He's always been welcome to bring his friends home, just as you have. Don't let Matthew give you the wrong idea about Catholics, Laura. We're human beings, you know. All too human, some of us."

She wasn't missing the chance to emphasize the fact of her Catholicism, Vincent thought, and was suddenly overwhelmed by an enormous emptiness: the black-haired girl sitting primly on the sofa, the grey-haired woman rather too obviously putting her at her ease, the blotchy-faced man now surreptitiously inspecting Laura's legs, weren't people he wanted any part of or, worse, weren't a species he wanted any part of: and, a small sneering voice said, if God had died for them, that only demonstrated His bad taste.

Matthew rose abruptly and went over to the cocktail cabinet. "Can I get you a drink, Laura? You don't mind me calling you Laura, do you?"

"Of course not, Matthew. But I won't have a drink if you don't mind."

Vincent saw his mother nod in approval. "I could tell you didn't like drink," she said. "Not that I can visualize – " she brought out the word with a flourish – "my son Vincent giving his friendship to a girl who was a drinker. It's our curse, Laura. My father always used to say that if it weren't for drink the Irish would be masters of the world."

"He put away a lot of the hard stuff himself," Matthew said, pouring himself a whisky.

"My father drank like a gentleman," his mother said. "Like an Englishman, he used often to say." She was keeping her temper, Vincent noted, without any difficulty; normally the slightest reflection on the memory of her father was the occasion of a fierce quarrel. "You used to live in his house, didn't you, Laura? The home of my youth – " she sighed heavily but with genuine emotion. "Of course, it's not fashionable now."

"That's a fine thing to say, Mother," Vincent said. "You mean she would only live there because the neighbourhood had gone down."

"You're too sharp, Vincent. I was just being a little nostalgic, that's all."

"I wasn't in your father's house for very long, Mrs Dungarvan. A house isn't the same after it's been converted to flats, anyway."

"Daniel House," his mother said. "Ah, my father worshipped the Liberator. There were some who said he had a certain likeness to him." She snorted rather than laughed. "Of course a great many Irishmen could say the same. Daniel O'Connell had his faults, as perhaps you'll know." Again there was the interrogative tone as she looked towards Laura.

"It becomes romantic when it's a long time ago," Laura said. "Like people boasting of their ancestor being a king's mistress."

It was the right answer, Vincent thought, emerging dazed from the emptiness; she had made it plain that she was fully conversant with Irish history without being awkwardly explicit. His mother approved of her, she had appraised her hair and her clothes and her deportment and accent, she had given her a brief *viva voce* examination and she had passed with ease; what had she in mind next? He listened intently but she remained friendly, polite, pleasant, asking Laura about her job, her new flat, her taste in literature; she was in short, behaving like a true Rosslea.

Not until Maureen had come in with coffee and sandwiches did he remember what his father had said once about his grandfather Rosslea. It had been at the time when his father had been seized by the notion of setting up in business on his own; what precisely had happened between his father and his grandfather he'd never known, but his father had come back late and slightly drunk one night and had said, staring at the fire: "The cunning old bastard. The cunning old bastard." It wasn't a word his father was in the habit of using, but he had repeated it and said with a gloom utterly foreign to him: "I'll work for others all my life, Vincent. He drew me out, the bloody old lawyer drew me out, so pleasant and understanding and smiling, I was talking away like a fool and then all of a sudden I realized what I'd said. He'd make the Pope confess to being a Methodist, he would, smiling away there – "

Maureen sat on the arm of his chair. "Drink your coffee whilst it's hot, Vince," she said. She lowered her voice. "She seems to be getting on like a house on fire," she said. "Honestly, I could have kicked myself when I realized – "

"Could you?" he asked. "Could you, Maureen?" With a burst of affection he saw her colour, and felt a vague longing for things somehow to be different, to be less devious, to know where he stood. Maureen would never be able to deceive him or anyone else, except perhaps Matthew. She had no secrets, she couldn't hide her feelings: then with a twinge of premonition he saw her look at Laura and he spoke quickly. "Did Matthew get over his trouble?"

She turned her head slowly towards him. "What trouble?"

The sense of involvement suddenly became too much. And at the same time he felt an odd pride, cold, amoral, unhappy. I have slept with these two women, he thought, and I came from that woman's womb, and only two of us know about it and if more than two know about it the whole home will be pulled down into ruin…

"You know what trouble," he said sharply.

"For the time being," she said. Matthew had poured himself another whisky and was talking to Laura and his mother, his face animated. "He soon forgets, does Matthew. He's full of plans again, he's going to make his fortune, he's always off seeing men on business."

"Like my father."

"Your father had a good job at Silvington's. He liked to dream, but it was just a game with him. Ah well, the Dungarvans will muddle on, no doubt."

He had nothing more to say to her: he looked at the shabby untidy room with a kind of horror. Her gaiety had been induced by sexual curiosity as Matthew's now was induced by alcohol; all the qualities he had admired in her still existed, but they were of no use to him. She was a package deal; she came with a house, with children, with bad tempers and burnt toast and bills on a wet Monday morning: he didn't have to see her again, he could pretend that what had taken place on the grey carpet in front of the fire, the blue cushions underneath them that were now on the sofa where Laura sat, hadn't counted as more than a venial sin, was hardly worth telling at confession.

"Silbridge," he heard his mother say. "That's where my son Paul's wife comes from."

"I don't go there very often," Laura said. "If it weren't for my parents I'd never go there at all."

He went over to Matthew. "A small one, Matthew," he said.

He seemed to detect an expression of triumph on his mother's face, but couldn't discover the reason for it. Obscurely he felt that Laura needed help.

"My sister-in-law doesn't go there much either," he said. "In fact, she keeps it pretty quiet. Describes it as being near Doncaster, which is about as accurate as describing Charbury as being near Harrogate."

"You haven't met Paul and Jenny, have you, Laura?" his mother said. It was as if Vincent had not spoken. "You'd like them. Paul's a solicitor, he takes after his grandfather Rosslea. Jenny was a librarian like yourself."

"I met her at the Library School," Laura said. "We were in different years, though."

"It's a small world," his mother said. Vincent suddenly remembered her, nearly two months ago, delivering what she had supposed to be the *coup de grâce*; why, he wondered, was she speaking as if she'd discovered all this for the first time? "Jenny's a convert. She's very devout. It's often the case. Paul says he often wishes she'd stayed a heretic, then he could have a good lie-in on a Sunday now and again and perhaps have a little meat on a Friday."

"I had a time when I used to think of becoming a Catholic," Laura said to Vincent's surprise. "When I was in the South. But I suppose I was just being romantic about it because I was rather unhappy at the time."

"Yes," his mother said, "one does have this longing for certainty, for some kind of assurance. You'd feel things, of course, you'd apprehend reality with the heart, as I would, as I'm sure Jenny did. But Vincent now sees it up here – " she tapped her forehead. "Aren't I right, Vincent?"

"I'm afraid you are, Mamma," he said. "I'd advise Laura to keep well out of the clutches of the Scarlet Woman myself."

"They wouldn't have me, anyway," Laura said lightly.

"Oh my dear, what nonsense. The Church is there for all who have the gift of faith, and most of all for those who need her. But you're exactly the sort of person She would have." She offered Laura a cigarette and then Maureen.

"No, thank you," Maureen said. Her face had turned pale. "Don't let my mother-in-law convert you, Laura. It's bad enough being born one sometimes."

"Baptised, not born," his mother said. "It's an important distinction."

"I know," Maureen said. "Dead ignorant, that's me." She stood up and began to collect the cups and plates. "You must come again, Laura. You know your way here now."

It was the signal for dismissal; it was reasonable enough, Vincent thought, it now being nearly midnight, but it was perhaps a little abrupt. Then he looked again at Maureen's face; it had turned paler even as she was speaking. He was aware that his mother had noticed it, aware too that she had noticed his concern; at all costs he had to keep those pale blue eyes from probing any further. He looked at his watch ostentatiously. "Good Lord, none of us'll ever get up tomorrow," he said. "Come on, Mother. I'll drop you on the way…" As he shepherded his mother and Laura out of the house Maureen smiled at him; the smile was all the more disquieting because of the pallor of her face and the hand that was now, he could plainly see, holding the chair for support.

When he stopped the car outside Laura's flat she kissed him lightly on the forehead.

"Don't come in," she said. "It's too late."

"There's nothing wrong, is there?" He looked up at the first-floor window where a light had just been switched on.

"No, darling. I'm tired, that's all."

"I'm sorry you were submitted to my family at such short notice."

"I enjoyed it"

"You're just saying that to be polite."

"No, no," she said, so vehemently that he was startled. "I'll never tell you lies. Sometimes I won't tell you the truth, but I won't tell you lies, not even little ones."

"I'm sure you won't," he said gently. Even inside the car it was cold once the engine had stopped running; he pulled up the collar of his sheepskin coat. "I'll see you on Saturday, shall I?"

"I'm going home. But come and see me at the library if you like." She opened the door of the car; he could see a faint glitter on the pavement.

"Watch your step," he said. "It's going to be frosty. I'll see you to the door – "

"No," she said. "The neighbours are watching. My Catholic neighbours. Remember?"

"The Holy Family," he said, and was amused to see her frown.

"How long is it since you've been to confession?" she asked abruptly.

"Laura for God's sake – "

"Don't mind me. It's the general atmosphere created by your mother." She stood by the door for a moment in silence. "Vincent, how many children did you say they have, again?"

"Three. Kevin's two, Michael's six, Eileen's eight. Why do you ask?"

"Idle curiosity. Only I was thinking that perhaps I wish I'd missed just for once. I wish I were in trouble. Pregnant. Do I have to spell it out? Good night, Vincent." She slammed the car door. He could not be certain but as she walked up to the front door she seemed to be crying.

Sixteen

"The sun roof," Paul said, pointing upwards with his pipe, "was one of the selling points. They must have seen me coming. We've had this house for three years and we haven't used it three times."

"You could cover it in," Vincent said. Whenever he visited Paul he was always taken out into the garden to look at the sun roof and Paul's comment and his own reply never varied.

Paul grunted. The noise meant that he was reserving his opinion; it also meant, Vincent thought, that he didn't think that anyone else's opinion was of much value. He waited for the second grunt; it came after a long silence, and they walked down to the swing at the bottom of the garden, where Shane was pushing a screaming Bernard higher and higher. "Steady on there," Paul said. He looked at the house: against the grey sky its grey stone seemed queerly unsubstantial. A light came on at the window under the sun roof and simultaneously the sound of draining water; the lines of the house sharpened, the stone became solid. Bernard had ceased to scream now; Shane was pushing him with an exaggerated slowness, watching Paul unblinkingly. Paul smiled at him and ruffled his hair which, recently cut, had the appearance of fur, bristly yet soft. "Can we watch TV now, Daddy?" he asked, enduring the caress rather than welcoming it.

"You ought to get some more fresh air."

"It's wrestling, Daddy. And Bernard says he feels cold." The swing stopped. The two white faces looked appealingly at Paul as if, Vincent thought, begging for a crust to save them from starvation.

"Get yourselves off to the idiot's lantern, then." The boys ran into the house; as they passed by the lighted window Vincent noticed that their faces were rosy, not pale; it had been a trick of the light, the approaching dark made all faces pale and sad.

Paul bent down to pick up a toy cutlass. "Come back" he shouted, but the boys were already in the house. "Little devils," he said. "They leave everything lying around and then they cry because they can't find them." He swung the cutlass round his head. "They have it made," he said. "They have more toys now than ever we had in the whole of our lives. They don't know what to do with them all and that's a fact."

"I wonder what happens to old toys," Vincent said. "I didn't break mine and I didn't lose them and I didn't give them away. But they've all gone."

"Parents give them away," Paul said, "If they didn't, they wouldn't be able to move for the damned things. And they want a dog now, if you please, as if there weren't enough bloody dogs in the neighbourhood. When they're not washing their damned cars, they're taking their damned dogs for walks…" He looked at the lighted window. "I wish I could get some help for Jenny. It's practically impossible in Harrogate. There must be someone who'd do with the money."

"If there were, they wouldn't tell you."

"The sun's going in," Paul said. "If it was ever out." One might as well not speak, Vincent thought; other people's voices were for Paul simply irrelevant interruptions of his non-stop monologue.

The baby was sleeping in the pram as they went into the drawing-room. Paul turned up the gas-fire and switched on a table-light. "It looks a bit more cheerful now," he said. "Not that the baby cares. He just eats and sleeps. When he cries you let him cry and he stops. It's not like it was with Shane. The first year neither Jenny nor I ever had a full night's sleep. You

201

bachelors don't know where you're well off." He looked at the eggshell blue stippled wall and frowned. "Little grubby paws at work again," he said. "I told Jenny that colour was a mistake."

"Dark colours are depressing," Vincent said, not caring very much.

"That's all very well, but we've got all this light beech stuff now. You're lucky, I tell you." He looked round the big rather sparsely furnished room with an expression which was presumably intended to be rueful – the man weighed down by possessions – but which succeeded only in being complacent.

"That's what I wanted to see you about," Vincent said.

"You're not setting up on your own, are you? Not that I'd blame you. Mother's a wonderful woman but she's a bit too bossy at times – "

"You know what we were talking about earlier on. Laura."

Paul relit his pipe, using at least half a dozen matches. "That's for you to work out," he said finally. "We don't want to quarrel about it, do we?"

"Paul, I simply want your advice. I'll pay you six and eightpence, if you like."

"I'm not the right person to come to, Vincent. I'm not an expert on Canon Law. In fact I'm not much of an expert on any branch of the law. I'm a run-of-the-mill solicitor, that's all. Honestly, you'll get all the information you need from a little CTS pamphlet, and I can't add any more to that. The dear old Catholic Truth Society knows far more than I do." He walked over to the pram. "I don't see why you can't find yourself a nice Catholic girl." He stroked the baby's cheek. "That's my son, my fine little son, he'll grow up big and strong, so he will…" He put his handkerchief to his nose. "My God, he niffs a bit, though."

He returned to his arm-chair and picked up his pipe; Vincent went over to the table where the drinks were kept, scarcely able to speak.

"Count up to ten," Paul said, "and pour yourself a drink. And one for me too."

"I don't want a drink," Vincent said. He looked at Paul's cardigan, originally loosely fitting and now tightly stretched. "You don't either. I want to know what chance Laura has of getting an annulment."

"About as much chance as I have of being elected Pope," Paul said cheerfully. "In theory, if the marriage was never consummated it's null and void. But if he got in by the front door, even only once... Are you telling me he never did? And are you certain of it? It's a serious matter, Vincent, a most serious matter."

"Supposing he had been – all right as a man?" Vincent asked hesitantly.

Paul laughed. "Vincent, that proves it. Someone's lying. Or let's say someone's not being very precise. Stick to one story. Remember those boys in Rome – not that you need go to Rome – are sharp as needles. Supposing, just supposing, her husband could – well, put it in every inch of the way. But supposing she wanted children and her husband wouldn't have them at any price. Then – but you'd have to prove it – the marriage could be declared null and void. Not automatically, but there'd be a chance. Legally, of course, she's in a mess. She committed perjury, you see. And you'd have to persuade her husband to admit to deceiving the Court too. And the co-respondent would be brought into it. And, for that matter, perhaps the people at the hotel. If only she'd got an annulment in the first instance, as she should have done – " He walked over to the table, poured out two small drinks and handed one to Vincent.

"What you really mean is that you can't help me," Vincent said.

"The only way I could help you would be to remove him from the face of the earth. And obviously that's not possible." He put his pipe down on the enormous metal ash-tray, originally his grandfather Rosslea's, which took up almost all the top of the coffee-table beside his arm-chair. "My God, Vincent, I'm appalled by your ignorance. You know what the Church says about annulment, and what the Law says isn't really very much different. But you think there's some way round, that the whole thing's just a rather cunning game." He wagged his finger at Vincent; the gesture was amazingly artificial, in accordance with what he felt a solicitor's outward behaviour should be; the next stage, Vincent thought, would be a starched wing-collar and gold pince-nez. "Let me assure you, Vincent, that even if you could persuade Mr Palworth to admit to what is after all a grave criminal offence, even if Laura didn't change her mind, which, after all, women do, you'd have at least four years to wait. But it might be longer. So much longer, in fact, that you might be past marriage by the time it was settled. And of course she'd have to become a Catholic first. And you'd have to keep well away from her, to be on the safe side." He smiled, his face for a moment the brother's rather than the lawyer's. "Matthew and Maureen say she's most delectable. They're privileged, of course; I haven't been given the pleasure of seeing her. She's got a little place of her own, hasn't she?"

Vincent looked away from him at Shane's First Communion certificate over the mantelpiece. "I expect she has," he mumbled.

"That's a rather shamefaced reply," Paul's voice was amused. "Come off it, Vince. You've been well, let us say rifling the pantry and don't try to pretend that you haven't. I can make a pretty near guess at the last time you went to confession. Are you not going to repent until Easter?"

"You're not guessing at all about confession. Mother told you, didn't she?"

Paul shook his head slowly; it was as if he were made of a substance which weighed more than flesh. "No, she did not, my dear little brother. I am not her favourite, for the simple reason that I escaped from her during the war. If only you'd been a year or so older or if only you'd gone to foreign parts and seen some action. Once you've seen a few men killed, it gives you a sense of perspective. I tell you this much, Vincent: Mother was very much against me getting married to Jenny. I was still too young, Jenny was a Protestant, I'd bring her grey hair in sorrow to the grave… I just took not a blind bit of notice. It's different now, of course; she and Jenny get on like a house on fire."

"We've gone a long way from the subject. What's going to happen to Laura?"

Paul yawned. "She can get married," he said, "but not, obviously, to you. Or she can live in a state of blissful chastity. I wouldn't waste any tears on her, if I were you."

"But I want to marry her."

"You talk like a bloody schoolgirl, Vincent. What ails you is that you've had it for the first time in your life and you're knocked for a six. You live among books and children, Vincent, but I don't. I hear things every day that you wouldn't honestly believe possible – they come to me as if I were a priest, but they've got to give me a much fuller story than they give a priest. Why, I had a dirty old devil in yesterday who divorced his first wife to marry his secretary – the secretary was thirty years younger than him – and when his second wife, if that's what one calls her, was ill after she had a baby, he had the old wife come to stay to look after her. He used to take them both round the pubs with him. This is my Mrs Number One, he'd say, and this is my Mrs Number Two. And now his prostate gland is going on strike and he doesn't trust Number Two. So he wants to make a new will, so she can't remarry when he dies. Actually, what he really wants to do is to have a chastity belt locked on to her for life. He talks a lot above love. All the Protestants do. They know no more about it than the animals." He lowered his voice. "I'll tell you when you find out about love. When you have children. Believe me, until then marriage is very nice but there's nothing so wonderful about it. One little golden casket's very like another."

"I've heard all this before," Vincent said. "You won't help me and that's all there is to it."

Paul grunted; at the third grunt Vincent knew that the subject was closed. "It's time Jenny finished in the kitchen," he said. "I keep telling her not to bother, but she will insist on preparing you a Methodist meat tea." He opened the drawing-room door. "You can smell it now. Baked beans is what we get normally. By the way, have you seen Matthew recently?"

Vincent shook his head.

"I hear that Maureen's joined the pudding club," Paul said.

"That's nice," Vincent said. "He's one ahead of you now." It was true, he thought, about the icy hand around the heart; there was a coldness in his chest now and a difficulty in breathing as he calculated the time of conception; whether it was his or wasn't from now on he'd always be a hair's breadth from disaster. There was no guilt; but that would come later, just as pain came after a battle wound.

"You'll never get your money back now," Paul said.

"I don't want it." He found that he was shouting and waving his fists. "I don't want it back, do you hear?"

"Steady on," Paul said. "You'll wake the baby." He went over to the pram. "Quiet, my darling Larry, quiet my king." The baby's red face twitched, his eyes opened; Paul gently kissed his forehead. "They're so helpless," he said. His face was made of flesh now, worried and tired, the bone near the skin; as he continued to coo endearments at the baby he seemed to gain a dignity he hadn't possessed before.

Jenny came briskly into the room bringing with her a smell of soap and talcum powder and eau de cologne; for her, Vincent thought with amusement and something like respect, tea for a visitor was always a ceremonial occasion.

"Tea's nearly ready," she said. "The meringues seem to have come out properly, it's a miracle." She went over to the baby. "Has he been good?" She grimaced. "No, not really. Fetch the baby's basket in from the morning room will you, Paul?"

When Paul had gone she looked at Vincent with a severe expression on her face. "Did I hear you shouting?"

"We weren't quarrelling, love. I just told him that I wasn't bothered about a loan I made to Matthew."

She smiled. "He lays down the law a bit, doesn't he? But he means well, Vincent. He can be a bit clumsy at times, that's all. Laura's a good girl, Vincent, she'll always do the right thing in the end…"

"The question being what the right thing is," he said.

Paul appeared with the basket. "Stand back," he said. "I'd leave the room if I were you, Vincent, or you'll be put off marriage for life."

Vincent opened his mouth to speak but as he watched them bending over the small squirming body he did not dare to speak. It was as if he had thrown something valuable away and could not find it again; it was now in the hands of Paul and Jenny and a word from him could take it away from them too. He turned abruptly away and went into the morning room to sit between Shane and Bernard on the big shabby sofa. Shane put his fingers to his lips, his eyes on the sheriff as he walked out of the saloon, his hands on his Colts; but Bernard moved closer to him, and Vincent put his arm round his shoulders, grateful for the unquestioning and undemanding affection.

Seventeen

As they walked out of the auditorium into the foyer with its faded red carpet, Vincent had no desire to speak and no desire for company, grateful though he had been originally not to go to the concert alone or with a companion of his own sex. The music still filled him, he had escaped for over two hours from the world of moral judgements: the grey sea broke on a rocky shore, the night had fallen over the great forest, he was well outside time because he was outside himself and, being outside himself, could see that he was made in the image of God. He was carrying the music like a full cup. Laura beside him in her bright red dress was scarcely a companion but an ornament, something to be worn like an opera cloak; what he really wanted to do was to go straight home, fold the garment away as it were, and then play records until the small hours. He could so easily spill all that the cup contained, the taste of it couldn't even be guaranteed to compete with the street outside the concert hall, the traffic and the Saturday night drunks and the black façade of the concert hall and the off-white concrete of the new department store across the road, crammed with goods which, whether cameras or televisions or radios or gramophones or dresses or shoes or suits or women's underwear or trains, were all displayed so as to look larger or brighter or tougher or softer or, quite simply, gayer than they actually were, as if the kingdoms of the earth were being offered one, as if, he thought – the cup already wavering – these things were the reason for one being here.

If he could reach his home immediately, then the cup couldn't spill and couldn't overflow, no matter how much more music was put into it; or even if Laura would say the right things, be in the right mood, then it would be possible to walk the two hundred yards to the car park, to drive Laura home, to make the journey to his own home over roads along which he'd driven too many times before for them to be other than intolerably depressing; he would make the journey and still be outside Charbury, still be outside himself, still be outside the middle of the twentieth century, if only Laura were what he had first taken her to be.

"I'll take you home," he said to her.

"I told you not to use that word," she said.

"I'm sorry. I'll take you to your flat."

"I'd like a drink first," she said.

"There aren't any very good pubs in the centre. They tend to have fights on a Saturday night."

"I wouldn't want to mix with any low people, Vincent. We'd better go to an espresso bar."

"I could give you some coffee at my house."

She stopped. "No, Vincent. You're in enough trouble already on my account. And now you've told your brother all my little secrets I'd feel – well, rather awkward. You didn't handle that very well, did you?"

"We've been chewing it over for the last two weeks now, Laura. Can't we just drop it? I was enjoying myself – "

"Yes, I could see you were. Your feet aren't touching the ground, are they? You're well away into those old Northern mists, aren't you? Bloody Sibelius is just what you like, and bloody Delius, and bloody Palestrina, all the cold boys – "

"They're not cold," he said, but as he marshalled his arguments he knew that it was useless: it was not his taste in music they were arguing about.

The Nevada was crowded; he made as if to turn away but she pulled him forward. "Come and sit with the common people," she said. "Come with your brothers in Christ, Vincent." She caught Jack Moonan's eye and within a minute they were sitting at a corner table which as far as Vincent could see had not been there when he came in; he smiled at Laura and she said sharply, "He's doing it for me and not for you. Excuse me." She put her raincoat down on her chair and walked over to Jack Moonan; he said something to her in a low voice and she came back to the table, her face for a moment sallow and tired and yet curiously excited.

"What's that all about?"

"I was asking him if he had any Gauloises. And ordering our coffee, since you don't seem very keen on doing it."

"For God's sake, don't nag. I don't know what's got into you – "

"I'll tell you what's got into me, Vincent. I'm twenty-seven, and every month I put off having children is going to make it more difficult for me to have children. I'm such a dope that when you told me you were actually going to do something about our marriage, I believed you. And then you come back and it's impossible at first, and then it may be possible if I do this and that and the other, and with luck in five years – I don't want to wait, I don't want to keep on being a woman on my own, I want a baby, I want more than one baby – "

"This is it, then. You've found someone else, haven't you?"

"I wish I could. But I happen to love you. I haven't been with very many men, you know. After I was divorced, I tried, I tried really hard, perhaps I even fancied myself for a while as a *femme fatale*; but *femmes fatales* shouldn't get the dirty end of the stick, and I always do. I don't honestly feel I'm going to love anyone else but you, but there's no future in it. And in a way sleeping with you is nearly as bad as sleeping with Robert. *You* don't have all the fiddling about to do, naturally, and you don't have, every damned month, the worry and then – I can't help it – the disappointment."

"We'll be married soon. You must believe me – "

"But I don't believe you. What I believe is that pretty soon you're going to find a nice little Papist virgin and then I won't see you for dust. In the meantime, I go on commiting murder. Yes, murder. That's what the priests would say, and they're right."

The music had gone now; there was the smell of hot milk and cigarette smoke and the Wells Fargo and the Wanted Alive or Dead notices and the plastic shotguns and revolvers and the shrill voices communicating with snatches of song and comedians' catchwords and advertising slogans: the music had told him lies. God didn't have bleached hair, God didn't wear winkle-pickers or a leather jacket, God wasn't laughing for no good reason, God wasn't appealing to him with a shaking voice for something he couldn't give; he looked at her agonized face and tried to feel compassion but could only feel distaste, as for the pimples on the face of the youth at the table opposite. She had lost her identity, she could offer him nothing but involvement in the same sort of existence that the people in the Espresso Nevada had been sentenced to at birth; what she had offered hadn't been a gift, but had to be paid for. She lit another cigarette: he wanted to knock it out of her mouth but instead took her hand and tried to put some warmth into his voice.

"Don't upset yourself, we'll work something out." He tried to think of something more to say; but the longer he looked at her the less he wanted to speak to her; it was the word *murder* he couldn't take, if he spoke it would grow real, it would be as if Moonan, watching them intently from behind the counter, were to take down the plastic shotgun on the wall above him and to aim it at him and to fire real bullets: murder, murder, murder, the bayonet through the womb and his hand on the bayonet.

"Perhaps I've already worked something out," she said. "There's something I haven't told you." She paused and took a drink of coffee; he found himself following suit, as if the familiar action would somehow make what he was about to hear less unpleasant. She put down her cup, but still did not speak; suddenly, appallingly, he was visited by love, he put together the pieces of evidence and they added up to only one thing, and there was no need to assume warmth; a simple decision on her part had transformed his whole life. "You needn't be frightened to tell me," he said. "We'll get married immediately. I do love you – "

To his surprise, she was laughing, and laughing so loudly that heads were turning to look at her. "No, no, Vincent, that's not it, though isn't it a shame I hadn't thought of it before?" She stopped laughing, but there was still a smile on her face, fixed, artificially bright, as she continued. "No, Vincent, I'm not pregnant. But you Papists are wonderful really you are. That went straight home about murder, didn't it? And then you thought you weren't a murderer after all. Really you ought to wear badges like the yellow star of David and then a girl would know to steer clear of you... I've heard from Robert, that's all. He's still in Birmingham and doing very well. He's not actually making the stuff any longer but selling it, so he gets much more money. Not that I care. He wants to try again; he still loves me, you see."

"When did you hear from him?"

"A week ago. He's phoned too. I've told him he's wasting his time. But he won't take no for an answer. He seems to have changed. He said something about a psychiatrist but the line was very bad. So that alters everything, doesn't it? I can't very well ask him to do his best to make his marriage null and void. Not now. Though as your clever brother very clearly perceived, there never would have been much likelihood of him co-operating."

"It's very strange that he should choose this time to make his overtures."

She put her head on one side with an expression on her face for which, if she had been one of his pupils, he would instantly have punished her. "I haven't approached him, my dear. But someone else has."

"What do you mean?"

"Someone wrote him a letter."

"Who?" He had a strange feeling of vicarious guilt, of having, through his own negligence, put someone else in the dock.

"I don't know. Robert says it wasn't signed, but he thinks it was a woman."

He recovered himself. There was, he reasoned carefully, the world of the policeman and the magistrate and the judge, of the truncheon and the cell and, eventually, the noose. Once in that world – and the writer of an anonymous letter was bound to enter it – there was no escape. With all her stupidities his mother would never risk being pulled down into that world. She knew the law. "I'm sure that he got no such letter," he said. "He's made the whole story up. Where would she get Robert's address from? Whoever she is."

"Why should that be a problem?" She shook her head slowly. "Oh, God, what a snob you are. Everyone in your family knows where Robert's parents live. You think that you're the only person in the world with any brains. His parents are in the phone book in any case. It could hardly be easier."

"I don't believe it. She'd never be so idiotic. She'd put her name to it – "

"You're frightened to speak her name, aren't you? It's another of your secrets. You've got a lot of secrets, Vincent, stored away like bombs. Perhaps if you see the letter you'll be able to say who it is. But I don't think you'll tell me."

"I can't see what doesn't exist," he said coldly.

"The letter said we were having an affair and Robert had better come back to me before it was too late. How would Robert know about us if he hadn't been told?"

"There still doesn't have to be a letter."

"If Robert still has it, you could ask him to show it to you. Perhaps tonight."

"Say that again."

"You could ask him yourself. He was here tonight. That's what Jack just told me. I don't know where he is now, of course. If he's running true to form, he'll have got hopelessly sloshed, but he says he's given up drinking."

"Highly commendable," Vincent said. "I suppose he thinks that giving up the booze settles everything. You're going to say that you still love him, aren't you?"

"No. I can't ever love him again. But he was my husband, you know. *Is my husband*, I should say. If he's changed, if he has, as you'd put it, a sincere purpose of amendment, you ought to be encouraging me to go back to him. You're a dog in the manger, aren't you?"

"I'd better take you home," Vincent said. He gestured at Jack Moonan who shook his head. "Our coffee seems to be paid for," he said. "What exactly was your motive for that?" But she was already putting on her coat and he had to run to catch her up as she went down the street in the opposite direction from the car.

"Wait," he said, catching her arm. "What have I done wrong?"

"If you don't know, I can't ever make you understand," she said.

"Come to the car."

"I will if you let go of my arm," she said in a high voice, hurt and whining. Inside the car she started to cry. "You're a fool," she said. "He'll be waiting for me."

"All the more reason for me to come with you."

"It's a mess we've got ourselves into," she said. "A dreary hopeless mess."

"That's a sin," he said. "Despair. You damn yourself in this world and the next." His spirits were beginning to rise; he was at last to meet the faceless villain, the man who stood in his way was about to become a human being, he was about to undergo an experience which, whether desirable or not, was a basic one, one which even bore some relation to music; it couldn't, whatever the musicians said, feed upon its own guts, it had to be about the basic things, or even simply about the climb to Marlcliffe, the journey which he had anticipated being bored by; he wasn't frightened of Robert being at the flat but of his not being there, of the battle being cancelled; he wondered what it felt like to hit a man and realized that he had never done so; Paul and Matthew had killed, if not as many as they hinted at, at least more than once, but he, living in the most violent century in history had lived within a charmed circle. What he was feeling was scarcely ennobling, but he was feeling, he was alive; and then, as he came nearer to the flat, he began to dislike himself. There was no difference between him and the drunkards brawling down in the city at this moment, he thought; except that they were less culpable, knowing no better and not being themselves.

"You'd better let me out here," Laura said. "I know he'll be there."

"He might attack you. Then what would it look like?"

"Robert? He's the gentlest person in the world. That's the last thing I'm afraid of."

"I'd better meet him just the same."

"He'll go away if I tell him to. In the morning – "

"Shut up." He saw a narrow lane to the left and turned down it and stopped on the grass verge. He kissed her fiercely, his hand reaching down the front of her dress; she submitted to the kiss for a moment, then pulled herself away abruptly. "I don't want to," she said. He kissed her again; she hit him on the face. "Next time I'll hit you somewhere else," she said. "Besides, we're not married. And I'm not prepared. You've never thought about these unpleasant details, have you, Vincent? I've sheltered you, just as everyone else has. But this is a good time to tell you…"

He started the car, her voice continuing remorselessly, only ceasing when he drew up beside her flat. He had not listened to her; but he knew that later he would remember every word; he had not felt like this since the day some twenty-three years ago when Matthew had told him in hoarse whispers where babies came from; he had refused to believe Matthew then and now he wanted to refuse to believe Laura.

There was a white Jaguar saloon parked outside the front door; as they passed it he saw a man inside slumped over the steering wheel.

215

"It's him," Laura whispered. "Go away now. Vincent. I'll be all right."

"He's drunk."

She shook her head. "He's having a catnap. Robert can sleep anywhere any time. He's very proud of it." She spoke as if the sleeper were her child; he felt for the first time the stirrings of jealousy. Robert's face was pillowed on his arms but under the light of the street lamp Vincent could see his fair, close-cropped hair and his thin neck and the gold signet ring on his left hand; he would know him again, he thought with hatred. He looked down the deserted street; it ran straight for about two hundred yards down a slight incline, then sloped more steeply until it joined the main road. He peered into the car; Robert twitched slightly but did not move.

He felt Laura's hand on his arm. "Take me inside."

He followed her dumbly; when they were inside the flat he found that he could not stop his teeth chattering.

"You can't know what was in my mind," he said.

"I don't want to know." She put a match to the fire, her back towards him; when she rose she did not turn to face him. "I can't be any good for you. The worst of it is, that I wouldn't have cared. He's driven a hundred miles to see me and I don't care. I hoped at first he was drunk, because then it would have been an ironclad excuse not to see him. But he isn't. When you've lived with a man for three years you develop a sixth sense for things like that. He's sober and he means what he says."

"You're not going to let him stay here." The fire was already burning brightly, his jealousy was dwindling; what he had felt so strongly outside was, he persuaded himself, only the most evanescent of notions; even if Laura had not taken him inside he wouldn't have touched the handbrake.

"That's my business. Would you like him to drive back and fall asleep at the wheel in real earnest?"

"I won't pretend that I'd shed any tears over it."

"No, you wouldn't." She turned to face him. "That's why I love you."

"Then what's all the fuss about?"

"It isn't as simple as all that. I don't want to be too close to you. And yet I do, you're so hard and you smell so nice. Soap and wool and even the cold outside." She moved to the other side of the room and looked at herself in the big gilt-framed mirror which hung on the wall. "You even look a bit like me. If we were married, we'd look more and more alike. But I haven't noticed you rushing along for a special licence yet."

The doorbell rang. "And now you really had better go." She smiled. "As soon as he comes in. Mumble some excuses."

As she walked out of the room he noticed how tightly her dress fitted around her buttocks; together with desire came, irresistibly, an urge to hurt her. "Before you let him in," he said, "tell me one thing. Did you put that dress on specially?"

The doorbell rang again; he caught hold of her wrist, appalled and delighted by its thinness. "Let me go," she said.

"You've a nice bottom," he said. "It's as flat as a boy's, but of course it's fuller than a boy's. I'm only surprised you didn't put on a pair of slacks. That would really have made him gloriously happy."

She clawed at his face with her free hand, her face contorted; he pushed her away, hoping that she would fall, but she recovered her balance and ran to the front door. He went to the studio couch and sat down, breathing heavily. Without the benefit of alcohol, he thought, with a heavy self-satisfaction, he had attained the state which everyone wished for: he was free of the fear of consequences. They told me that sin was ugly, he thought, but it isn't true. I was happy when I looked inside his car for the handbrake, I was happy when I hurt her deeply, I am happy now as I look up and see him standing over me, because along with the after-shave lotion I can smell fear.

He stood up; Robert was as tall as he was but the heavy fawn duffle-coat could not disguise his weediness. He had a pale skin and large brown eyes which darted backwards and forwards from Vincent to Laura and then to the open bedroom door; Vincent went over and closed it.

"It's time you went home," Robert said. He had a small, delicately curved mouth: the outline seemed too perfect a cupid's bow not to be artificial and then at the second glance too perfect not to be real. But the hair, Vincent thought, was definitely touched up; it was as if the colour, evenly yellow, had been put on with a spray gun.

You heard what my husband said," Laura's hand was on the telephone.

"Laura, you can't be serious. You love me – "

"Love. Love, he says." She was not addressing him or Robert but someone who wasn't in the room. "After the things you've said to me. I can't love you any more, you're a filthy hypocrite, you're the lowest of the low, a dirty Mick murderer – "

"Laura, listen to me." He took a step towards her; Robert grabbed his arm. The touch triggered off a blind hatred, there was a pleasure greater than anything he had ever experienced as he hit Robert on the mouth and saw him fall down. "Don't touch me," he said. He raised his foot. "Who sent you here, you bastard?"

Laura knelt down beside him. "You're not hurt, darling," she said. "Mr Dungarvan's demonstrated his virility now, and he's going home. Going home to Mother. He's a mummy's boy; you see. Don't answer him." She looked fiercely at Vincent. "You stupid animal," she said. "You stupid brawling animal. You know a woman wrote to him from Charbury. Who did you think it was?" She dabbed Robert's mouth with her handkerchief, cradling his head on her lap.

"I won't bother you again," Vincent said. To his horror he found his knees actually beginning to give way, there was no strength left in his body. Robert's mouth was bleeding more profusely now; Laura's handkerchief was soaked red. Neither of them spoke, but Robert twisted his head round to watch him go.

When he reached his car he realized that he had not asked Robert for the letter. It was not necessary, he thought; without having seen it, he knew exactly what the handwriting would be like, a teacher's round hand like his own but more open and more inclined to flourishes – there was no good reason for her attempting to disguise it, since Robert was hardly likely to take it to the police. She would be waiting for him now, ready for the sort of quarrel she most enjoyed, the big scene with good on one side and evil on the other. She would be eager too to learn of the success of her stratagem, consumed with curiosity but in no position to ask him outright whether Robert had received the letter. She wouldn't be given that satisfaction; if she found out, she would have to find out for herself.

That was it, he thought; say nothing. He stood for a moment taking deep breaths of the cold night air and then suddenly was seized by a griping pain in the belly which left him dizzy and retching. "Oh, God," he said aloud. "God pity me." But he could not stop remembering the expression in Robert's eyes; there had been fear there, and shock, but most of all there had been acceptance. The small white square of cambric had been soaked red with blood; it was as if he had hit himself.

Eighteen

The room now seemed to have come into its own, to have dropped all pretence: its purpose had never been to provide a space in which people could live. The brown and red stippled walls, the heavy dark furniture, the black vase with the beech leaves, the big wooden crucifix on the wall, had all been chosen to set off the light oak coffin which stood by the window. There had never been a time when this house was unfamiliar to him; his grandparents had come to live here when they were first married fifty-eight years ago, his grandfather and his father and his uncle had gone on ahead and now his grandmother had caught up with them, no matter what the Bible might say, and when he left this house he would never enter it again.

Still on his knees by the coffin, Vincent started to cry. It was an unexpected relief to give way to an emotion of which he need not be ashamed; when Paul put his arm round his shoulders he felt almost resentful.

"Joe Monaghan will be here any minute," Paul said. "Don't be so upset, love. She's where she wants to be." He nodded towards the photograph of his Uncle Matthew. "She once told me that when he was killed she wanted nothing else but to be in the grave with him. And then his wife and the baby – " He put his hands to his eyes.

"It's more than forty years ago," Vincent said. "It's all over now." He stood up and kissed his grandmother's cold forehead.

"It isn't to me," Paul said with sudden passion. "It isn't to me." He knelt by the coffin, his lips moving; Vincent watched him with a curious feeling of envy, knowing why the thought of the dead baby moved him: it was as if death had reached out to touch his own child.

"There couldn't have been any pain," he said, half to himself. "She didn't wake up, that's all."

Paul stood up, dusting his knees. "If it's a long illness, they say it's a merciful release," he said. "If it's quick they say there couldn't have been any pain." He shivered. "There's a bitter wind outside," he said. "I hope to God Shane doesn't get bronchitis again." He looked at the empty fireplace. "It was only last week there was a roaring fire there. You'll not see another, Vincent, the whole street's coming down."

There was the sound of a car in the street outside; Vincent parted the curtains and saw the hearse. "Monaghan's here," he said.

Paul did not seem to have heard him. "I never thought she was so small," he said. "No bigger than a child – " He put hands to his eyes again; Vincent took his arm and led him out of the room.

As he looked around the church he found a certain comfort from the presence of so many of his relations, even a tribal pride; nearly sixty years ago a man and a woman had gone to bed together at Number Ten Pelham Street and here, against all odds, were their children and their grandchildren and their great-grandchildren: they only all came together for weddings and funerals but they came to what was, after all, their family chapel. And, just as his grandmother's house had come into its own for her death, so did St Maurice's come into its own. The thick walls, the small high windows, the darkness and the coolness, admitted death without demur, perhaps even deceived death into the belief of victory; the profusion of memorial tablets, the realism of the Stations of the Cross, were proof enough that here there were no illusions about death being a friend. Jesus' face was human: as He took up the Cross He was shocked at its weight, even the grain of the wood was palpable; and when Veronica wiped His face there was not upon it the lightning sketch of the stories but blood and sweat. The handkerchief didn't seem very big but women's handkerchiefs never were; suddenly a similitude struck him, and he looked away towards the priest in his black vestments: if he had to begin thinking like that, where would he end?,

Death had come into the church, death was listening, as pleased as if the ceremony were to commemorate death and not eternal life; a voice was crying out of the depths but what guarantee was there that it would be heard, why should the Lord's ears be attentive, if the Lord observed iniquities, what else was there to be done but to endure it? The women's faces around him were dry-eyed; they only weep at weddings, he thought bitterly. He glanced at his mother, her eyes were moist and he felt betrayed, shocked as a child would be at adult weakness. *And breathe the air of Paradise;* but had it been Paradise that his grandmother had ever wanted, hadn't it rather been not to be hurt past all endurance? And now the trap was going to close, now death was going to be contradicted, now death was going to be told that what lay in the coffin wasn't worth having, that there was no victory. But the fire wouldn't be lit in the front room again, and soon her house would be pulled down and the whole street with it; and if the street only stood because she was alive, what of the city now and what of the world? *The just man will never be forgotten; no sentence of doom will he hear to haunt him.* Vincent looked at the sixth station again and, despite himself, remembered his fist driving into Robert's face.

He put his missal down and listened to the sound of the Latin rather than its meaning, hoping to lose himself, hoping for what had always come before, the defeat of death: *et lucis aeternae beatitudine perfrui,* and enjoy the happiness of eternal light. Eternal light dispensing the darkness and death scuttling away like a cockroach; but it was the choir, it was the music, it would have been the same if it had been Laura's body they'd been singing about, and if it was her body that he had in mind then death had won, there was only dust in the coffin and not an immortal soul. After a while he opened his missal again and forced himself to follow the Mass; when the priest broke the Host there was a moment of sharp physical hunger and a bitter longing to be in his place, a sense of having thrown a chance away, of having ordered, so as to speak, the wrong meal; and for a moment the bread was flesh and he understood, and then, aridly, there was only Father Rothlin, Thaddeus Rothlin aged fifty with a smooth red face and short bristly black hair, and Thaddeus Rothlin who always smoked cheroots except during Lent and who was, so his grandmother had always said, a relation by marriage, was drinking, from the chalice. His intellect took over again, the sergeant re-dressing the wavering ranks, and he had no doubt as to what was happening on the high altar; but there was no joy in the realization of the miracle, merely a dumb acceptance.

When he came out of the church Maureen ran up to him, her face glowing. "Vincent, wait a moment. Matt's got to run me back after we've been to the cemetery, the woman who's taking care of the kids..." Her voice trailed away as she looked at Vincent's mother. "Come over to see us," she said. The black coat, the black mantilla, the black high-heeled shoes and dark stockings, the glowing face, the newly tinted blonde hair, had a sharply erotic effect; regardless of his mother's watching eyes, Vincent found himself moving nearer to her. "I've been busy," he said.

"You're not so busy now," Maureen said. Then her face changed. "It's no use standing about in the cold," she said. "I've got to be careful now. Any time, Vincent. And you of course, Grandma."

"That was an afterthought," his mother said as Maureen walked off to Matthew who was talking quietly with his Uncle Peter. "And she shouldn't be running about like that–" an expression of surprise, faintly comic in its completeness, came over her face. "It's Laura," she said.

Vincent's throat became suddenly dry; as Laura drew level with him he couldn't speak but had to content himself with putting out his hand; more, he thought to himself, like a policeman than a lover. Over the smell of chocolate from the factory there was this morning the smell of mint and of malt, faintly nauseating in its sweetness; there was, too, the smell of Laura, different from what it had been, clean but tired and even frightened. "I didn't know you were here," he said at last. "There's a seat in the car."

"I've got to go back to work. I was sorry to hear about your grandmother; Vincent." She turned to Vincent's mother. "No one will mind me going to the funeral, will they, Mrs Dungarvan?"

"God's house is open to everyone," Vincent's mother said and, making a gesture which was entirely out of character, pressed Laura's hand. "You're very welcome, my dear."

It was as if St Maurice's were her private property, Vincent thought sourly. "Are you sure you won't come, Laura?"

Laura shook her head, her face expressionless; puzzled, Vincent climbed into the car.

"There's a good girl," his mother said as the funeral procession moved off. She sighed noisily. "I'd say that she felt the grace of God despite herself. Are you not seeing her so much lately?"

There was no hint of mockery in her voice; Vincent repressed his anger with an effort. "I'm seeing her tonight," he said briefly. Make what you want of that, he thought childishly: we'll see who's the cleverest in the end. But why did Laura come to the funeral having refused twice to see him again? Behind every action there is a motive; she wasn't the sort of person to act purely on impulse. And then, as they reached the cemetery the problem was solved; and but for the occasion and for the presence of his mother, he would have laughed aloud at his own stupidity.

But as he waited for Laura outside the Reference Department that evening the notion of Laura as the coy mistress blowing hot then cold seemed with every minute more cheap and shoddy. It wasn't that she couldn't change her mind, it wasn't that she couldn't regret a decision; but she wouldn't have chosen such an elliptical way of announcing that she would after all see him, that Robert hadn't changed, that the marriage couldn't be made to work again. She would have told him directly, she had her pride but she also had her own kind of honesty. What kept him waiting on the draughty landing reading over and over again the syllabuses of local societies (his own name, he was amused to note, was down on the Newman Association list of speakers) was simple curiosity; why had she bothered to take time off to attend the funeral of an old woman she had met only once?

The first rush of students came out, chattering like starlings, as undifferentiated as starlings in their uniform of jeans and sweaters and duffle-coats; then, more quietly, the staff and last of all, Laura, a small black book under her arm, alone.

"Laura."

She looked at him blankly then, recognizing him, pushed the dark hair back from her forehead and smiled.

"I thought you'd come here."

"Can I see you?"

She nodded.

"We'll go to the Nevada," he said, taking her arm.

She pulled her arm away. "No. Jack Moonan would think it odd."

He felt his temper rising. "I don't really care what a café proprietor thinks of me," he snapped.

"No, Vincent, you don't. In fact, you despise him. There aren't many people whom you don't despise."

They stopped by his car. He took out the ignition key. "I could take you home," he said. "To your flat, that is. Or to the Country Club…"

She pointed to the Weavers' Arms across the road. "That will do," she said.

225

"You can't go there. It's a really low dive. We'll go to the Railway Hotel." He took her arm again.

"Vincent, I'm not a prisoner being taken into custody. I don't want to go to the Railway Hotel. You'll have to drive me there and it's miles away from my bus stop."

"I'll take you to the bus stop."

"No, you'll say you may as well take me to my flat. It's the low dive or nothing."

He shrugged his shoulders and followed her into the Weavers' Arms.

"I warned you," he said as they sat down in the lounge, looking in distaste at the blotchy-brown wallpaper and the iron tables, and the old twitching-faced woman muttering over a glass near the fire. There was a smell of cooking and stale tobacco and, above all, poverty: later there might at least be the appearance of conviviality, a hubbub which had a kind of vitality, but at half past seven on a Wednesday evening, it was open simply because the law required it.

"We won't be here long," she said. "It'll do you good, Vincent." She lit a Gauloise; the old woman by the fire sniffed suspiciously in her direction, then smiled at them, showing ill-fitting false teeth. "Poor old thing," Laura whispered. "Buy her a drink, Vincent." She laughed. "It surely can't be Vincent de Paul you were named after," she said

"All right, you've made your point. Why did you come to St Maurice's this morning?"

"I liked your grandmother. It was a mark of respect." The landlord shuffled in, breathing heavily; Vincent ordered two whiskies and, feeling slightly embarrassed, whatever the lady in the corner would like for herself. With an expression of something near to surprise disturbing the folds of his face the landlord shuffled out and reappeared with the drinks. "And have one with me yourself," Vincent added; as the landlord accepted the offer he could see that the expression was one of approval. No matter who came into the pub that evening, he realized, no harm would come to him or Laura; she knew, and always would know, what was the right thing to do.

"Respect," Vincent said. "Respect. Was that all? You hardly knew her."

"I used to see her sometimes when I had the afternoon off mid-week."

"You didn't tell me."

"You seem shocked. As if she – or I, come to that – didn't exist when you weren't around. But I asked her not to tell you."

"Why?"

"Perhaps I had some crazy idea of getting closer to you, of being able to understand you better. Or perhaps it's just that I liked her because she was so calm and relaxed. She told me a lot of things about you and your mother and your father. And I still don't understand you."

"No one ever understands anyone else. Why did you come this morning? It's no use with Robert, is it? You'd like a man again, wouldn't you?" He was appalled at his own vulgarity; more appalled, he thought with a kind of pride than Laura was; but he couldn't stop himself, remembering her nakedness, remembering the whispered confidences, remembering again this time without any guilt, his fist crashing into Robert's mouth.

"I went because I wanted to go to Mass," she said. "And because of her too. Vincent, can't you see that other people want some sort of reassurance too? Do you think that God's exclusively yours? It's so awful, this feeling that you're just a body, of having nothing to think about but the body; because then there isn't any love."

"You don't love Robert," he said obstinately.

"I have to," she said. "Whether I like it or not. He's all right now; he's not so anxious about it." She looked at him, anxiously. "I've hurt you," she said.

With the sudden pang of jealousy there came the memory of his feelings when at the age of fifteen he'd heard that Louise Conlon was to become a nun. She had lived in the next house but one, a plump, dark-haired girl who always seemed to be laughing, who laughed naked in his secret dreams: the thought of her being of her own free will eternally inviolate had come as an insult to his masculinity, as a cold rejection. The feeling had passed because as always his intellect had come to his rescue, had told him that Louise had chosen something else, not coldly, but passionately.

"It doesn't matter," he said. "Don't worry about me." There was self-pity in his voice; deliberately he set out to play on her feelings. "I loved you. I still love you. I never have had any other woman but you and if you won't have me I don't want any other woman – "

Then he saw the pity in her eyes and stopped abruptly.

"Don't, Vincent. Please don't. I'm not going to listen any more."

"You win," he said. "You win."

She gasped as if she had been struck. "You fool," she said fiercely, "neither of us wins."

Nineteen

Maureen had put on a great deal too much rouge and the blue dress was too closely fitting for a woman three months pregnant: unavailingly he reminded himself of the pregnancy, of what was now inside her growing more easy to kill as it grew larger. She was Maureen no longer, but the vessel of life; the child could have no guilt but the guilt we were all born with and that would be washed away, and perhaps he'd be asked to be godfather again, and standing there in the church would solemnly renounce Satan and all his works on behalf of the child.

He wouldn't be able to bear it, he told himself; there was a limit to deception, there was a limit to betrayal. And then as she leaned towards him and he saw for a moment the shape of her breasts and the tiny beads of sweat on her upper lip from the heat of the fire, he knew that there was no limit, that now Laura had left him there was nowhere else to go; and if Matthew, now sitting on the arm of Delia's chair talking about the vicissitudes of the wool trade, was so stupid as not to see what was going on, that was Matthew's own funeral. *Giver of peace and lover of charity, bestow on your servants true unity in our will:* there could at least be no scandal about the child, it would be indisputably a Dungarvan. This is sin, this coldness in the heart, this mean lip-smacking enjoyment; it falls from the sky like the snow and if I tried to escape it I should be run down, a scream and then the still bundle of rags is proof enough that the splendid promises won't be kept.

"You're not talking very much, Vincent," Delia said, leaving Matthew to finish his sentence apparently for the sole benefit of the cocktail cabinet.

"I think I've the 'flu coming on," he said. "If not something worse."

"Come nearer the fire then," Maureen said, making room for him on the sofa beside Harry Bandon. He hesitated: his mother looked up from her knitting, her eyes narrowing.

"It'll pass," he said. "Seven days if I take treatment and a week if I don't." He walked over to the bay window which overlooked the road and looked out. Under the tall electric light standards the snow had a pale blue tinge; there was no moon but it was as if the moon shone from the earth as far as the eye could see. There was a story he had once read about a lamp-post in a wood between the worlds; he had a brief longing for adventure, for some sort of austerity, for release from the bed with the electric blanket switched on an hour beforehand, from the hot drink last thing at night, from comfort and three square meals a day, from the personal relationships like overheated rooms, from the tedium and the pain, from the stink of mortality. It's death I want, he thought, I love the look of the snow because it covers the green and the brown and the black, because it forces life indoors, because it makes it possible to imagine an empty world, a world given a fresh start. The snow wouldn't stay; already in places the tarmac was beginning to show like rotting flesh through a bandage; but with luck there would be heavier falls before the winter was out.

He sat down beside Maureen and as he felt the warmth of her body through the thin dress he felt a half-sick desire for her, he began to devise ways of meeting her. Worst of all, looking at Matthew, a glass of beer unregarded beside him, lighting a new pipe with the expenditure of a great many matches, he began to hate him because of his stupidity, his wide-eyed trustfulness, even for the fact that since he'd seen him last, he seemed to be drinking less and his face was thinner and smoother, his eyes clearer, he had against all odds recovered command of himself. And there was a new carpet, the suite had new loose covers, the fourteen-inch TV had been replaced by a seventeen-inch model; Matthew was climbing back into the ring, he wasn't going to be able to feel superior to him any more.

Maureen nudged him in the ribs. "You haven't been near us for months and then you sit mum all evening," she said. "Where's your drink?"

"I think Vincent would rather have a cup of tea," his mother said, laying down her knitting.

Surreptitiously, Vincent looked at his watch. Even Delia seemed subdued this evening. Matthew had returned to his monologue on the wool trade and she was answering him in monosyllables, not even attempting to extract the promise of a cheap cloth length from him. Something had gone sour, the quiet family evening was a little too contrived; sooner or later all topics of conversation would run out and the TV, at which Harry Bandon had been glancing longingly for the last half-hour, would be switched on. An hour and a half of TV, punctuated by tea and biscuits, a little more conversation and the quiet family evening would be over.

"I'll make the tea," Maureen said. "I'd do with some myself. Matthew keeps me off the hard stuff now."

She rose and Vincent stood up.

"You see?" she said to Matthew's back. "Vincent has manners."

Harry Bandon started to rise; she shook her head. "No, no. It's only my husband I want to get at. And you sit down, Vincent." She gave him a little push; it was as if her hands had no bones in them. "It's the gesture I appreciate."

"Vincent is very accomplished at gestures," his mother said. "I read once that there were two kinds of good manners, social and natural. Vincent is very good at the social kind." There was a small spot of colour high on each cheekbone. "Have you heard of the courtesy of the heart, Harry?"

Harry mumbled something about Nature and gentlemen, his face bemused; he wasn't, Vincent reflected, quite sure who was being criticized. But Delia knew, and Maureen knew. Delia had again ceased the pretence of listening to Matthew and was waiting eagerly for the quarrel to begin – anything to break the monotony – and Maureen was frightened of what the quarrel might uncover.

"My mother's addressing the question to me really, Harry," Vincent said. "The answer is that of course I have." He held open the door for Maureen and, keeping his tone casual, sat down beside Harry. What pleased them? What were they interested in? How did one communicate? "I see you've got a Renault Dauphine," he said.

Harry's face came to life; it was as if Vincent had asked him about his child.

"They're marvellous this weather," he said. "Better traction you know. More weight on the back wheels and you don't have any power loss. But what I really want is the Gordini – "

Delia, who apparently had given up the attempt to disguise her lack of interest in the wool trade, called out: "You buy one of those things and you'll be off rallying again. I know you."

"Women," Harry said. "They're never content until they stop you doing what you like doing."

"They're all the same," Matthew said. "You'll get used to it, lad." He switched on the television and Vincent felt the tension perceptibly relax. Independent suspension all round, lightweight cloth is no use for this climate, improved traction, three speeds or four speeds – one talked so that one didn't appear to take too seriously what was happening on the TV screen, one didn't need to put any effort into the talking because at any moment something exciting on the TV screen might claim one's undivided attention. Emptiness was swallowing him up, cars were running him down, bolts of worsted and mohair were entangling him; if he died now there couldn't be hell because there was no sin nor heaven because there was no virtue: only limbo, the cosy emptiness with the fire that wasn't meant to burn you and which could be quenched at the turn of a little patent lever. Only his mother kept herself apart, sitting upright in a hard-backed chair knitting furiously.

"You're making too much noise," a child's voice said; Eileen stood at the door in a pink nightgown, her feet bare. She came over to Vincent. "Make them turn it down, Uncle Vincent," she said, pointing to the television.

"Go back to bed." Matthew's voice was sharp; Vincent felt a pang of sympathy. Two years ago, even a year ago, she would have been made a fuss of, caressed, scolded with an amused gentleness if scolded at all: but now she was eight, well past the age of reason and her childhood was running out.

He stroked the dark tousled hair. "Do what Daddy says, love."

His mother rose from her chair. "Come on, Eileen, you're a big girl now."

"You take me up, Uncle Vincent."

Matthew shrugged, his eyes returning to the television. "You've been elected, Vincent. Tell her if she comes down again I'll skelp her."

His mother subsided into her chair; as Vincent took Eileen's hand he was aware that he had done the wrong thing; he half-carried the child up the stairs, kissed her perfunctorily, and walked downstairs slowly, reluctant to re-enter the room. He paused for a moment by the radiator in the hall and adjusted his tie in the mirror on the wall; it was one of the few occasions on which he wished that he smoked, that he was able to disguise his nervousness with a cigarette. He heard Maureen's voice call his name, but did not turn round: she called it again and he went towards the kitchen, dragging his feet like a boy walking up for punishment.

"What is it?"

"You've finished with that Laura, haven't you?" Her eyes were gleaming.

"Yes."

"Oh, God, I'm so glad – "

There was the sound of quick impatient footsteps along the passage; the door was flung open and his mother walked in, rather in the manner of a policeman making an arrest.

Maureen's voice suddenly altered, becoming flat and matter-of-fact. "Was that Eileen making a nuisance of herself?"

"I thought I'd give you a hand," his mother said to Maureen. "You'd think that Delia would have made the offer but there she still is, showing her big fat legs and smoking like a chimney. Don't worry about Eileen, Vincent was the same at her age. She just can't bear to be left out of anything." She looked around the kitchen, her glance taking in all the signs of a recent tidying-up; the colour scheme of the kitchen was predominantly white, a white that with some nine years' hard wear was in places grey and brown and black.

"You can't keep a house tidy with three young children," Maureen said, plugging in the electric kettle. It had a frayed flex, just as the cupboards had loose handles and the taps defective washers and the curtains less material than was needed for them to meet in the middle; here, Vincent recognized wryly, was the fecklessness against which his mother fought an unceasing battle. He himself deplored it and yet at the same time felt its slatternly charm; it was in his blood too.

"I'll cut the bread if you like," his mother said to Maureen.

Maureen handed her the bread-knife, the handle towards her. She had recovered herself now as she brought out the cheese and butter and potted meat; as Vincent left the kitchen she said in a dreamy voice: "Eileen loves her Uncle Vincent, Grandma. She misses him when he doesn't come."

"She's very like him," his mother said.

He did not hear Maureen's answer but as he returned to the sitting-room he had a premonition of disaster so complete that for the first time that evening he was not bored, but suddenly surprisingly thankful to talk about nothing more disturbing than wool and cars and interior decoration and to watch the faces on the television screen.

On the journey home his mother was silent, but once when he stopped at the traffic lights he glanced at her and saw that her lips were moving; he was tempted to ask her what was the name of the God to whom she was praying, but knew from past experience that the consequence would be that he would lose his temper and finally, his throat sore from shouting, would humbly beg her to break her silence. And then, as they walked into the house, he remembered that only twice had this been his experience. His quarrels with his mother had been intense enough, but they hadn't taken that particular course; he was deputizing for another man. As he looked at her he saw that she was breathing heavily and that her face had an expression, indecently incongruous under the grey hair, of childlike greed: she was excited, she was enjoying herself. I am the meal you're going to sit down to, he thought; he backed away from her as if the eating might be physical and said coldly: "I'm rather tired, Mother. I'm going straight to bed."

He was half-way up the steps when her hand caught his arm, holding it painfully tight. "You're not going to bed until you've heard what I'm going to say. I've kept silent for too long!" Her voice rose to a scream.

He slumped into a chair in the drawing-room, his hands over his eyes. He heard her footsteps go out of the room and return; there was a heavy thud and the click of a switch. She had brought in the portable electric fire: he began to laugh. "You're going to reprimand me in comfort, aren't you?" he asked.

"Vincent, answer me one question. One question. What's going on between you and Maureen?"

"Nothing. And if you ask me that question just once more, I'll leave the house, late as it is." There was still the feeling that someone else was standing in his shoes; he felt his flesh crawl with an old horror that was none of his making but was what he had been born with.

"You used to nearly live there once, and I used often to wonder what the attraction was. Matthew's your own brother, but he's not your kind. God knows who is. Even Paul isn't, he's not quite clever enough, he hasn't read enough. I've seen the superior smile on your face when he's been talking, meaning no harm, but not putting things as neatly as you, perhaps because everything isn't a game to him. I've noticed a lot more than you think I've noticed, but I've bit my tongue and I've prayed for God to give you understanding and perhaps some notion of love. I hoped once you might be one of God's holy priests, I thought that that's why you walked on your own, I thought at least you were pure – "

"You're surprised that I'm a man? Is that it?" He disliked the sneer in his own voice; but now the truth was coming out, the sore was being revealed, it was too late for self-control. He looked at the picture of Campion's execution and was shaken to find that momentarily it had become as real as a Press photograph; he rubbed his eyes and the doubleted and ruffed figures were puppets again, the martyr's eyes were rolling upwards like a blues singer's. And then he saw that the smoke from the cauldron was still convincing, as solid as the smoke from the cigarette which his mother had just lit.

"I know you're a man. The Church doesn't want eunuchs. I know Laura was a cheap wife for you and I know now that she's gone back to her husband. I wasn't sure until tonight, because you haven't told me anything."

"Say that again, Mother. You weren't sure that Laura had gone back to her husband?"

"Of course I wasn't. How could I be?" Her voice was merely irritated, the tone of high drama had disappeared.

"I suggest you're lying."

"I'm not the liar. Oh God, God, God – " her voice rose higher at each repetition of the name – why can't you be merciful and take me away? This is my son, this is my clever son, my favourite, my high hope, seducing his brother's wife – " she stood up suddenly over him pointing her finger accusingly – "cuckolding his own brother and then preparing to do it again. God will not be mocked, I tell you! Are you going to deny it?"

She sat down again and after a pause picked up her cigarette again. Vincent repressed a wild desire to laugh. "I've always had my suspicions," she said in a quiet voice, "but when she invited Laura to her house, well aware she'd be bound to meet me, I began to wonder. And I saw the way she looked at Laura, and a little voice inside – " she pointed to her breast – "told me, *she's jealous*. Clever as you are, you didn't notice, because you had what you wanted, and that's all you cared about. And then Laura came to your grandmother's funeral, and I saw Maureen's face. She can't hide her feelings. She was ashamed, she couldn't face Laura – "

"Mother, this is the most complete rubbish – "

"Is it? I saw you tonight in the kitchen, I heard what you said. *Every word*."

"About Eileen," he said quickly.

"About Laura. Oh God, why did you let that man take her away from you? Why don't you get her back?" She put her hands to her head, ruffling her hair grotesquely, rocking backwards and forwards in a grief that was completely without artifice. "He isn't a real man, is he? She's a good girl, she has the grace of God in her, and better go with her than wreck your brother's home and break his children's hearts."

"You lying old bitch!" he shouted. "I wonder that God doesn't strike you dead! Who wrote to Laura's husband in the first instance? If it hadn't been for you he wouldn't have turned up again." He stood up. "I'm leaving in the morning. I can't trust myself to say another word to you." He was aware of himself as being not without dignity; another man, he thought, would have hurled bitter reproaches at her.

"You can leave as soon as you like," she said quietly. "But what makes you think I wrote to Laura's husband? I know nothing about it. In fact, I haven't the faintest idea what's been going on this past month if not this past four months, and I'm afraid to ask. I pick up hints from you now and again and I piece them together, but I can't tell whether I'm right or wrong. But what in God's name is all this about letters?"

He sat down again, looking at her with a reluctant admiration. "You don't give in easily, do you, Mother?" The untidy quarrel, highly charged with emotion, the ranting and raving melodrama, had become, if not exactly drawing-room comedy, a scene from a novel by Henry James, civilized and complex, the nastiness and rawness kept under fur wraps.

"I've done nothing to give in about. I only want to know just what it is that's kept my son away from confession for four months. And I want to know about this letter I'm supposed to have written."

His temper began to rise again. "Oh, God, you damned hypocrite, how can you sit there and pretend you don't know? You wrote to Robert telling him I was having an affair with Laura and he'd better come back before it was too late. I never saw the damned letter. I don't like even thinking about it. Laura told me the gist of it. She doesn't lie, even if you do. And it worked, though you couldn't have been sure, it must just have been a shot in the dark. Now you know!" His voice rose to a scream.

"Yes, I do. So Laura went back to her husband. I never quite got it straight about him – " she grimaced in disgust – "but I suppose he's pulled himself together somehow. He is her husband, after all. Is he living with her now?"

"He comes to see her at week-ends. His job is in Birmingham. Not that I want to talk about him. Or her."

"So you think I'd write an anonymous letter?"

"Mother, I'm tired to death of going over the same ground. You wanted to break it up between Laura and me – " he shrugged his shoulders – "and you broke it up. Never mind how you did. In a way I don't blame you – " he was astounded to find himself shrugging his shoulders again – "but that's irrelevant. I've had enough, I've had my lot. Even if I'm entirely in the wrong, I can't take any more. I'm going to pack my bags now, and tomorrow I'll find somewhere in Charbury." He began to shrug his shoulders again and checked himself; in another moment his nerves would be entirely out of control.

"You'll have to go a great deal farther than Charbury," his mother said. She had not moved whilst he had been speaking; her stillness seemed with every moment to accumulate into immovable decision. "I didn't write that letter." She raised her hand slowly. "May God strike me dead if I did."

She was speaking the truth; Vincent, watching her hand drop back slowly to her lap, asked hoarsely; "Then who was it?"

She smiled. "Your grandfather Rosslea always had his heart set on your being a lawyer. And he was a clever man. But he didn't know you as well as I did. Vincent hasn't the right sort of mind for it, I said, he'll never be interested enough in other people. It's all here – " she tapped her forehead – "but that's not enough. You've told me who it is, Vincent, and you've not known you told me. You've hanged yourself."

"It was Jenny, wasn't it?"

Her stillness vanished in an irritated gesture of contempt. "Don't be a fool. Jenny's only interested in her husband and children. She doesn't give a toss about you. I doubt whether she'd have you in the house except for Paul's sake." The contempt in her voice seemed to increase but her voice remained quiet and unhurried. "You'll not keep anything from me, Vincent. Many's the time your father has tried to lie to me, sitting in this selfsame room in that selfsame chair. But I got it out of him in the end, out of his own mouth he'd always condemn himself. And then in the end he'd still deny what he'd done. Until finally, he was found out and it was no use him denying it."

Against his will, her eyes held him, the blue twin set and navy skirt were the robes of the prophetess. "It couldn't be anyone else

239

but Jenny," he said weakly. "Let's leave it now, Mother. It doesn't matter any more."

"It matters very much. My poor son. My poor son who thinks he's so clever. It was Maureen. Your brother's wife."

"Why should it be Maureen?" He was only playing for time now, the revelation could be staved off no longer.

"That settles it, you see. It couldn't have been anyone else. It wasn't me, and it certainly wasn't Jenny." She stopped as if unwilling to continue, suddenly looking older than her years.

"What's settled?"

She closed her eyes. "That's enough, Vincent. Oh, God, I'm so tired. Do you know – " her tone was incongruously chatty for a moment – "that everything comes round to the same thing in the end? Everything repeats itself?"

"Mother, I'm not listening to serial stories. What is settled? And why on earth should Maureen have written that letter?"

"That's just it." His mother's eyes were still closed.

"Maureen means absolutely nothing to me."

His mother's eyes opened. "That's what your father used to say. He used to say it about them all. *She means absolutely nothing to me, I don't even like her…*"

"If Maureen didn't want me to marry Laura, then what of it?"

What his mother had said about his father suddenly became clear to him; he turned fiercely on his mother. "My God, have you gone mad? Can't you leave even the dead alone? First Maureen, then my father – I wish to Christ he were still here and then this house would be less like a morgue – " He remembered his last leave in the Education Corps, being shown round the Hibernian Club and the Irish Club and the Knights of St Columba, his father as much the centre of attraction as Vincent was; and he remembered too, on the night his father had taken him out, returning to a darkened house, the tiptoeing upstairs (*I don't know what mood your Mother will be in*) and his mother on the landing in her dressing-gown and the smile vanishing from his father's face.

"He wasn't in it all that much," his mother said. "You think he was a good man, don't you? He was a stupid man, as stupid as you. I knew about him as I know about you and Maureen. And you try to wriggle out of it, just as he always tried to wriggle out of it and you only make matters worse. If it hadn't been for you telling me about that letter I would never have been quite certain. But I am now."

"If it was her then all it means is that she didn't want me to marry Laura," he said obstinately. "You're so sharp you'll cut yourself."

She closed her eyes again and leaned back as if to recruit her energies.

"I kept it from you about your father all these years," she said. "I knew you thought the sun shone out of him. And I thought you had a vocation. I thought you'd make up for what he'd done. I was wrong. And now you'll have to go away, a long way from here, because if you stay you'll see Maureen again and if you see her again you'll commit adultery with her again." Each word seemed an effort now; he had the feeling that she had set herself a task and now was nearing the end of her allotted time.

She opened her eyes. "Maureen wrote that letter to stop you marrying Laura. She wouldn't have done it if there hadn't been something between you." She sighed, looking at him intently and dispassionately. Something in her face reminded him of his Grandfather Rosslea explaining the complexities of Balkan politics. "A man will stop another man from getting a woman even if he knows he doesn't have any chance with that woman. But a woman only does it because she intends to have that man for herself." She shook her head. "You might have made a priest. You wouldn't have made a bishop. You're Gerry Dungarvan's son, not mine. Your father's son, God help you. Mind you don't end as he did." There was no trace of love in her voice now.

"What do you mean?"

"He died with a woman. The same woman you cast your eye upon one night at the Hibernian Club of all places. In the act, in the act of adultery, in mortal sin, that's how your fine father died. Now you know. His pals did a grand job of hushing it up, but I found out. I've lived with it all these years and now you can live with it for a change. And perhaps if you remember it it'll keep you from the same death."

"Death," he said stupidly, "death. I thought you'd bring death into it. My father. My father. You haven't left me with anything, have you? Did you hate him as much as you hate me?"

"Hate him?" she said. "Hate him?" The tears suddenly ran down her cheeks, scoring paths through the face-powder. She did not attempt to dry them but ran her hands through her already dishevelled hair again, a middle-aged woman ravaged by grief. "I loved him. You fool, you cold fool, I loved him."

Twenty

He dawdled for a moment looking at the records in the window of W H Smith's, the collar of his sheepskin jacket turned up against the east wind. Each time the door opened there was a gust of warm air and the smell of newsprint: the records all seemed to be about love, love in the Pacific, in New York, in Paris, in the Rocky Mountains, in Park Lane, love with health in its cheeks, hair shining, teeth white, Eros newly bathed and depilated, saying *cheese* for the photographer; but still, he thought, turning away to trudge on through the slush, the terrible and irresistible god. In Robert's voice when he'd telephoned there had been a note of hysteria – *you must come, for Christ's sake, I know you must hate me* – and he'd told Robert to calm down, he'd tried to put him off, having settled down with *Live and Let Die*, an indulgence he'd been saving up for just such a February afternoon; but the pleadings had become even more hysterical and finally he'd been driven out of the warm room as much by curiosity as by pity.

When he went into Rodger's Tearooms the string trio was playing selections from *The Student Prince*; despite himself he found that his spirits were rising at the warmth, at the smell of toast and coffee and chocolate, at the oak panelling and at, above all, the music, rich and creamy, with a solid melodic line, the best confectionery of its kind.

He saw Robert at the far end of the room, smoking a cigarette in a long holder, staring into his teacup as if trying to read his future. He sat down beside him, rubbing his hands briskly.

"It's a wretched afternoon," he said. "Sorry if I've kept you waiting." He beckoned the waitress. "A pot of tea, please. Better make it for two. And two toasted teacakes, and cakes." His high spirits mounted still further as he scrutinized Robert's face; in the weeks that had elapsed since he'd seen him he had perceptibly grown thinner and at the same time puffier in the face, and the blond hair seemed even more obviously tinted. On one cheek there was a patch of dry eczema which soon, to judge by the way in which from time to time he rubbed his eyes, would spread. Vincent smiled, knowing that the smile was the worst possible kind of smile, seeing with a small twinge of malicious pleasure Robert's hand fly to his cheek.

"How are you, Robert?"

"You needn't gloat," Robert said surprisingly. He looked away from Vincent; the large brown eyes, that were as wasted on a man as the small delicate mouth was, flickered from person to person desperately. And suddenly the music seemed to Vincent a joke in bad taste; Robert was not rejoicing in his youth, but looking for sympathy, looking for a face that wasn't a stranger's.

"I'm not gloating," he said gently. "Why do you think I'm here?"

"Because I'd have bloody well come to your house otherwise," Robert said waspishly. "And I'd have let your mother know a thing or two, you bloody hypocrite."

"She isn't in. But it wouldn't have made much difference. I'm leaving Charbury as soon as I can."

"I wish you were leaving this earth. Christ, if you had any idea of how much I hate you and people like you." He pulled out a yellow Paisley handkerchief of the same shade as his tie. There was a smell of eau de cologne. He dabbed his forehead and carefully refolded the handkerchief. "You're an animal, Vincent.

An animal that pretends to be a human being. I've known dogs I liked better than you."

Vincent bit into a piece of toasted teacake. "I bet you have. But don't you think you'd better tell me what you wanted to see me about?"

Robert leaned forward. "Haven't you got any feelings, you bastard? Do you think I wanted to see you to eat bloody toasted teacakes and drink tea? You've been sleeping with my wife, that's why I want to see you. Or are you really like an animal? Do you walk away afterwards like a dog or a cat?"

"I haven't had anything to do with her since you reappeared. I'm sorry I behaved badly then, but I'm only human." The tea had infused now; without thinking he poured out two cups. "I can see now there's no future in it for Laura and me."

"She's not one of the Elect. Not good enough for you." There was in Robert's voice a genuine indignation; he wants his rights, Vincent thought with amusement, even if he's not sure what those rights are.

"She's married. To you. Until the day you die. We don't under any circumstances recognize divorce."

"That's very handy." Robert dabbed his forehead again with his handkerchief, this time not refolding it as he put it back in his pocket. "But you're lying to me. I suppose you'll have some way of squaring it with your conscience, though."

"For God's sake get a grip on yourself. I've told you for the last time I haven't touched Laura since you came back."

Robert's face was twitching, the patch of eczema seemed to be growing redder. "It's nearly two months ago. I can only come at the weekends. You're here all the time."

"So are a thousand other men. There isn't anything else I can say. Laura has decided to go back to you, and there's nothing I can do to make her change her mind. I don't admire her taste, but no doubt she's doing it from a sense of Christian duty."

He paused; there were tears in Robert's eyes.

"You bastard," Robert said. "You cruel bastard. You knew what would hurt me, you knew what would go right home... Yes, that's it. A sense of duty..."

"You must have appealed to precisely that sense of duty often enough," Vincent said, aware of enjoying the exchange intellectually. "You can't have your cake and eat it too. You choose either to be ruled by emotion or by reason – "

"Shut up," Robert said. "I'm not one of your pupils. Answer me my question. Have you seen Laura? Have you seen her during the last" – he paused, his lips moving silently – "six weeks?"

"Do you want the truth?" He was tempted to tell Robert that he had slept with Laura; though he had tried to be cool and reasonable, jealousy was now literally making him physically ill: he had put Laura out of his mind, he knew that he couldn't have her but the thought of another man having her was suddenly unbearable. In another minute he would either hit Robert or scream abuse at him; he began, to select epithets, the filthiest he knew, and as he rehearsed them the jealousy began to pass.

"That's what I've come here for," Robert said, so quietly that Vincent had to lean forward to catch the words.

"It's wisest not to answer some questions," Vincent said. "There's been enough trouble as it is." He put five shillings on the table. "Pay the bill. I'm going – "

"Stuff that." Robert's whole body seemed to stiffen, his eyes to narrow, the small chromium table knife to become, instead of an unregarded part of the tea-service, a potential weapon conveniently close to his right hand. "Have you seen Laura? Yes or no?"

"You've had a quarrel with her, haven't you?" He was surprised at the quality of his pleasure, which every moment added to; revenge was as sweet as the cliché said but it was a varied sweetness, a cumulative sweetness, differently coloured layers piling up one after the other, a sundae for adults.

Robert's hand went to the knife, as Vincent knew it would, put it aside, then clenched hard. "Don't muck me about any more. Or

246

there *will* be a nasty scene. *I don't care what happens to me any more.* Can you understand that?"

Vincent shook his head.

"You should. If you don't, who will?" It was an appeal for help, the note of menace had vanished; it was with an effort now that Vincent kept his face blank. The string trio was playing *Golden Days* now; he was astounded to find himself taking the music at its face value, allowing himself the luxury of regret and hopeless longing. He heard Robert's voice, angry and cold again.

"Are you going to answer my question, or shall I knock your teeth in? *Have you seen Laura?*"

He saw that the threat was genuine, that Robert had reached the breaking-point; but he could not resist delaying his answer; the cherry on the sundae, he thought, viciously watching Robert's face growing more and more apprehensive, eager to know the truth and at the same time desperately frightened of it.

"Yes," he said. "I've seen her." He stood up. "That's what you wanted to know."

"You slept with her, didn't you?"

"You asked me if I'd seen her. I've told you." I'm telling the strict truth, he said to himself, watching Robert's face redden then grow pale again.

"High and dry," Robert whispered. "High and dry. Have you ever heard that expression? I do love her. I love her more than you." Now his expression was accusing; Vincent looked away from him.

"So you say,"

"That's enough. I asked for it. Now I'm going to get it." The brown eyes were looking round the room again; this time, Vincent thought, they'd given up the search for sympathy before it had begun. "You'll not tell me the whole truth, will you? It wouldn't hurt so much if you did. But I'll tell you one thing before you go; it'll happen to you. You can't imagine that it will, but just you wait. *Just you wait.*"

That evening, waiting his turn for confession at St Maurice's, Vincent painstakingly reconstructed the conversation. The sin had been there, the consciousness of it had driven him here at last, the guilt had been too much to carry. Now that he was here he found his first feeling of panic evaporated; he had fled into the church as if pursued, but now he knew that there was all the time in the world. The quietness was purposeful, the operation would take place and the operation would be successful, God would cut out the cancer, and there was no panic and no pain now. There was no such person as Maureen, there was another man's wife. There was no such person as Laura. There was another man's wife. There had been anger, there had been sloth, there had been pride. Neglect of my morning and night prayers. Presumption: *it's a long time until Easter.* He looked behind him at the two adjacent doors of the confessional, one for the priest and one for the penitent, and remembered when at the age of eighteen he had, in his nervousness, gone into the priest's door. He was in control of his life now, and yet it was as if events had taken control of him; even here he was frightened, high and dry, dry and empty, wanting to be the West Indian bus conductor on his left, wanting to be the shabby old woman shuffling out of the confessional now, wanting to be anyone except Vincent Dungarvan: *envy of another's spiritual good*, he said to himself, and then, all the time in the world suddenly running out, he was in the confessional: Bless me, Father, for I have sinned it is four months since my last confession; the venial sins quickly then the flat statements: once with the first, more than once with the second, it was out now, it was finished with; no, Father, I won't sin again, she has gone back to her husband now. I saw him today, Father. I wanted to hurt him. He thinks I've been with her again. I said... I'd seen her. But I wouldn't tell him anything more – "

The voice behind the grille said sharply: "Well, my child? Was that the truth? Had you seen her?"

"Yes, Father."

"Did you – have relations with her on that occasion?"

"No, Father. But I wanted to hurt him, I wanted him to believe it was still going on…"

"Don't see him again. And most emphatically not her either. It's most unwise, And remember: you are bound to love everybody, but you cannot always like them." The voice was reassuringly brisk. "Now make a good Act of Contrition…"

The burden was lifted, he had been given what he had asked for; but as he came out into the street he could not rid himself of the memory of Robert's twitching face as he left him sitting alone in the café. The snow began to fall, but it was melting almost before it touched the ground; in this black street it never had the chance to be white, to make the long façade of St Maurice's, broken only by the bell-tower and the entrance, more like a church and less like a factory.

If it was a factory, he thought, looking for his Uncle Matthew's name on the memorial tablet by the entrance, it had done the job he had specified. There was no guilt; to feel guilt now would be a kind of heresy. You – Vincent Dungarvan, the West Indian bus conductor, the shabby old woman – all paid for what you wanted in the same coin. But as he opened the door of his car he had for a moment the uneasy feeling of having been given more than he should, of having been given too much. He'd paid with a ten-shilling note and been given change for a pound; but it was too late to go back now: it isn't as if so big a firm can't afford if, he thought, smiling to himself at the aptness of the image.

Twenty-one

"I've a good mind to sell this house when you've gone," his mother said. "It's too big for one old woman."

"You're not old," Vincent said, looking up from *The Lord of the Rings*. It was ten o'clock now and she'd hardly spoken yet; he put the book down. She wanted to talk, or rather to gossip; this past two weeks almost every evening had taken this shape. There had been no quarrelling: his receiving Communion had settled that. At confession that evening there had only been the problem of finding enough sins to make his visit worthwhile: he couldn't, he thought, very well say that his sin was to be neither hot nor cold, to wish neither to hurt nor to be hurt, to wish only to do his job and, increasingly, to escape into fantasy.

"I might come down south with you," his mother said. "I don't know how I've stuck it out this winter."

"It isn't over yet," Vincent said as a gust of rain drove against the window.

"You'll not like being on your own," his mother said. "I don't think you even know how to boil an egg."

"I'll soon learn," Vincent said indifferently.

"You don't need to go so far away as Berkshire," she said.

"I don't even know whether I've been shortlisted yet. Where do you want me to go?"

"There's plenty of jobs in Yorkshire." She passed him the *Catholic Herald*. "Here's a job at St Bede's. And look, I've marked this one at Ampleforth – "

"I've seen it, Mother. They'll certainly not have me at Ampleforth, I'm not clever enough. In any case I want a change."

"You're not strong, Vincent. The Dungarvans don't make old bones. You'll not last five minutes without someone to take care of you."

"Does it matter?" He felt her concern reach out to envelop him, her thin face was so foolish with love that it was as indecent as if she had bared her breast for him to suck.

"It matters to me. That's wicked talk, Vincent, that's cause for confession. No matter what your sins, your mother still loves you. A mother doesn't ever stop loving her children. When you were little and you were naughty I used to punish you, and you'd always think I'd stopped loving you because I was angry. That wasn't so. I punished you *because* I loved you…"

He was reminded of the chapter he had just been reading; the house was his grave, the grave above the ground, the pebbledash and brick barrow; and it was as if, he thought with hatred, the long bony hand of the Barrow-wight, the guardian of the tomb, were crawling towards him and he had no sword.

"You wanted me to leave Charbury," he said. "We'll not go over that ground again." He had found the sword now, and at the risk of dispelling the warmth and the quiet he had to use it. "If I stay there'll be trouble. But in any case I would have gone. I'm in a rut here."

"You're tired of your home," she said, the familiar edge returning to her voice. "Or is it that you want to be out of my sight and doing exactly as you please?"

That's just it, he thought: to be out of your sight in a small flat in a strange city and answerable to nobody. The alternative would be more evenings like this, a lifetime of evenings like this; and then, he thought, the special seat at the Hibernian Club, another old bachelor teacher like Boots Ardrahan shuffling to his appointed place every evening, the eyes glancing at the wrist watches; you can set the clock by Doom Dungarvan. He smiled at the nickname which he had overheard O'Hara using that morning; it was at least an improvement upon Boots.

"I seem to have done exactly as I pleased in Charbury," he said, still smiling.

"You have paid in full," she said entirely without irony, giving each word its full value.

"I haven't. Someone else has."

"I haven't the least idea what you're talking about, Vincent."

"My God, it's only ten days ago. Your daughter-in-law has a miscarriage, you lose your grandchild before he's born, and you say you don't know what I'm talking about. People noticed, you know. You've only been to see Maureen once since it happened. Just once. If it were Jenny, it'd be a different story, wouldn't it?"

"She has sufficient relations of her own," his mother said calmly.

He thought of Maureen's white face, old without make-up, and the hair grotesquely streaky, the bleach growing out; when he had visited her she had only answered him in monosyllables and when he had taken her hand she had pulled it away.

"She might have died," he said. "And you don't care."

"Don't remind me of her," his mother said. "I've had enough heartache over that one to last me for the rest of my days." She frowned at him. "Haven't you too?"

"I haven't had a miscarriage."

"We'll not talk about that. A miscarriage is a misfortune, not a punishment."

"It'll do until God thinks of something better," he said bitterly.

"I had three," she said. "And a still birth, and that's the heaviest sorrow of all. But you'll not hear me complain – " The doorbell rang. "My God, who can that be at this hour?"

"I'll answer it," Vincent said, but his mother was already going out of the room; she opened the front door and Vincent heard her gasp in surprise.

"Laura. What's the matter?"

Laura's trench-coat was dripping with rain, her head-scarf so wet that it was impossible to determine its colour; as she leaned against the porch, panting as if she had been running, he was overwhelmed by pity and, irrelevantly, by the memory of Maureen's hand pushing his away.

"Something dreadful's happened," she said. She did not seem to see Vincent. His mother made no move in invite Laura in; her voice was curious rather than compassionate: "What is it, Laura? It's very late – "

He pushed his way past his mother and took Laura inside, his arm round her waist.

"The taxi's waiting," she said. "If you won't have me, I'll go back." She leaned against the wall, her face white. When he had helped her to take off her trench-coat there were large dark patches on her dress; she submitted to his ministrations without speaking, her eyes fixed appealingly not, he realized with surprise, on him but on his mother.

"I'll pay off the taxi," he said. "Mother, can't you see that Laura's soaked to the skin?"

His mother came towards Laura, her face sullen. "If you'd phoned, Laura – " she began, then stopped; Laura's arms were hanging loosely by her side, her mouth was parted as if gasping for breath, she had not taken off the wet headscarf.

"Mary pity women," his mother said, and unfastened Laura's headscarf. "We'll get you into something dry. Vincent, you heard what Laura said. Pay off the taxi." She took Laura's arm and led her upstairs, saying something to her which Vincent didn't catch; he went out into the rain, glad of the fresh air, glad even of the physical discomfort of the rain soaking through his thin slippers.

When he returned to the empty sitting-room, there was a moment of anti-climax when he scarcely knew what to do with himself; but the excitement persisted; he had an absurd desire to sing and dance, to make some acknowledgement of the fact that he had just let life in, that unexpectedly there had been an amnesty and not only for him, that upstairs there were footsteps and doors opening and water running, and more than one woman's voice. Whatever terrible thing had happened, whatever reason Laura had come for and even if this was the last time he saw her, he'd been made aware of the world outside the house and he was not going to lose that awareness. He had asked a girl out for a drink five months ago, he had for once in his life acted out a desire, and now everything had changed. He closed *The Lord of the Rings* with a snap and replaced it on the shelf. He had thought once that everything moved so quickly and violently that he was helpless, he had thought he was being used. But it was he who had asked Laura out for a drink, it was he who had started it all. The gun, he thought, didn't fire itself; I needn't be frightened of or astounded at the noise.

He had been sitting for nearly half an hour when his mother came into the room, her face flushed. "She'll be down in a minute," she said. "The poor girl. The poor girl. She's been walking around Charbury like someone demented, not knowing where to turn."

"What's the matter?" he asked. "Why did she come here?"

His mother turned her face away from him.

"Her husband's dead. He killed himself, God forgive him. Sleeping tablets." She lifted up her hands. "Oh, God, what a terrible thing. He was only thirty-three."

"I'll take her home when she's recovered."

"Is that all you can say?"

"It's only a fortnight ago that I saw him." He began to feel a little sick but took a deep breath.

She turned abruptly. "She's staying here tonight. You can sleep in the spare room. Mind, you're not to let that girl down or I'll kill you. I'll make her something to eat now. I dare say she's had nothing." She stopped at the doorway. "Vincent," she said softly. "I'm sure it wasn't her fault. Be kind to her." She was, he realized, issuing no further orders; she was asking him a favour. It was as if she weren't quite sure of the favour being granted, he thought, his sense of guilt deepening as he saw the door close behind her slowly and gently as if she were frightened to slam it. Had she seen the blood on his hands? He had a sudden picture of Robert washing down pill after pill, the dry bitter taste, the furniture, the ceiling, the floor changing shape, expanding and contracting, the sleep pouring down his throat, thick and glutinous at first then sharpening and hardening, filling throat and nostrils and lungs like granite chippings: before the end there would be the frantic desire to breathe air again but then it would be too late. There would be no actual blood but there was blood on his hands as much as if he had used a knife instead of those few words in Rodger's Tea-rooms. Not even a few words, he thought: I make a bad confession even to myself, I murdered Robert with silence. I murdered him and I went to Communion the day afterwards.

Laura came into the room and looked at him hesitatingly, as if unsure of her welcome. His mother's blue quilted dressing-gown was two sizes too large for her and her face had been washed clean of make-up; her eyes were swollen with tears. He put his arms round her and kissed her forehead gently, feeling compassion and nothing else. This was how he would see her in years to come, except that the dressing-gown would not be so long nor of that particular shade: this was, so to speak, a dummy run, an exercise with blank cartridges; if there was compassion now there would be love later.

"You know, don't you?" she asked.

"My mother told me."

"Did she? She's very kind, Vincent." There was no irony in her voice but there was no emotion: he had the feeling of something being about to break, quietly, dryly, irretrievably.

"Laura," he said, "listen to me. If it was anyone's fault it was mine. I saw Robert – I lied to him, yes, I lied, I lied in a clever way. I wanted him to think I'd slept with you. That is, slept with you since he came back." He paused: it was important to make it clear what had happened at Rodger's Tearooms, to make a good confession. The familiar feeling of relief was coming to him now, the guilt was being disposed of by the fact of admitting it. Then he saw that she was not listening; she was waiting to make her own confession, he was on the wrong side of the grille.

"I know," she said. "He wrote to me. I got it this morning. He'd often talked about killing himself before, so I didn't really take it seriously. His mother told me, Vincent. I had the day off and I came to the flat and the phone was ringing. I hung up on her and I went out. I couldn't bear it, and I walked miles in the rain and there isn't anybody living anywhere. There are no lights, Vincent, and I walked and walked and got wetter and wetter, and then I came here because there wasn't anywhere else to go. She blamed me. Vincent, she blamed me." She moved away from Vincent and pulled the dressing-gown together at the neck, her head turned away from him as if, he thought, to make up for the fact that she could see his face clearly and the light was on.

"I thought I was pregnant," she said. "I know I'm not now, but I thought I was then. And it would have been his child, Vincent, it couldn't have been anyone else's."

He gasped as if struck, jealousy for a moment replacing guilt, and then recovered himself: his own feelings had no place here, it was only Laura who mattered. "Go on," he said gently. "He was your husband, after all."

"I told him because I was fool enough to think he'd be pleased, that we could start again properly. I didn't love him but I thought perhaps a child would make a difference. You have to love a child, haven't you? And then you love the father of the child in the child. I was trying, Vincent, I was trying because Robert needed me and I thought he'd changed. And I told him and he raved like a madman. I was a filthy cow, it wasn't his child. I had to get rid of it –" she shuddered. "I had to get rid of it, I had to murder my baby, I was a cow, a filthy cow." She put her hand to her belly. "That was the word he used the most, it made me feel sick here. I was a filthy cow, I had to murder my baby. And I told him it was his, I yelled and shouted too. I think I convinced him and then – and that's what I couldn't bear – he said it made no difference, that

I still must get rid of it, that he didn't want a child. His own child, Vincent, he wanted his own child murdered. What sort of man is that?"

"He couldn't help it. He didn't know what he was saying." Vincent put his hand on hers, shocked by its coldness.

"I didn't care whether he could help it or not, because I couldn't help what I said. I called him filthy names too. I said he wasn't a man, that he'd never been a man, that even when he did it it was a mess, that he was a rotten pansy, that I loathed him – and I knew with every word that I was ruining him as a man, and I didn't care. I said if he were a man he'd be able to make love there and then, I asked him to prove it – and that did it, that drove him straight out and I never saw him again. And he needn't have died: that's what's so terrible and so ridiculous, it's just the way things would go for Robert. Because I found out yesterday that I wasn't pregnant."

"You didn't know what would happen," Vincent said. "No one does." He put his arm around her shoulders gently. I met Robert twice, he thought: the first time I struck him, the second time I helped to kill him.

"Vincent, he was in a trap. One way or the other he couldn't get out. But what more can I do than say I'm sorry? Where does it end?"

"It ends here," Vincent said. The door of the confessional closed behind the penitent; but, he thought, the priest is a penitent too, we absolve each other as soldiers once did on the battlefield.

"You're going away," Laura said, her voice drowsy; he saw that she had reached the limit of her endurance.

"Hush," he said. "I'll not go away without you." He held her more firmly as he felt her body relax against his; we have told each other the truth, he thought, and now we begin from here, sitting for a moment in silence as the Russians do before a journey. When his mother came into the room he did not take his arm away from Laura's shoulders.

JOHN BRAINE

THE CRYING GAME

Young Frank Batcombe, fresh out of his middle-class, Yorkshire home, now belongs to the mod, sexy, brutal London scene. A rising star in journalism, good-looking, smooth and on the make in every way, he has two major schemes in progress: one is to create a scandal that will ruin a Labour politician and gain instant renown for himself; the other is to escape marriage to a girl he believes is carrying his child. The question is – could Frank simply be a half-decent man in a rotten environment?

'A cautionary tale of swinging London…' *New York Times*

'A kinky, mod, kaleidoscope scene of bright-plumed 'birds' and opportunistic bastards who will do anything to get ahead… Shocks and hypnotises at the same time' *Publishers' Weekly*

'Compulsively entertaining' *Sunday Telegraph*

John Braine

The Pious Agent

Xavier Flynn is a fervent Catholic and a ruthless professional killer working in a secret government department. His investigation of a revolutionary group who plan to sabotage one of Britain's leading industrial companies takes him from amorous embrace to deadly encounter in this dynamic, riveting thriller in which Flynn must use every ounce of his nerve and know-how to stay alive.

'The plot is fast and furious…' *The Guardian*

'…a spy thriller of unusual pungency and abrasiveness –
an extremely exciting book' *Scotsman*

'…a secret agent very different from all the rest' *Daily Express*

'…more convincing and exciting than James Bond'
Illustrated London News

JOHN BRAINE

THE QUEEN OF A DISTANT COUNTRY

When writer Tom Metfield realises with huge dismay that his novels have become mere recordings of his personal experience, his attempt to remedy the situation leads him to Miranda – once a distinguished novelist who has swapped her glittering career to be a solicitor's wife in a Yorkshire seaside town where Tom spent his youth. He is intrigued to know why Miranda has sold out on her dreams and settled for far less than she could have accomplished. In exploiting her character and lifestyle, Tom finds himself, reluctantly, delving into his own.

'A novel of real unforced style and feeling' *Times Literary Supplement*

STAY WITH ME TILL MORNING

A loving wife, three beautiful children, a perfect marriage and a nice house in a fashionable Yorkshire village – what more could a man ask for? But middle-aged Clive Lendrick feels that something is missing, and what begins as a harmless flirtation could lead to more than he bargained for in a tale of a charmed life radically distorted by temptation.

'A powerful, sexy book' *Sunday Mirror*

'His best work since *Room at the Top*…dealing with the swerves and switches of lust, with sexual chicanery, and its devious relationship with affection' *Observer*

'A novel of quiet but formidable strength and impeccable craftsmanship' *Sunday Telegraph*

John Braine

The Two of Us

After the period of marital turmoil related in the stirring prequel *Stay With Me Till Morning*, middle-aged Clive and Robin Lendrick have reached an uneasy calm in their curiously enduring relationship, compounded by Clive's recent heart attack. All they really want is 'a quiet life', but trouble once more rears its ugly head with the arrival of Robin's former lover and a challenge to Clive's authority within the family firm. Can their weary relationship weather another storm?

'Mr Braine writes with an authority and confidence that are wholly beguiling...his ability to establish the details of how people live, to catch the tone and flavour of life as it is experienced, gives his fiction that quality of vitality, so hard to define' *The Scotsman*

'Compulsively readable' *Sunday Telegraph*

Waiting for Sheila

I don't like her, I don't trust her, and I never have done. I love her – there's an enormous difference.

Jim Seathwaite, General Manager of Droylsden's department store, is self-assured, smartly dressed, methodical and dynamic. But when he comes home to 11 Medway Close, Sugar Hill, the real Jim Seathwaite takes over – a muddled dreamer with troubled memories and guilty secrets, who begins to comprehend that only one thing rules his life – Sheila, his wife. Jim has a problem and only Sheila can settle it – but at what cost?

'Rises to wonderfully evocative heights' *Listener*

'Utterly believable' *Daily Express*

OTHER TITLES BY JOHN BRAINE AVAILABLE DIRECT
FROM HOUSE OF STRATUS

Quantity		£	$(US)	$(CAN)	€
	THE CRYING GAME	6.99	11.50	16.95	11.50
	ONE AND LAST LOVE	6.99	11.50	16.95	11.50
	THE PIOUS AGENT	6.99	11.50	16.95	11.50
	THE QUEEN OF A DISTANT COUNTRY	6.99	11.50	16.95	11.50
	STAY WITH ME TILL MORNING	6.99	11.50	16.95	11.50
	THE TWO OF US	6.99	11.50	16.95	11.50
	WAITING FOR SHEILA	6.99	11.50	16.95	11.50

ALL HOUSE OF STRATUS BOOKS ARE AVAILABLE FROM GOOD BOOKSHOPS
OR DIRECT FROM THE PUBLISHER:

Internet: **www.houseofstratus.com** including author interviews, reviews, features.

Email: **sales@houseofstratus.com** please quote author, title and credit card details.

Hotline: UK ONLY: **0800 169 1780**, please quote author, title and credit card details.
INTERNATIONAL: **+44 (0) 20 7494 6400**, please quote author, title and credit card details.

Send to: **House of Stratus Sales Department**
24c Old Burlington Street
London
W1X 1RL
UK

Please allow for postage costs charged per order plus an amount per book as set out in the tables below:

	£(Sterling)	$(US)	$(CAN)	€(Euros)
Cost per order				
UK	2.00	3.00	4.50	3.30
Europe	3.00	4.50	6.75	5.00
North America	3.00	4.50	6.75	5.00
Rest of World	3.00	4.50	6.75	5.00
Additional cost per book				
UK	0.50	0.75	1.15	0.85
Europe	1.00	1.50	2.30	1.70
North America	2.00	3.00	4.60	3.40
Rest of World	2.50	3.75	5.75	4.25

PLEASE SEND CHEQUE, POSTAL ORDER (STERLING ONLY), EUROCHEQUE, OR INTERNATIONAL MONEY ORDER (PLEASE CIRCLE METHOD OF PAYMENT YOU WISH TO USE)
MAKE PAYABLE TO: STRATUS HOLDINGS plc

Cost of book(s):———————— Example: 3 x books at £6.99 each: £20.97

Cost of order:———————— Example: £2.00 (Delivery to UK address)

Additional cost per book:———————— Example: 3 x £0.50: £1.50

Order total including postage:——— Example: £24.47

Please tick currency you wish to use and add total amount of order:

☐ £ (Sterling)   ☐ $ (US)   ☐ $ (CAN)   ☐ € (EUROS)

VISA, MASTERCARD, SWITCH, AMEX, SOLO, JCB:

☐☐☐☐☐☐☐☐☐☐☐☐☐☐☐☐☐☐☐☐

Issue number (Switch only):

☐☐☐

Start Date: **Expiry Date:**

☐☐/☐☐   ☐☐/☐☐

Signature: _____

NAME: _____

ADDRESS: _____

_____

POSTCODE: _____

Please allow 28 days for delivery.

Prices subject to change without notice.
Please tick box if you do not wish to receive any additional information. ☐

House of Stratus publishes many other titles in this genre; please check our website (**www.houseofstratus.com**) for more details.